A NEXT GENERATION NOVEL

LIBERATE US

J.M. WALKER

IBSN: 978-1-989782-35-4

Liberate Us (Next Generation, #8)

FAMILY TREE

Angel and Genevieve "Jay" Rodriguez
(Grit, King's Harlots #1/Grim, King's Harlots #3)
Angelica "Gigi"
Ryder
Meadow

Asher and Meeka Donovan
(Stain, King's Harlots #2)
Aiden
Ashton

Coby and Brogan Porter
(Rude, King's Harlots #4/For You, King's Harlots #7)
Zachary "Zach"

Dale and Maxine "Max" Michaels
(Numb, King's Harlots #5)
Piper

Vincent "Stone" and Creena Stone
(Rust, King's Harlots #6)
Luna
Vincent Junior

Greyson and Eve Mercer
(Greyson, Hell's Harlem #1)
Jaron

Tray and Zillah Lister
(Tray, Hell's Harlem #2)
Beatrix "Bee"

John and Beatrix "Trixie" Butcher
(Hell's Harlem Series)
Cyrus
Samson "Sammy"

AUTHOR NOTE

I know a lot of readers don't like knowing possible triggers ahead of time, but I know a lot of readers DO need to know in advance. And that is perfectly understandable! So I thought I'd do something a little differently this time for the warning in this book by giving YOU the choice to read the trigger warnings or not.

Please see the link below that will take you directly to my site and it will include a more detailed warning.

<u>Please be advised that it WILL give some spoilers.</u>

https://www.aboutjmwalker.com/liberate-us-trigger-warnings

This is NOT a light and fluffy romance.

Final warning: This book deals with certain topics that may be triggering for some. Please read with caution.

DEDICATION

To porn and that porn star who has no idea who I am but inspired some of the scenes in this book.

Keep it up.

PROLOGUE

Amber

I WANT YOU NAKED and kneeling on the bed with your ass facing the door. I'm going to fill every inch of you with so much cum, it's going to be leaking from your pores. Get ready, baby, because I'm going to spend the night fucking you until you can no longer breathe.

I shivered as I read the text. Every inch of me came alive with anticipation. Not knowing when *he* would arrive. Would it be in a few minutes? Hours? Longer? I never knew and I liked it that way. We preferred it. The not knowing. The buildup leading to the final explosion. It was more exciting when things were left to chance and not planned.

Sammy Butcher and I had been sleeping together for a while now but every time with him was new and exciting. It always left me wanting more. No matter how many times he fucked me within an inch of my life, my craving for him never dwindled. He knew it and took advantage of it.

The first night together he broke my table.

The next time, he damn near broke my soul.

What we had was fun but at the same time, it was dangerous as hell. Because even though he was a dick most times, I still texted him when I needed to feel him deep and powerful inside of me.

He knew that no matter what, I couldn't get enough of him. I often wondered if something was wrong with me. I should know my worth and want to be treated like a queen. I did but I also liked to be fucked dirty against a wall. Or feel that delicious slice of pain as his palm connected with my cheek when he was deep inside me. He figured out rather quickly that I gave as good as I got. Both of us enjoyed that delicious slice of pain but at the same time, I liked to be held and protected too. I knew Sammy would never hurt me and take things further than I liked.

"Pick a safeword."

A safeword. A single word that would stop it all. He liked to try and make me use it, but I never did. I often thought he was challenging me in a way.

Most would think what we had was degrading, maybe it was, but I always consented. He was rough, powerful, took exactly what he wanted and gave it back to me in ways I never experienced before. He took care of me without even knowing it. Without even trying. I knew I was safe in his clutches. Even when his hands were wrapped around my throat. He made me realize that the dark side to sex was intoxicating with the right person and that it was okay to embrace it as long as we were safe.

While he threw vile words at me because he knew I liked it, he held me after. It was a contradiction in a way. With him being rough and vulgar during the act and then soft and gentle after. The after was my favorite. Always.

Placing the phone on my nightstand, I stripped and crawled onto the bed.

The sound of the door leading to my apartment closing sent a thrill rushing through me. I was so damn thankful I gave him that key because I liked not knowing when he would arrive. If I would be in the shower and have him join me unexpectedly or be sleeping and wake up with him beside me. Both of us liked not knowing.

LIBERATE US

But it looked like I wouldn't have to wait too long for him.

I replayed his rules over in my head.

No kissing on the mouth.

Tell him if it gets to be too much and use my safeword if I needed but I never did because he knew that I could take it. That I could take him.

All of him.

ONE

Amber

Some time before…

WHEN I PULLED UP in front of Rouge, I almost kept going. Motorcycles of all different shapes and sizes littered the parking lot. A sense of trepidation washed over me, knowing who was going to be within those walls. Walls that had been my safe place for as long as I could remember until *he* tainted them with his never-ending mood swings.

I knew he was there because I could sense him. As much as I didn't want it to happen, my heart fluttered at the possibility of going toe to toe with Sammy Butcher once again. Maybe tonight would be the night that he would actually talk to me. Only a handful of words had passed between us ever since I'd met him. I wished that he would talk to me instead of giving me one of his signature scowls. But maybe this was what he liked and how he wanted it.

"What the hell do you want, Sammy?" I demanded, placing my hands on my hips. I had only just met him a few days before and all he had done since, was glare at me. Every time I stood on that stage, he looked my way. A dark shadow would pass over his face. I would smirk, knowing it pissed him off every time I walked up to the pole and began to dance. And he would only stare at me. But that was it. He didn't do or say anything, and it was enough to drive me mad.

"You'll figure it out, Red." Sammy pushed a loose strand of hair behind my ear. The touch had been so gentle, especially coming from someone like him, I was momentarily shocked as a result. He frowned, noticed what he had just done, and that familiar scowl appeared on his face once again. *"Just hurry the fuck up. My dick and I are getting impatient."*

Although I had been called Red ever since I was a little girl, when Sammy used it, it did funny things to my belly. A vibrant shade of crimson covered my tresses. But I wasn't like a lot of redheads. I didn't have a single freckle on my pale skin. I remembered as a child how I would dab tiny dots on my flesh with a black or brown marker. I felt different without them. I could never hide because my hair always gave away my location. I was always found. By them. By everyone. By *him.*

When I pulled into the parking lot, a sense of relief left me that my space hadn't been taken. Not that it was ever assigned to me technically and it was a free-for-all, but I liked parking in it. It was closest to the door at the side of the building. I could get in without being seen and leave just the same.

I had been working at Rouge for a couple of months now and I considered the staff part of my family. Even my mom welcomed them into her life with open arms.

Killing the engine, I went to reach for my bag when a rough tap on the window made me jump. My head whipped around, my stomach twisting at the dark shadow standing by my car.

"Open up." Although the deep voice was muffled, I knew instantly who it was. I tried denying it but even my body knew. It reacted to him. Always. Especially when he was in one of his moods. "Red, open. *Now.*"

Was this it? Was Sammy going to finally tell me exactly what he wanted instead of glaring or scowling at me or beating guys within an inch of their lives just for breathing the same air as me?

LIBERATE US

I knew he wanted sex. I wasn't stupid. But I also knew that there was more to it than that and I was determined to find out.

My jaw clenched, a hot shiver racing down my spine over the fact that I would have to come face to face with Sammy sooner than I would have liked. It was too early in the evening for this shit.

Grabbing my bag, I shoved my phone into my back pocket and pushed open the door, not caring in the least if it hit him.

He grunted.

I smiled.

Once I stepped out of the car, Sammy was right there. In my space. He was too close. Way too close. So damn close that I could smell the leather of his cut. I could see the light smattering of dark scruff on his strong jaw but what I couldn't see, was any warmth in his dark eyes. Whatever emotion he felt was long gone and destroyed by something tragic that had happened to him. I knew because I felt the same.

Most guys I had ever been with, drowned themselves in cologne. But not Sammy. With him, it was leather. Leather, sex, and man. Pure hard man.

Taking a step toward him so I could close the door, my shoulder brushed his chest. As soon as I closed it, I was shoved up against it.

My breath caught in my throat as I stared up into angry eyes. I had no idea what Sammy's issue was with me. Maybe he wanted me like I wanted him, and it was new, so it pissed him off because he didn't know how to deal with it. It was how I felt anyway.

I noticed then how his hair had grown in some. He still kept the sides shaved but the dark, almost black, tresses were a little longer than normal on top. My fingers itched to run through it.

Never being this close to him before, I could see that his nose was a little crooked. In the dim lighting of the streetlight, I also saw a faint white line in his left eyebrow where there had once been hair but now, it was a scar. Maybe it was from getting punched after saying something stupid.

As we stared each other down, I couldn't help but think back over the few interactions we've had. He came into Rouge with his crew, ordered a few beers, chatted with the other girls and owners, and that was it. He never once approached me. Not since I started working here. Not since I did my last dance.

Why now?

Sammy's hand was around the base of my throat, holding me up against the side of my car. A wicked glint flashed in his dark eyes. He pushed harder, forcing me up onto my tiptoes.

A gasp escaped me, something foreign rushing through me. Questions danced in my head but no matter what, I couldn't voice them. No words left my lips as Sammy held me up against my car. It was later into the night, so it was dark enough that no one would catch us unless they walked by. But people making out, or even fucking in the parking lot, had been a normal thing. It was never *my* thing but now with Sammy's firm grip on me, I was beginning to rethink that.

We had been going back and forth for awhile now, skirting around the idea of what could possibly come out of whatever we were doing. Which was nothing at the moment. We hardly spoke but told all with our eyes. He looked at me like I was the worst person he had ever met, and I looked at him like he was the ending to everything I thought I knew.

He drove me insane.

I drove him mad.

An electric current snapped between us, forcing his head lower. The muscle in his jaw ticked, begging me to touch it but I feared that if I did, Sammy would walk away for good. So I kept my hands to myself. For now.

He took a step closer, his pelvis pressing up against my lower belly.

I shivered at the thickness hidden beneath his jeans. I wasn't a stranger to sex. Especially not when I used to strip for a living to make ends meet. But I had never experienced someone as intense as Sammy. His name almost didn't seem hard enough for him. His last name was Butcher. I was surprised he didn't just go by that.

Sammy released me, much to my surprise, and trailed his knuckles down the center of my chest. The lower they went, the harder my heart raced.

LIBERATE US

I clutched the strap of my bag and as much as I wanted to run, I couldn't help but get lost in his stare instead.

As his fingers delved lower, he watched me. I wasn't sure what he was looking for. For me to tell him to stop? For me to say hurry the fuck up and do it already? For me to run? I wasn't sure what he wanted but I wouldn't do or say any of those things. I wouldn't push him away but I wouldn't pull him closer, either. I wouldn't tell him to hurry up but I also wouldn't tell him to stop. No matter how much I was confused by his dislike for me, even if he never actually said it himself, it was there, looming over our heads like a single cloud in the sky. It was our little reminder that although both of us hated any sort of emotion, we embraced the hate. We wrapped it in our fingers and choked the fuck out of it. Much like I wanted him to do to me.

As his hand delved lower, his fingers skirted across my abdomen, over my hip, and around to my ass. Just when I was about to ask him what he was doing, he pulled my phone from the back pocket of my jeans. He swiped his thumb across the screen, a frown settling between his brows. After a couple more seconds, he handed it to me.

I took it, staring up at him.

He reached out, pinching my chin and tilting my head back. His dark eyes moved back and forth over my face. "You need me, you know where to find me." Instead of waiting for me to respond, he stepped away from me and began walking toward the club.

I couldn't help but watch him, wondering what the hell that was about. My jaw tingled from where he had touched me.

My phone buzzed a moment later, forcing my eyes to the small screen.

Unknown number: It's Sammy. Put a lock on your damn phone.

I drew in a sharp breath but did as I was told.

Mc: You know, you really need to learn your manners and how to say please. I don't like being told what to do.

9

Sammy: I have manners when they're warranted, Red. And yeah, I bet your beautiful fucking ass that you do in fact like being told what to do.

I huffed, about to put my phone away when another text came through from him.

Sammy: I gave you my number because I'm sick of this shit. You want to fuck, text me and I'll drop everything and be right over.

My body burned. Yes, God yes, I wanted that. I wanted all of that. I wanted to know what he felt like. I wanted to run my hands over every single hard line of him. I wanted to put a smile on his face and warmth in his eyes. But most of all, I wanted him to make me scream his name.

Me: Playing nice finally, Sammy?

Sammy: Careful because trust me, you do not want to push me.

Me: Your idle threats are cute, Sam, but you don't scare me.

Sammy: I don't want to scare you. I want to break you instead.

I read his words over and over before responding.

Me: What'll happen if I push you?

As I sent the text, I stepped into Rouge. When I reached the main area that was an open space with tables surrounding a large stage, my phone buzzed again.

Sammy: Keep pushing, Red, and see what happens.

LIBERATE US

I rolled my eyes.

Sammy: Don't roll your eyes at me, pet.

My back stiffened. My head snapped up, finding dark eyes staring directly back at me. Sammy was sitting in a booth to my left. From where I stood, he was the only one I could see. He sipped at his beer, keeping his gaze locked with mine.

He watched me like he could see right through me, and I wasn't sure how I felt about that. I felt naked every time I was around him, which wasn't very often. He was always with his crew. The Hell's Harlem Motorcycle Club. My late husband was a member of the same club but in a different chapter in another state. It seemed I couldn't get away from them, even if I tried.

Clearly, I had a type.

Arms suddenly wrapped around my middle.

I stiffened.

Sammy's eyes darkened, that scowl deepening on his face. Before I knew what he was doing, he was up and out of his seat and stomping toward me.

TWO

Amber

I WASN'T OVERLY SURE why I was surprised that Sammy reacted the way he did when another man touched me, but I was. Especially when Sammy pushed the guy away from me before I could even see who it was. Not that I needed to because no matter where I went and who I was with, a certain individual always showed up and I didn't need to actually see his face to know who it was.

But before I could stop him, Sammy had Will Hodges up against the wall. Will apparently thought it was funny and laughed.

"Something funny, fucker?" Sammy growled, pushing his forearm into Will's jugular.

"Yeah," Will grit out through clenched teeth. "Just think it's funny that you think she's actually worth it."

I glared at him. As much as I didn't actually want to stop Sammy, I went up to them and grabbed Sammy's arm. "Stop."

"Yeah, stop," Will mocked not attempting to push Sam away either.

Before they caused a scene, I pushed my way between them and shoved Sammy back, separating them. Just when I thought he was going to leave and not even bother, Sammy grabbed my hand, pulling me back toward him.

"What are you doing here, Will?" I demanded, ignoring the fact that my hand was in Sammy's, or that I was standing so close to him I could practically feel his heart beating in my own chest.

"I came to say hi," Will told me, running a hand through his longer black hair that hit just below his ears. His piercing green eyes locked with mine, his full lips pulling up into a smile that forced a small dimple to pop in his left cheek. A dimple that reminded me so much of his brother it was unreal. The two had been a year apart but you would never know. They were so damn similar in looks that you would think they were twins.

"What are you doing here?" I asked him, my breath catching as Sammy ran his hand up my forearm and enclosed his fingers around it, pulling me into him. That single movement made my hand bump his crotch. My mouth went dry as he pushed his pelvis into my touch, almost as if he was letting me know that every inch of him was mine if I wanted it. The movement had been so subtle, no one would even notice. But I did because I knew that Sammy didn't do anything by chance. He had motive and a reason for everything.

"I came here..." Will crossed his arms under his broad chest, his eyes flicking above my head. "You can leave."

Sammy grunted, leaning down to my ear. "Did you want his arms around you, Red?"

"No," I whispered.

"Did you want him to touch you?" he asked, his lips brushing over the shell of my ear.

I swallowed hard, shaking my head. "No, I did not want Will to touch me," I said, keeping my eyes locked with someone from my past who I really wished would leave me alone.

Will narrowed his brows at me. "She's lying."

"Doesn't matter if she's lying or not. You do not put your hands on someone without their permission."

I looked up at Sammy.

"Don't give me that look, Red." He gave my ass a pinch. "I know you want my hands on you."

I snorted. "But have I actually ever said that?"

"No, you haven't but you've never pushed me away either. Have you?"

He got me there. "True."

Sammy winked.

That single act made my heart flutter.

"You here for a reason?" Sammy asked Will, not looking away from me.

"Yeah, I'm here to talk to Red but I can see that she's clearly busy."

Will's words pulled my attention back to him.

"I'll see you soon." He nodded once and made his way toward the entrance of the club before disappearing out the double set of doors.

As soon as I could no longer see him, a breath I didn't realize I had been holding, left me.

"What was that about?"

My head whipped around, finding Sammy's brother coming toward us. I had never officially met him, but I knew of him. He had been coming to the club with Sam and a few of the other members of Hell's Harlem.

"Fucker touched Red without her permission," Sammy growled, running his finger along the side of my hand that was still touching his crotch.

Cyrus glanced at me before looking back at his brother. "You need to stop beating up every man who breathes the same air as she does."

I shifted on my feet. "I should go get ready for my shift."

"No." Sam hooked his pinky around mine. "Who is he to you?"

I sighed. "My brother-in-law."

"You're married?" Cyrus shook his head. "If you hurt my—"

"What? No. God, no. I'm not married anymore. My husband died if you must know, but I haven't even had this conversation with Sammy yet." I turned toward Sam. "I'm not married. I'm widowed."

"I'm sorry for your loss," he said gently.

My stomach twisted. "Don't be." I wanted to add that my late husband wasn't worth the sympathy but refrained and kept that thought to myself.

Sammy's eyes searched my face. "What does Will want with you then?"

"He was a biker. Was in the same crew as Aaron, my late husband, before he went rogue. I'm still friends with some of the guys, so Will tries to get me to give him information from time to time, but I always refuse. I know what happens to snitches. That's not me."

"I'm going to call Jaron. Fucker shouldn't be here without first notifying us." Cyrus went back to his table, leaving me alone with his brother.

Sammy's eyes burned into me, probably wondering if I was telling the truth or not. I was, but in all fairness to him, he didn't know me well, so I wouldn't blame him if he thought I wasn't.

"I can feel you staring at me," I murmured.

"I'm wondering if you're telling the truth or not," he said, taking the thought right out of my head.

"Trust me, Sam. I have no reason to lie. I married young because I was stupid and didn't know any better." A bitter taste filled my mouth, but I pushed those thoughts aside. I couldn't have this conversation with Sammy yet. If ever at all. "Aaron died four years ago and I've been single ever since." I was pushing thirty and had no intention of ever getting married again, let alone falling in love. "There's no one stopping us from fucking. You don't have to worry about another big bad biker cock blocking you." I patted his chest. "It's me. I'm choosing not to fuck you." When I took a step away from him, his hand wrapped around my upper arm.

"How close are you with Will?"

I looked up then, being met by dark eyes I had fantasized about for months. "Why?"

Sammy's brows narrowed. "Feeling defensive?"

I shoved out of his grip, pushing him back. "You know—"

LIBERATE US

Suddenly, Sammy wrapped a hand around my throat and pushed me back against the door that led to a storage room. He reached around me and opened the door, shoving me into the room.

"What the hell?" I demanded, pushing against his chest.

"Stop." He slammed me up against the door, closing it behind me.

"No, Sammy, you stop." I stepped down on his foot, pushing him back with all of my strength.

He stumbled back. "Amber."

I glared at him. "You can't put your hands on me whenever you feel like it. You can't demand things of me, talk down to me, treat me like you do, and expect—"

"Shut the fuck up." Sammy grabbed the collar of my shirt, pulling me toward him and shoving me up against the door. "I am not him. I am not your husband. I am not anyone you've ever been with."

I scoffed. "What, Sammy? Are you going to say you're better?"

His lips twitched. Was he actually going to smile for once? He removed his hand from my throat, brushing his thumb along the length of my jaw. "I'm not better. People come into our lives at different times for different reasons. They are not better. I am not better. I am just here."

"That's the thing." I swallowed hard, knowing my next words would probably change things. "You *are* better. I can't explain it, but you are."

Sammy opened his mouth to respond when a hard knock sounded on the door behind me.

"Red, Candace is looking for you," came a feminine voice from the other side.

"Coming," I called out. I turned to open the door when a hand slapped against it beside my head.

"Text me, Red." Sammy's mouth brushed along the shell of my ear causing a shiver to ripple down my spine.

"If I don't?" I threw at him.

"You will because I'm sick of fighting this. I made the first move by giving you my number. Now it's your turn." He stepped away from me and opened the door.

Before I could give him any sort of answer, I left the storage room and slowly blew out a breath.

As I neared the bar, Shawnee Drake placed a pitcher of beer on a tray resting on the bar top.

"For the guys?" I asked, slipping onto a stool.

"Yes." She placed a single bottle of beer on the bar top beside it. "For you."

I laughed, picking up the bottle and pulling back half of it before resting it back down. "Thank you."

"That bad?" She asked, blowing a loose strand of blond hair out of her eyes.

"I don't know anymore." I chanced a glance at Sammy. He was now sitting with his brother and a few other guys in a booth across the room. He looked up, his eyes meeting mine. He nodded once.

I gave him a small wave, wondering what we were doing. A part of me wondered why I was keeping him at arm's length and thought maybe I should just get it done and over with. Then another part knew. He could break me. Literally.

"Well, I can tell you that I've never seen him look at the other girls like he looks at you."

"I don't know." I shrugged, picking at the label on the bottle of beer I was nursing. "He's hard to read."

"He is." Shawnee's lips pulled into a thin line. "I don't know, baby girl, but just be careful. We don't need a repeat of...well...just be safe."

I nodded, giving her a small smile. "Thank you. I will." I slipped off the stool and grabbed the tray as Shawnee placed another pitcher on top of it, along with several mugs. "Wish me luck."

She laughed. "I'm not sure it's luck you need. Probably a little cock."

I snorted. "I'm not sure it's so little," I told her, remembering how Sammy had my hand pressed up against his pelvis earlier.

Shawnee threw her head back, a laugh booming through her. "God, I love you."

I winked, blew her a kiss, and headed toward Sammy's table when a dark shadow loomed over me.

I jumped, almost bumping into a large man.

"Sorry, pet, didn't mean to startle you."

I opened and closed my mouth, but no words came out. The guy was big. Around the same size as Sammy but older.

"Red, we need our beer," a deep voice called out from the table.

"Excuse me," I whispered, stepping around him and heading to the table of men.

When I reached the table Sammy was sitting at, I looked back at the mysterious stranger. He was at the bar, talking to Shawnee. She laughed every so often, flung her hair over her shoulder and smiled widely at him. Either she knew him, or she was just having fun flirting with him. I wasn't sure.

The older man looked my way over his shoulder, then winked.

My face heated at being caught staring.

"Red."

"Yeah yeah, hold your horses." I placed the tray of beer on the table, finding several pairs of eyes looking back at me, but the pair that set my blood on fire looked like he was ready to kill the man who spoke only a handful of words to me.

"You have your beer. Anything else I can get you?" I shouldn't have been so curt, but Sammy's staring had me unhinged.

"No thank you."

"I'm fine."

"And you?" I asked Sammy directly.

"Not sure you can give it to me," he answered.

I rolled my eyes. "Did you need anything else from the bar or kitchen?"

His lips twitched. "You on a platter would work for me."

I snorted. "In your dreams, buddy." Before we both got caught doing something in front of his friends at my place of work, I made my way back to the bar.

"You okay?" Shawnee asked, stuffing a piece of paper into the back pocket of her jean skirt.

"You got his number?" I looked around the room, not seeing the stranger anywhere.

"Maybe." She winked.

Before I could ask who he was, I saw Sammy stomping toward me. I braced myself, ready to face his wrath head-on and calling him out on his shit in front of his friends. When he stood a foot away from me, I lifted my hand. "Stop."

His brows narrowed but instead of listening to me, he took a step forward.

"Sammy." I backed up, my heart suddenly picking up speed. "I...I..."

He grabbed my hand, pulling me down the hall and away from the viewing eyes of his friends and the people I work with.

"Don't." I pulled my hand from his and lifted both, to ward him off.

"I'm not going to hurt you." He pulled me against him, pushing me back until I hit the wall.

"What if I want you to hurt me?" I murmured, the words leaving my lips before I could even stop them.

A low rumble left from somewhere deep in Sammy's chest. He pushed his pelvis into me, pressing all of him up against all of me.

"Everything I do will be because you want it." He lowered his mouth to the side of my throat. "I will push you. I will break you. I will bend you to my will." He licked and sucked at my skin. "Ask me why?"

"Why?" I whispered, shaking against him.

"Because." He gave my earlobe a gentle bite. "I know it's what you need." He kissed my cheek. "Text me, Red. I'm sick of waiting," he said, pushing away from me and taking a step back. He turned to head back down the hall, but I needed to know. I needed to know what the hell we were doing.

"Wait," I blurted.

He stopped, looking at me over his shoulder.

"What are we doing?"

"Nothing yet." When he didn't say any more and we only stood there, staring at each other, I couldn't help this need for him vibrating through me.

He tilted his head, staring at me.

"Sam, I…" I snapped my mouth shut, chewing my bottom lip.

"I know, Red." He turned and headed back down the hall from where we came.

I slid down the wall until I landed on my ass. He knew. He said he knew. But how could he know when I didn't even know what I was going to say. The handful of encounters I had with Sammy were already enough to knock me off my feet. Literally.

"Did you need me to get Corbin to kick them out?" Shawnee asked, her shoes coming into my line of sight.

"No." I shook my head. "I'm fine. Thank you."

"Are you sure? I don't give a shit if Sammy's attracted to you. You say the word and we can make them leave. And…"

I looked up then, being met by my friend's concerned stare. "Continue."

She sighed, pulled her long blond hair back into a ponytail, and tied an elastic around her hair. "I just worry about you. I don't want you to end up with another guy like Aaron."

I laughed then, rising to my full height. "Trust me. Sammy may be an ass, but he is nothing like Aaron."

"And how do you know that?" she asked, stepping in line with me as I neared the room that held change rooms, costumes and anything else the girls needed to spice up their routines whenever they danced.

I thought a moment. How *did* I know that? It wasn't like I knew Sammy really. I knew he was brooding, possessive and overbearing but I didn't really know much about him other than that. "I guess I don't actually know."

"He's made the other girls cry," Shawnee pointed out.

"I know." I pushed open the door that led to outfits of all different colors. "Have you heard from Gigi? She's supposed to be teaching us a new routine." Gigi Rodriguez was a former ballerina who hurt her knee after falling on it the wrong way. She taught us a routine a while ago that we did for Candace, our boss, and she loved it. A few tears were shed but she appreciated it nonetheless.

"Stop trying to change the subject."

"Listen." I turned toward my friend, someone who had been by my side since we were kids. "I'm attracted to Sammy. There I said it. What he wants is strictly just sex. No emotions. No commitments. Just pure sex."

Shawnee frowned. "Is that what you want?"

"It's all I can handle now, but Sammy is not Aaron. How do I know this? I don't know exactly but with Aaron, there were red flags almost instantly that I missed or ignored." I shrugged. "I was young and naïve. You know how shy and awkward I was growing up. Aaron was the first boy who noticed me, and I fell in love almost instantly." I sighed, not liking to think ill of the dead but the bastard got what he wanted. I never even had a chance to divorce him before he died. It was like that fact alone made it seem like he still had his clutches in me.

"Just be careful," Shawnee said gently, pulling me from my thoughts.

"I will. I'm going to organize this room finally like Candace asked, so you girls don't have to do it."

"And so you don't have to see a brooding biker?" Shawnee laughed lightly.

"Yeah."

She came up behind me, wrapping her arms around me from behind. "I love you, Amber, and I can understand being attracted to him but if he hurts you, I will gut him like a fucking fish. I stayed back and minded my own business with Aaron, but no more." She spun me around. "You hear me?"

I wrapped my arms around her, pulling her against me. "I hear you."

"Good." She gave me a squeeze and slapped my ass.

I yelped, jumping away from her. "Seriously."

She laughed. "I'll leave you alone. Just make sure to lock the door behind me."

"I will." I followed her to the door and closed it behind her once she left the room. Clicking the lock into place, I looked out at the room before me. As much as I thought I could distract myself from thoughts of Sammy, I knew that it would be almost impossible. I also knew that I would text him. Eventually. Maybe not tonight. Or even tomorrow night. But it would happen.

He knew it. I knew it.

It was only a matter of when.

THREE

Amber

IT HAD BEEN A few days since I'd seen Sammy and Will. Both of them got under my skin in very different ways. Sammy for the good and Will for the bad. Very bad. Every time I saw him, it reminded me of how stupid I'd been as a young girl. I wanted attention. I craved it. I didn't grow up with a father, so maybe that was part of my issue. Aaron wanted me. Will wanted me. Two guys. What more could a girl ask for? But the way they wanted me was unhealthy. I just didn't know it at the time.

Even though Aaron was no longer around, I felt like he was at times because both he and his brother had been so much alike. It was unreal. They weren't twins, but they were close, and their personalities were quite similar. But if I had to choose between both of them, as much as he had hurt me over the years, I would have chosen Aaron every single time. There was something off about Will. Always had been.

It was now Thursday evening, and I had the night off. I was sitting on my bed with my laptop in front of me, getting ready to video chat with my mom. It had been a routine we did often, at least twice a month, sometimes more if life allowed it.

Getting comfortable, I turned on the computer and waited for it to load. I sent my mom a quick text, letting her know that I was about to video call her. Once the laptop was booted up, I called her through Facebook and waited for her to answer.

When she finally did, I couldn't help but smile. My mom was more than just my mom. She was my best friend. Between her, Shawnee, and the other girls at Rouge, I had the best friends a girl could ever ask for. While I had known Shawnee the longest, I was close with all of them.

"Hi, baby girl," my mother greeted, pulling her long red hair back into a messy ponytail.

"Hi, Mummy.'" I sat back against the headboard and grabbed my glass of red wine off the nightstand. "How are you?"

"What's wrong?" she asked instead of answering my question and grabbing her own glass of wine. A deep frown appeared between her perfectly arched eyebrows. I swore the only way you would know that she was in her fifties was by the laugh lines at the corners of her eyes and mouth. Other than that, Andrea Bishop hardly had a gray hair on her head.

"You didn't answer my question," I pointed out, delaying my response as much as I could.

"I'm fine. Now tell me what's wrong?"

I sighed. "Have you been chatting with Emma again and getting her to read your Tarot cards?"

She laughed. "Nah. I just know my daughter. Is it a boy?"

"He's a man, mom." I rolled my eyes. "Definitely not a boy."

"So, tell me then, what's the issue?"

"I don't know." I took a sip of my wine, mulling over what I wanted to say. "Truth is, I have no idea. He's intense. He's also a biker."

Mom raised an eyebrow. "You sure that's a good idea?"

I groaned, throwing my head back against the headboard. "I don't know. The attraction is there. It's not like it was with Aaron. I think I only married him because he was the first guy who showed me any interest. It was just bad. He was bad for me. But Sammy...I think he's bad for me too but in a completely different way."

"What do you mean?"

"I don't know. I don't think he would ever hurt me. I haven't gotten any red flags with him like I did with Aaron. Sammy is just...well...he's Sammy." And Lord help me, but I loved the way he looked at me.

"When was the last time you had any fun?"

"You're my mom." I frowned. "You should be telling me to stay safe, keep out of trouble, and that Sammy is bad for me."

"Listen, I don't know who Sammy is, but I know you and I know Shawnee. Does she know about him?"

"Yeah. She does," I said, unsure as to what Mom was getting at.

"Okay, well I know that she would never let you end up with someone like Aaron again. You almost lost your friendship because of him." She lifted her hand when I went to speak. "I'm not done."

I sighed, taking a sip of wine to stop myself from saying something I would regret.

"I know what happened with Aaron wasn't your fault. You were young and in love."

"And dumb," I added, taking a bigger sip of wine that time.

"No, not dumb, just inexperienced."

"You're being nice, Mummy."

"Maybe." She gave me a small smile. "Is he nice to you? This Sammy?"

"He has his...yes, he's nice to me." There was no way I could tell her that the few times he had been a dick to me, turned me on. It was a kink not a lot of people understood. "As much of an ass as Sammy can be, he's still nothing like Aaron was." My late husband was nice in the beginning but boy, did he ever have me fooled. At least with Sammy, I knew where I stood with him. He wanted sex. End of.

"That's good at least."

Mom and I continued chatting for another hour. I found out she was seeing someone too but never gave me his name. She wanted to make sure there was something there before giving me any information about him. She also wanted to make sure he was worthy of meeting her daughter.

A half hour later, I was getting ready to hang up with my mom when Sammy's words from the other day rang into my head. He was sick of waiting. Well so was I.

I sent him a quick text, not even re-reading what I had written, knowing I probably sounded nervous or worse. Desperate.

"Did you text him?" Mom asked, trying to pour wine into her glass when the bottle was clearly empty.

I laughed as she pouted. "I did."

"Good girl. You go enjoy him and I'm going to continue getting drunk by myself."

I blew her a kiss. We said our goodbyes and I told her I would see her soon, when I would drive up to spend a week with her. I couldn't wait to see her but for now, I would do what she suggested and have some fun.

When my phone buzzed, I knew that this would be it and my world was about to change. I just wasn't sure if it would be for the better.

(Sammy)

I never wanted her. Not in the way one would think. She deserved better. Far better than someone like me. I was angry. Hated mostly everyone around me except for a select few and even then, their happiness pissed me off most days.

I was elated for them. I really was. But I didn't have that same happiness. Not that I went out looking for it or anything.

Amber Bishop was the exception. She was my undoing. She broke down the walls I had spent years building. I masked my pain with humor and crude remarks, but she saw right through me. Even when I was mean to her, she would cross her arms under her chest and stare me down. Every time I told her exactly what was on my mind, whether it be nice or not, her cheeks would turn a nice shade of red and her eyes would darken. My words, no matter how hurtful or to the point they were, turned her on. Because she knew I didn't mean them. Which was the truth.

The things I was into and the women I had sex with bordered on the more extreme version of kink. But I made sure it was safe, sane, and consensual. Always.

If they wanted me to slap them around, bruise them, or mark them up, as long as an agreed upon safeword was used if it got to be too much for them, I was game. But unfortunately, a lot, if not most, women couldn't handle me. But I knew that Amber could. Part of that scared me and was probably why I was avoiding the mere idea of fucking her.

I had spent months skirting around that shit. Of finally being with her like I knew both of us wanted. Did I have feelings for her like my brother accused me of having? I wasn't sure, but at the moment I didn't care. What I did care about was what her soaking wet pussy felt like as it squeezed a release out of my dick. That was the only thing that mattered at the moment. The rest could wait because again, it didn't matter. Feelings got people hurt. Emotions had people killed. My parents were no exception. Was it the reason I had closed my heart off to everyone? Maybe. I didn't know. But if Amber kept pushing, I knew, because I wasn't stupid, I could fall for her. She would then leave me like my mom left my dad. I would break. Just like he had. I knew it wasn't exactly the same since my mom had been killed, but I couldn't handle going through what my dad did. And then he went off and got himself killed too.

It didn't help. None of it helped.

My phone took that moment to ding. I braced myself, expecting some sort of bad news like we seemed to have been getting for what felt like forever, when my eyes moved across the small screen. My dick lengthened, threatening to burst against the zipper of my jeans.

Red: If you're bored and want to come over, you can. Don't feel like you have to, but my door is always open. Or it will be once you get here.

I raised an eyebrow. Even in her text, she seemed nervous.

A second text came in which included her address.

Shoving my phone in my pocket, I flicked the smoke to the ground and butted it out with my boot.

Straddling my bike, I drove the distance it took to get to Amber's apartment. My body stirred the closer I got. These feelings were new for me. I had never sought out a woman, gone to her apartment, or even wanted to be friends with her instead of just fucking. But unfortunately for me, my big mouth got in the way most of the time and I had no idea how to speak to Amber. She had me flustered. She unraveled me. Completely and utterly, I was a mess. Because of her. I said shit that would usually get me slapped, but she gave it right back to me instead. But I found that I wanted her hands on me. It was something I never wanted before. Most of the women I had been with never even had a chance to touch me. But they never complained when they limped away from my bed.

When Amber's apartment building came into view, I kicked up the throttle and sped toward the pussy I had been craving for months. Nothing curbed this want, this *need*. And I knew nothing would until I got exactly what I wanted.

Once I finally reached her apartment, I pulled into the large driveway, parked in some empty random spot, not caring in the least if it was meant for someone who lived there. If I got a ticket or towed, it would be worth it as long as I had a taste of Amber.

I needed her to beg.

I needed her to scream.

But most of all, I needed her to look at me like I was the only one who mattered.

Jogging to the front door, I entered the building, searched her name on the list of residents who lived there, and stabbed the button once I found her.

"Hello?" came her reply, seconds later.

"Let me in," I demanded, my voice curt.

A buzz sounded, the lock clicking free.

Get ready, Red, I'm coming for you and once I've had you, I'm never letting you go.

FOUR

Amber

I WASN'T ACTUALLY EXPECTING Sammy to come over. It wasn't like he had ever given me any indication that he wanted more out of whatever it was we were doing. Not until recently anyway. At first, I thought he hated me. I thought maybe he had known Aaron and Will and didn't like the fact that I had taken up stripping to make ends meet. But when Will approached me and I realized that they, in fact, did not know each other, I figured there was more to it than that. Something I didn't know but was sure about to find out.

It was only sex. It would be only sex with Sammy. It was something that I realized I needed at the moment. I had already been married once. I didn't need hearts and flowers, and I definitely didn't need a relationship. Having a few flings since my husband died should have curbed the itch, but it didn't. Then I met Sammy so many months ago and no one else even came close to what I wanted. There was something about him I craved. There was a darkness to him I wanted to wrap myself up in. I was always drawn to the darker side of sex, but Aaron was having none of it and made me feel like a freak instead. So, I shoved those fantasies aside. Until now.

Besides giving me his phone number, Sammy never hinted, never said more than a handful of words to me either. Not until just the other day. My body still burned from the couple of times he had his hands on me. How he said he wouldn't hurt me. Maybe he was right, but it didn't mean I couldn't be cautious just the same.

But now he was here all because I sent him a booty text. God, what the hell was wrong with me?

I didn't have long to stew when a hard knock sounded on the door. It made my heart jump to my throat. Even his knocks had attitude.

Taking a deep breath, I headed to the door and clicked the deadbolt free.

The door opened before I had a chance to open it myself.

Sammy forced his way into my apartment, much like he had forced his way into my life months ago. He was an asshole, but I couldn't help the way my body reacted to him. It had been so long since I had spent the night with a man. Maybe that was why my body wanted him before my brain could catch up. Either way, while Sammy's eyes roamed down the length of my body, I couldn't help but sway toward him.

His eyes snapped to mine, a cheeky grin spreading on his handsome face.

Giving myself a shake, I swallowed hard and started backing up. "Do you want a drink?"

He shut the door, clicking all of the locks back into place. When he was done, he looked at me over his shoulder, his eyes once again, roaming down the length of me.

I took another step back.

He followed, not answering my question and zeroing in on me like a predator about to catch his prey. Just the mere idea of him ripping me apart, sent a shiver down my spine.

"Why now?" I asked, needing to know since we had been going back and forth for months. Maybe even longer.

"Why not now?" he asked, taking another step toward me.

"Because it's not like you've hinted at anything. I've tried talking to you, being your friend, and you've been nothing but an asshole this whole time." I jumped when I backed up into the edge of the dining room table.

Sammy smirked, his dark eyes locking with mine. "You calling me out on my shit, Red? It seems to me that you haven't hinted either. I made the first move by giving you my phone number. The rest was on you."

"It was about damn time." I tried backing up even more but with the table blocking me, I ended up sitting on the edge, and he got closer to me.

"Really?" He chuckled, closing the distance between us. "Were you impatiently waiting for my cock?" He placed his hands on the table at either side of me, his mouth mere inches from mine. A little closer and I could finally feel what his kisses were like. I bet they were deep, consuming, and aggressive.

His dark eyes twinkled. With him being this close, I could see some gray in his light beard.

His eyes dropped to my mouth, something flashing in the dark orbs, but much to my dismay he only leaned down toward my ear. "Tell me how much you've wanted my cock inside of you this whole time."

I snorted, faking a yawn. "Seriously, is this how you get all the ladies to drop their panties for you?"

He leaned back, staring at me. "Careful, Red."

I placed my hands against his chest. For half a second, all I could do was picture him naked but that was quickly replaced by the brat in me who wanted to play with him. Of course, I had wanted his cock inside of me this whole time, but I also wasn't one to drop to my knees so quickly either. If my late husband taught me one thing, it was to be strong and sure of myself. Even though most times I didn't feel that way.

"What do you want?" Sammy asked me.

"You know what I want,' I said softly. but did he? Did he actually know what I wanted? After all of this time, after years of going through each day because I had to and there was nothing better for me to do, did Sammy actually truly know what I wanted? Because if he did, I hoped he would tell me because I sure as hell had no idea.

"Tell me, Red." His mouth brushed along the shell of my ear. "Tell me if you want my cock deep inside you. Tell me if you want my mouth on you. Licking you. Sucking that little clit until you squirm and cream all over my face. Tell me if you want me to fuck your beautiful tight ass. Tell. Me." He growled those last two words, and I swore it turned me on more to hear him become unraveled.

"And if I don't want all of that?" I turned my head, our lips lightly brushing against each other.

Sammy stiffened, his handsome face suddenly morphing into a deep scowl. He wrapped his fingers around my throat. "No. Kissing," he growled, pulling me against him and off the edge of the table.

I swallowed hard at the mere intensity rolling off of him. "What's wrong, Sammy? Afraid you'll fall in love with me?" I knew my mouth got away from me sometimes, but this man needed to learn that he wasn't always in control.

Before I could say anything else, Sammy spun me around and bent me over the table. He pushed his arm against the back of my neck, pinning me down. "I would be very careful if I were you."

"You know, threatening the woman you're about to fuck doesn't make you more of a man."

"Oh my beautiful Red, I'm going to have so much fun tearing you apart," he murmured, licking along the shell of my ear.

I shivered at the threat hidden beneath his deep voice.

"You like that," he murmured, keeping his arm against the back of my neck. "Me threatening you. Me promising you hours of pleasure." A swat landed against my ass.

I gasped.

"I wonder how much pain you like." His palm landed against my ass cheek once again. "Like that, baby?"

"Yes," I whispered, figuring there was no point in denying it.

"Do you know what a safeword is?" he asked, running a hand down the side of my body.

"I think so." Truth was, I *did* know what a safeword was, but I didn't want to scare him away with how much I knew about the BDSM lifestyle before I got what I wanted from him.

"Choose one and if you use it, everything stops. I'll leave and you'll never see me again." His fingers slowly slid up the back of my thigh. "Choose a word, Red."

"What's your middle name?" I asked, my voice trembling.

"Tyler."

"Okay." I took a deep breath. "I choose Tyler as my safeword."

His fingers stopped in their path. "You sure about that?"

I swallowed hard. "Y-Yes."

He released my neck, running his hands beneath my tank top and cupping my breasts. "You feel fucking good." His kissed the spot behind my ear. "So good. I'm more of an ass man but with your tits...yeah, I could get used to these."

My heart sped up, his calloused fingers pinching my nipples.

He pushed the tank top up the length of my body, slipping it up and over my head before sliding it up my arms. Cool air washed over my naked skin, sending a flush of goosebumps erupting along my skin.

His mouth found the spot at the base my neck. When his lips were replaced by his teeth and he bit down, a shuddered breath left me. "Is there anything you're not into? Name-calling, being degraded, slapped...things like that. I need to know, Red."

I swallowed hard, my face heating as he listed things I had craved for years. "I'm willing to try anything at least once. Within reason of course. But no sharing. That's definitely a hard limit."

"Interesting that you know what hard limits are." He pinched my nipples, pushing his waist into the seat of my ass. "We can talk about that later but trust me, I'm not into sharing. I'm a possessive fuck and prefer to keep my woman all to myself."

A breath I didn't realize I had been holding, left me. I never knew what he was into, but I had seen women throw themselves at him. I just assumed he took them up on their offer. The fact that he actually asked me what I didn't like, broke down a wall I had built around myself. To communicate your desires with someone, even if they were a stranger for the most part, made me realize that maybe not all men were like Aaron.

"If I do something and you don't like it, tell me, Red." In a rough move, Sammy tied my tank top around my wrists. "You're going to be sore tomorrow."

A breathless laugh left me. "You're pretty sure of yourself."

"Nope." He chuckled. "But I do know my way around a woman's body and yours is no different."

I pushed up onto my elbows, looking at him over my shoulder. "Trying to turn me on by talking about the other women you've been with? Such a charmer, Sammy."

His dark eyes snapped to mine. Before I knew what was happening, his hand was in my hair. He pulled, whipping my head back at an odd angle. "You're a brat, my Little Red."

My body burned when he referred to me as *his*, but I laughed anyway, tried to play it cool, and pushed back into him. The feel of the thick bulge behind his jeans, sent a flutter of heat rushing through me. "Seems it turns you on when I don't give in right away. Doesn't it?"

Sammy didn't respond. He released my hair and hooked his fingers into the waist of my shorts. In a rough move, he ripped them down my legs, lowering to his knees behind me.

"Safeword."

I grinned. "Tyler."

He grabbed handfuls of my ass and winked.

(Sammy)

The brat in her turned the Dom in me on. Just like my brother, I had spent years looking for the perfect sub. Our lifestyle wasn't commonly known. My brother and I would go to a BDSM club a few hours away only to come home empty-handed. It never helped. This want. This need. This obsession to get that perfect pet.

But with Amber waiting, watching, allowing me that moment to take control of her pleasure and yet, still calling me out, I knew

LIBERATE US

I found the brat I needed. Even if it was just for tonight. I found that I wanted to test her limits and see how far I could take things.

"Sam."

The sound of my name snapped me out of it.

Lowering to the floor behind her, I grabbed her hips and pulled her toward my face in a rough move.

I had wanted to savor her, smell every inch of her but my mouth had watered at the sight of her. Her pink pussy glistened, begging me for everything I could give her.

When her cunt came into contact with my face, a growl left me.

She gasped, arching her back like a cat.

Hooking my arms around her legs, I lifted her onto her toes.

I bit and sucked, flicked and fucked her with my tongue. The sweet acidic flavor made my taste buds tingle.

Her moans and whimpers sounded around me, making me eat at her harder.

Slipping my finger between the crack of her ass, I ran the tip back and forth over that tight little ring I would eventually fuck.

"Sammy," she panted, rocking against me.

Pulling her harder against my face, I bent her over.

Her cries of pleasure became louder. Her body shook, her skin coating with a light sheen of sweat.

Thrusting a finger into her pussy, I coated it with her juices and ran it over the tight little hole between the cheeks of her ass.

She shivered, pushing back into me.

Wrapping my other arm around her thighs, I slid my finger back down to her soaked cunt and shoved it into her body. Flicking my tongue back and forth over her swollen clit, I hummed against her hot center.

"Fuck," I snarled against her pussy. "You taste like sin." I licked her all over, biting and nipping at her hot center. Shoving a second finger into her, I swallowed the surge of wetness leaving her.

"God, that feels good." Her thighs trembled, soft mewls leaving her when her breathing picked up.

When my name left her lips on a harsh scream, I growled against her pussy.

"Please," she whined.

Licking up the length of her center, I nipped her ass and thrust my tongue into the tight rim.

She gasped, pushing her waist into me.

Giving her one final lick, I brushed my mouth up her spine, making sure to wipe the lingering juices on my lips, along her skin.

When I was standing behind her, I fisted her hair. "Get ready, Little Red." I undid my belt buckle. "We're about to break the fucking table."

(Amber)

I shivered at his threat. Words that promised me endless hours of pleasure. I knew he was cocky for a reason. Hell, I had heard it from other women and was always left feeling jealous. Maybe he was making his rounds through all of us. Unless they were lying. I couldn't be sure. Either way, rumors were that he was good and knew how to use his dick.

Sammy bent over me, capturing my hair in his hand. "What are you thinking about, Red? Wanting to use that safeword already?"

I laughed. "Hardly."

"Then tell me," he murmured against my ear.

"Just thinking how you've gone through a lot of women I know." I probably shouldn't have been talking about this before things got even better, but he asked.

"They wish." He grunted. "Trust me, babe. I don't fuck where I drink."

"I don't know what that—" A hard swat landed against my ass, sucking all the air from my lungs.

"It means that I haven't been through all of your friends, Amber. It means that you are actually the only woman at Rouge that I'm about to fuck. The only one I want to fuck."

"Why all those rumors then? Why make the girls cry?"

His hand tightened in my hair, pulling my head back. "We gonna talk about the rumors all night or are you going to shut the fuck up and let me do what I know you want me to do?"

"Depends."

"On what?" He slipped a hand between my legs, running his fingers over my hot center.

I shivered at the gentle contact coming from a man like him. "Tell me why you go to the club all the time then. If you're not there looking to hook up with any of the women, you're there for another reason."

The sound of a tinfoil package being torn open, sent a shiver down my spine. "Why the hell does it matter?"

"Because, if you want my pussy—"

Sammy slammed into me, forcing a gasp from my mouth.

"Oh." I shook against him. "Fuck."

"You were saying?" He pulled my head back, slamming his pelvis against me. The thrusts were rough, bordering on violent, as he fucked me against my table.

My arms shook, my legs trembled at the brutal force of his cock thrusting in and out of me. He didn't even give me a chance to get used to his size. I knew he was big but now that he was inside of me, it felt like he was trying to split me in half.

"To answer your question, my Little Red." His teeth sunk into my throat. "I go to Rouge to see you. Besides doing club business with my brothers, I go to make sure you're safe and that you're not dancing. The girls cry because they're sad that they don't get my cock."

I couldn't believe his words. All this time.

"I know I'm an asshole, but I also know that it turns you on whenever I'm a dick to you." His hand moved from my hair to my mouth. He slipped his fingers between my lips, holding my head in place as his hips picked up speed. His fingers slid deeper down the back of my tongue, making me gag, which earned me a grunt. "I'm also learning rather quickly that you like when I'm rough with you." He pulled all the way out of me, shoving me face first against the table. "Isn't that right?" he asked, thrusting all of his inches back into me.

"Yes," I cried out, my words muffled by his fingers. "God, yes."

Sammy removed his fingers from my mouth, wrapped them around my throat, and bent over me.

"Please." I couldn't help but beg. The pleasure rushing through me was nothing like I had ever felt before. The tip of him hit that special spot inside me that had never been hit before. No matter how many guys I had been with.

Sammy ran his hands down my sides and back up before cupping my breasts. He grunted, slamming into me in rough moves.

"God, I can't," I whimpered, lifting onto my elbows.

He pushed into me as deep as my body would allow, forcing the table to move across the floor.

"Harder," I heard myself say.

A dark chuckle left him. He grabbed my hips, kicked my legs apart even more, and thrust hard and deep.

"Yes," I cried out. "Fuck."

"You like that." He grabbed my hair, pulling me upright and back against him. "Me fucking you like a little slut." He removed my tank top from around my wrists before cupping my throat. "So fucking tight, baby," he murmured in my ear. "So tight. You're going to suck all the cum from my body."

"Fuck me harder, Sam," I panted, needing the pain he promised.

With his nose pressed against my cheek, his hot breath fanned over the side of my face. He reached between us, smacking his palm across my ass. The sharp pain only heightened this need for him.

"You're my little brat, aren't you?" he murmured, ripping my head back even more.

"Yes." I reached behind me, needing to touch some part of him. He was still fully clothed, minus his dick which was currently inside of me. I latched on to his jeans, pulling him closer.

"Fuck, baby, you're going to make me come so damn hard, all that cream is going to break the condom."

A laugh left me. "God, so dirty."

He chuckled.

I realized then that it was a sound I liked. There was a side to Sammy that he never shared with anyone. He didn't smile or laugh often but when he did, it reached a part of me that no other man had ever been able to reach. Especially not since my late husband passed.

He bent over me, his hips stopping. His teeth found my shoulder, his tongue licking along the sting of his bite. He towered over me, covering my hands with his and pushing into me as far as my body would allow him. The movements picked up, forcing the table to scratch along the floor until it hit the wall. My hips were pressed up against the edge and I could already feel bruises forming, but I didn't care. Not in the least.

"Harder, Sammy," I begged. "Break my fucking table."

He grunted his approval, his lips brushing along the shell of my ear. His hips powered forward and back, tearing into a part of my body that hadn't been used in so long besides my own touch.

"If I get to be too much for you, tell me," he whispered in my ear. That was the final warning he gave before he shoved his fingers into my mouth. His index and middle fingers hooked into my cheeks, forcing my mouth open wide.

My breathing came out in short quick pants, drool dripped down my chin, but I found that it only turned me on even more.

Pulling his fingers from my mouth, he wrapped his arm around my chest and held me tightly against him. It was so tight, it was like he was trying to show me that I was safe with him. He rolled his hips, back and forth, side to side.

My whimpers turned into moans, my legs shaking at the brutal force of him fucking me. "Harder," I demanded, needing that delicious pain of being fucked good and hard.

He fisted my hair, holding my head in place. Hooking his other hand around my thigh, he lifted my knee onto the table, opening me even more to him.

Sammy stopped, pushing into me as far as my body would allow. With his free hand, he slipped his fingers into my pussy alongside his cock.

I swallowed a gasp at being stretched even wider.

"Hmm…" He licked up the side of my face, his hand in my hair, tightening. His fingers thrust into me once, twice, before he pulled them out of me and ran them over the tight hole between the cheeks of my ass. Instead of giving me a chance to take a breath, he shoved them into me.

I cried out, my eyes rolling into the back of my head.

Sam thrust his fingers in and out of my ass and began picking up speed with his hips. He powered forward and back. My body felt full, the slight pain of parts of him being in both my pussy and ass, ignited this yearning for more.

"God," I whispered, a shiver trembling through my body.

Sammy slipped from my heat, keeping a firm grip on my hair. He pulled his fingers from my body and began running his hand along my swollen center.

I moaned, pushing back into his touch.

His palm moved quickly back and forth over my swollen clit. "Come for me." He pulled back, landing a hard slap against my center.

A sharp gasp left me as the slice of pain forced my eyes open.

"What the fuck did I say?" he growled, slapping me again.

"Make me," I whined. "God, make me, please make me come."

"Do it." He ripped my head back, slapping his palm over and over against my throbbing clit.

I arched into his swings, needing more, needing him. "Yes, fucking hell." A release rushed through me, liquid spraying from my body while I screamed.

"That's it, my little slut." He thrust his cock back into me and wrapped his arms around my head. "Hold on, baby." He kissed my cheek. "I'm about to bruise your cunt."

FIVE

Amber

I WOKE GOD ONLY knew when.

When I rolled onto my back, every muscle and cell in my body screamed with protest. I had never been used like that before. I didn't even remember going to bed. Opening my eyes slowly, I blinked past the early morning light streaming in through my bedroom window and rolled back onto my stomach.

I was still naked, remnants from the night before coated on my skin. I must have passed out at some point, but I still didn't remember putting myself to bed. Unless Sammy did.

My thoughts traveled back to the night before.

Pleasure and pain mixed as one.

After Sammy finally had his own release, I still couldn't get over the fact that he had moaned my name.

"Fuck, Amber. So damn good." His body shook behind me, his cock swelling and spilling his pleasure into the condom.

Before I had a chance to even comment or say anything at all, he flipped me onto my back and dove his head between my legs.

I cried out, the scratchiness of his beard tickling my inner thighs.

He lifted his head, releasing me with a wet smack, then licked and sucked up the length of my body. His lips closed around my nipple, his teeth sinking into the budding peak.

I inhaled a sharp gasp, arching under him.

Sammy lifted his head, his dark eyes locking with mine. Much to my surprise, his palm connected with my face at the same time he shoved two fingers into me.

I whimpered, my back bowing off the table. He slapped my cheek again before wrapping his long fingers around my throat and finishing what he started.

I groaned into my pillow, my body burning as memories of the night before rushed through me. I quickly learned that he could go for hours and wasn't selfish. In the least. Not like Aaron. Not that I could ever compare them, but Aaron only made sure he got his own release and didn't care about my pleasure at all. With Sammy, he gave me more pleasure than I could ever handle. I had never known that I liked to be slapped. Spanked on the ass sure, but slapped in the face? My core clenched at the thought. I wasn't sure how Sam even knew I would like it. Unless he just took that when I told him I didn't like sharing but would try anything else at least once, literally. He tested my limits, but I had a feeling that I hadn't experienced half of what he had to offer.

I had begged him to stop at one point because I couldn't handle any more and he only muttered 'safeword' against my pussy. But I never used it because I didn't want him to stop and disappear from my life, like he originally threatened. So, I took what he gave me and embraced his rough mouth between my legs until he had me coming at least three times before he finally stopped.

I still couldn't believe I had spent the night before with him, but since we got what we both wanted, it was time to move on. Or that was what I was trying to tell myself anyway. Truth was, I wanted more. I wanted him.

Sammy Butcher officially ruined me for other men.

Rising to my elbows, I reached for my phone to see if I had any new emails or text messages and saw a text from Sammy.

Knowing him, he was probably thanking me for the fuck, but when I opened his message and my eyes moved along the words, I was not expecting to read what I did.

Sammy: I left a bottle of water and some pain meds with it on your nightstand, since I imagine you're sore.

He was right. I *was* sore. My eyes flicked to my nightstand, finding the water and two little pills sitting beside it. But where did he get them from? I didn't have a whole lot in my medicine cabinet, so I wasn't sure where he got the pills from. And how the hell could he be rough one moment and thoughtful the next?

Before I could stop myself, I called him.

"Miss my cock already?" came his deep reply that sent a shiver racing over every inch of me.

"Unlikely," I threw back at him.

He chuckled. "What's up?"

"Where did you find pain meds?"

"I knocked on one of your neighbor's doors," he said, like it was the most obvious answer.

Putting my phone on speaker, I placed it on the bed and went to my dresser. "Why would you do that?" I glanced at the clock. "It's not even eight in the morning."

"And? You needed meds and you have none in your place, so I had to get them somehow. By the way, why don't you have any meds?"

"Because they're expensive if you must know." I rummaged through my dresser for clean pajamas. "Apparently, it's hard to make good money by keeping your clothes on."

"Yeah, let's keep it that way," he grumbled.

"Why would you get me meds, Sam?"

"Because I knew you were going to be sore and before you say anything, it's not me being cocky. It's me being observant and learning your body. I also gave you multiple orgasms and by the way you creamed all over my cock and face, I imagine it's been a while for you." As soon as those words left his mouth, I heard a cough in the background.

"Where are you?"

"At the pharmacy."

I shook my head, unable to believe that he could talk so openly about sex like that. And in public too. "You don't embarrass easily, do you?"

He grunted. "It's just sex, babe. I think it would make things a whole hell of a lot easier for most people if they talked about it more."

"True." It never helped Aaron and me but that was in the past and there was nothing I could do about it now, so all I could do was learn from it.

"Gotta go, Red, I'll be there in ten."

Before I could ask why he was coming back over, the call disconnected. He would be here? He was coming back? I thought he fucked me, put me to bed, and left after, then move on?

I quickly took a shower and put on pajama shorts and a tank top. It didn't leave much to the imagination, but it wasn't like Sammy hadn't seen me naked already, so what was the point? Besides, the shorts were gray and soft, and the tank top was black and loose but also soft to the touch as well. They were comfortable and that was all I wanted.

I brushed my teeth, needing to make myself look at least somewhat presentable.

As I was throwing my long wavy red hair up into a messy bun, the intercom buzzed.

I went up to it and pressed the button. "Yeah."

"Let me in," Sammy demanded.

I pressed another button, bracing myself for whatever his attitude would be this morning and finished fixing my hair so it was off the back of my neck. Once it was up and I was satisfied the elastic could hold all of my hair, a hard knock sounded on the door.

I went to the door, checked the peephole to make sure it was, in fact, him and opened it.

He stood there in different clothes, holding a plastic bag and a cup of coffee.

"What are you doing back here?" I asked, stepping to the side so he could enter.

"These are for you," he said, handing me the bag and coffee instead of answering my question. "I didn't know what you took, so it's just black."

"Oh." I held the bag and coffee in one hand while I closed and locked the door. "Thank you but you didn't have to do this." I went to the dining room to place the coffee and bag on top of the table when I noticed that it was leaning on its side. "I guess we did break the table," I said, more to myself.

"I told you we would," Sammy said, coming up to my side. He took the bag from me and went into the kitchen.

I followed him.

"I'll fix your table and if it can't be fixed, I'll buy you a new one." He leaned against the counter, crossing his arms under his chest. His eyes roamed down the length of me, reminding me that I didn't have much on. "Next time, we're breaking your fucking bed."

"Next time?" I asked, taking a sip of the coffee, hope dancing inside of me. I went up to the counter to root through the bag.

Sammy remained close, turning toward me. "You thought I'd fuck you and leave?"

"You did leave, did you not? You're wearing different clothes." When I looked in the bag, my eyes widened.

"I slept beside you after I put you in bed. I eventually woke up because I couldn't sleep anymore. I saw you didn't have any pain meds, so I knocked on one of your neighbor's doors, got what I needed, and put them on your nightstand. After that, I went home to shower and change. I would have been back sooner, but traffic was shit."

"I..." I pulled out a bottle of Tylenol, a box of Band Aids, along with a box of tampons and a box of pads. "You did this. For me?"

"Yes. You didn't have anything in your medicine cabinet. Speaking of, did you take the meds?"

"Uh...no. I was kind of distracted by you being nice."

He mumbled a curse, pushed away from the counter, and left the kitchen.

While I went through the bag, I couldn't help the flutter in my stomach over how nice this was of him. It was thoughtful and while most would think it was lame, it was the sweetest thing a guy had ever done for me.

"Take these."

I jumped when Sammy stepped up behind me, holding his hand out in front of me. I took the two little pills sitting in the palm of his hand and stuck them between my lips.

"Here." He handed me a bottle of water.

I took a sip, swallowed the pills, and opened my mouth, sticking out my tongue. "Ahhh. Happy?"

He fisted my hair, tugging my head back.

I whimpered at the odd angle, my body flushing with heat.

"Next time I ask you to do something, it would bode well for you if you listened," he murmured in my ear.

"And if I don't?" I threw back at him.

"I don't think your ass will like the things I have planned for it if you don't in fact listen to me." He kissed my cheek and released my hair roughly. "You're also lucky that I like little brats who defy me."

"Well, you're in luck, Sammy," I said, winking.

"Drink your coffee." He shook his head. "I'll make breakfast."

"You don't have to." I took the bag from the counter. "Thank you for buying these things for me. You didn't have to do that either."

"I wanted to, and I also want to cook you breakfast." Sammy went to the fridge and pulled out a carton of eggs.

"Stop, Sam. Seriously." I grabbed the eggs from him. "If you want to fuck me again, just tell me, but you don't have to cook me breakfast."

"I don't know who the fuck hurt you but when I say I'm going to do something, I mean it. I said I was going to fuck you. I did. I said I was going to break your table. I did. Now I said I'm going to cook breakfast. Which…" He ripped the carton of eggs from my hand. "I'm about to do."

"Why?" I appreciated him being nice but there had to be an ulterior motive behind his actions.

"Because I'm hungry. We worked up an appetite last night and I haven't eaten anything besides your pussy in twelve hours. So, forgive me for wanting some food."

I searched his face, looking for a sign, an indication that there was another plan behind his being nice, but I couldn't find anything. I couldn't read him, and I wasn't sure how I felt about that.

"Listen." His brows narrowed. "I don't have an ulterior motive. Do I want to fuck you again? Yes. Will I fuck you again? Definitely yes. My only motive is to feed you, fuck, shower, fuck again, and maybe if you let me, get to know you a bit more too. Is all of that fine with you?" he asked, his voice curt and to the point.

I only nodded because what the hell could I even say to all of that?

"Good. Now that we got that out of the way, how do you take your eggs?"

(Sammy)

She had me unraveled. She had me feeling things I never thought my cold, closed off heart could ever feel. And when she defied me like a little brat, it stirred every cell in my body. I wanted to throw her over my knee and spank her ass, fuck her within an inch of her life, and then I wanted to hold her and comfort her after. Was this how my brother felt? We never really talked about our relationships or the women we fucked, but now that he had found the love of his life, I wondered if maybe I should ask him.

After I cooked Red breakfast, we were sitting in her living room, since we broke the table and all, and ate in silence. She was lucky she behaved or else I would have had her at my feet, eating out of a bowl off the ground. Some would think it was degrading, hell, most probably did, but we all had our own things we were into. Our own personal kinks. As long as no animals or children were involved and everyone was a consenting adult, I didn't give a shit what you were into.

When I had asked her the night before what she didn't like so I knew what not to do, her words opened up something in me. The fact that she was willing to try anything, within reason, at least once, was exciting. Besides sharing, and thank fuck for that. A lot of people didn't want to be called names or slapped. Some would even consider it a form of abuse. And it was, if it was with the wrong person. Sure, Amber and I didn't know each other completely and we just started sleeping together, but I needed her to trust that I wouldn't hurt her. Spank and slap her around, sure, but that was it. I took safewords seriously and if she would have used it, I would have stopped. Maybe not leave like I had said, but I definitely would have stopped doing what I was doing so we could talk about it.

Once I was done my food, I drank my orange juice and watched her over the rim of the glass. The outfit she was wearing left little to the imagination. The fact she felt comfortable enough to wear it around me, sparked this need for her even more. The gray shorts were short, showcasing her long toned legs. The black tank top was loose, but I could still see she wasn't wearing a bra with the way her tits swayed when she moved.

"You're staring, Sam," she mumbled, stabbing at the food on her plate.

She had also been the only woman who ever called me Sam. Some tried calling me by my full name, but it never ended well for them. My mother had been the only one who called me Samson. No one else deserved to let that name leave their lips and always got my fist in their face if they were a guy or my wrath if they were a woman.

Letting my eyes roam back down the length of Amber, I mentally patted my own back when she shifted in her spot on the couch.

"Sammy."

My eyes snapped to hers. "What?"

"I can feel you staring and it's distracting."

"Did you date at all after your husband died?" I asked, needing to get to know her more. I needed to find out why after all of these months, we were finally fucking. I needed to find out everything I could about the woman I had become celibate for and was beyond obsessed with.

"Uh..." She glanced my way. "No. Not really." She looked back down at her plate, moving the eggs around with her fork. I learned that we had something in common when it came to eggs. We didn't overly care how they were cooked. As long as they were in fact cooked and not snotty. I had laughed at the face she had made and ever since that moment, even though it had been something small, I could feel a wall breaking down between us.

"I spent some time having one-night stands," she continued. "But I found that guys aren't really appreciative of a woman who has more sex than them."

"What happened?" I asked, the hackles on the back of my neck raising that she had issues with other men she fucked.

"Nothing really. Not compared to...well...it doesn't matter." She took a breath. "A couple of them came to Rouge and saw me dancing. They didn't like that, called me names and tried making me feel worthless. They also tried to make me lose my job, but Candace is good to us girls, so she always sides with us first. Ronny and Corbin threw the bastards out."

"You stopped dancing. For me." I sat forward. "Why?"

She laughed. "It wasn't exactly for you."

I frowned at that. "What do you mean?"

"I had some issues with other men being a little too handsy. A couple of us girls did, so Candace made us keep our clothes on for awhile and if the men wanted us to strip, they would have to pay extra. Not sure how legal that is but I just did my job, so I never questioned her. And then when you beat up those guys..." She met my gaze again.

Back when I first met Amber, something about her called out to me. I saw a guy approach her, touch her when she clearly didn't want it, and my fists were flying against his face before I knew what I was doing. That happened a few more times before she finally stopped dancing and became a server instead.

"If you want to dance, Red, you dance for me. I'll even pay you if you need but I don't want you on that stage."

Amber sat back in her spot on the couch, crossing one knee over the other and staring at me. "You know, Aaron used to try to control me. While it worked for the most part, in the end, I finally realized that I deserved better. So, you can try and control me all you want, Sammy, but I promise you, I will defy you and I will push you."

Rising from my spot, I went up to her. "I want you to defy me, Red. But I promise that I won't push you to do anything you don't want to do."

She uncrossed her legs and spread her knees, allowing me between them.

"If you really didn't want to listen to me though, if you wanted to defy me like you say you do, you would still be dancing."

"Maybe." She reached for my belt, unbuckling it and lowering the zipper to my jeans. "If you really wanted to control me like you imply..." She stared up at me, lowering my jeans over my hips. "You would."

"Is that what you want?" I cupped her face, slowly moving my hand to the back of her head before grabbing a fistful of her hair.

"Yes." She licked her lips, her cheeks becoming rosy. "I need to be controlled but I also need to be defiant."

"You're a brat," I added, tugging her head back.

"If that's what you want to call me, sure." Her eyes dropped to my waist, my cock pointing directly at her. "God, you're beautiful."

I grinned, wrapping my free hand around my dick. "If you want to be controlled, remember your safeword." I tightened my hold on her hair, pulling her off the couch and forcing her to her knees on the floor at my feet.

"How do I know that if I use it, you'll stop?" Something flashed in her eyes. It was a hint of something that had happened to her. I knew because I had seen it in others.

Tugging her head back, I ran the tip of my cock over her lips, up the side of her cheek, and back down.

She stuck her tongue out as I ran the head of my dick over it, a tingle of pleasure sliding over my skin at the soft contact.

"This is where our trust begins, Red," I told her, lining the tip of my cock up with her mouth. "It can't grow unless we start somewhere."

She swallowed hard. "Okay."

"What's your safeword?"

"Tyler," she whispered.

"If your mouth is full of cock and you need me to stop, tap my hip. Understand?"

She nodded, her cheeks turning a nice shade of pink.

"Open. Wide." I tilted my head, giving her a wicked grin. "I'm about to make you cry."

Her breath caught but she did as she was told. As soon as her full lips parted, I slid my cock down the length of her tongue until the tip bumped the back of her throat. She gagged, her throat working me over as she tried breathing around me.

"Breathe through your nose, pet," I instructed.

She inhaled, letting it out slowly. A low moan followed soon after.

Holding her head in both hands, I tilted it back and stepped between her knees. "You want me to control you," I said and began thrusting into her mouth. "You want me to degrade you and dominate you."

Her nostrils flared, her eyes staring up at me. She whimpered, her tongue licking along the length of me as I pumped into her mouth.

"I need your submission, Red." I pushed my dick down the length of her tongue until it hit the back of her throat. Stopping, I held her head in place, her lips pressed against the base of me. "I know that submission is there. I can sense it. We can talk about that over time but for now, open those slutty little lips wider and take my cock like a good girl." I took a step back, tightening my hold on her head and forcing her to come with me.

She crawled on all fours, having no choice but to follow me.

Giving her a moment of reprieve, I stopped and pulled from her mouth.

She took a deep inhale, her cheeks coated with her tears.

"Had enough?" I asked, my voice low.

A hint of mischief flashed in her eyes. "Try me, Sam."

My cock jumped.

She caught the movement, a slow grin spreading on her face.

"Open that fucking mouth," I demanded, forcing her back onto her ass and stepping between her knees.

Her pupils dilated, her mouth widening as far as it would allow.

Locking my hands on her head, I braced myself and began fucking her face.

SIX

Amber

ONE NIGHT, I WAS at Rouge and sitting at the bar. I was waiting for my shift to start but was also mulling over what had happened with Sammy a few mornings ago.

After I gave him the blow job, he had lifted me onto my coffee table and went down on me once again. I could still feel the scratchiness of his beard at my thighs and center. I learned rather quickly that it was one of his favorite, if not his most favorite, things to do when it came to anything sexual. The happy wet noises that came from him during, turned me on even more. He had murmured how good I tasted. How he wished he could bottle up my scent. How tasting me made him hard as fuck. It made me feel good about myself, especially since we all struggle with moments of being insecure.

I could still feel his tongue deep in parts of me that had been neglected by a man for months. Deep in other parts of me that had never been used for pleasure before, but I realized rather quickly that if Sammy and I continued doing what we were doing, I wanted it all. We didn't have sex again, but the foreplay was just as good. If not more so.

After he had given me countless orgasms, he wiped his chin and ran his hand coated in my juices over my stomach and up to my breasts. In a way, it was like he was marking me. Especially when while he was doing it, he shoved his fingers into my mouth, wrapped his other hand around his cock, and came in a matter of minutes onto my stomach and pussy. I could still feel the burn of his palm connecting with my cheek as he rubbed his cum into my skin with his other hand.

I thought back to the intensity of his dark eyes. They were a chocolate brown but so damn dark, they looked almost black. I could barely see his pupils, but I knew he could see mine. Every time he demanded me to do something in that deep, dominating voice of his or even when he slapped my face and wrapped his hand around my throat, he would smirk. I couldn't control my body or its reaction when it came to him. But I also found that I didn't overly want to, either.

"Hey girl."

I jumped, finding Shawnee smiling and her shoulders shaking with laughter at my expense. "Sorry, I was daydreaming."

"No worries." She nodded once. "You okay?"

"Yeah." I scrubbed a hand down my face, lightly tapping my cheeks. "Haven't been sleeping well." I couldn't get Sam and my time with him out of my head, so that didn't help.

"Oh, I bet you haven't." Her smile widened. "So, tell me..." She paused, pulling her long blond hair back into a messy ponytail. "How was he?"

"Why do you think my crappy sleep involves a guy?" I asked, the back of my neck heating.

"Girl, your crappy sleep doesn't involve just any guy," she reminded me. "You spent the night with Sammy Butcher. Maybe multiple nights. I'm waiting for you to tell me that part. But he's the guy who has made most of the girls here cry. Except for me. He needs a pussy or a little more ink for my taste."

"And he needs to be older," I pointed out, remembering the guy I had bumped into the other night who had been talking to her.

Shawnee laughed. "Yeah, true. So enough about me and my daddy issues. Tell me how he was."

I sighed. "You talked to my mom, didn't you?"

"She called me right up after her video chat with you. She said that you texted some guy, asking him to come over. She also asked me about him and how he is with you. But of course, I haven't seen him with you a whole lot, so I didn't really know what to say."

I pushed the straw around in the glass tumbler that still had some cranberry juice and vodka left over in it. "He's fine with me. I know I don't know him well. I don't think anyone does besides his brother. But I promise you that he is not Aaron."

"You thought Aaron was a decent guy too in the beginning." Shawnee liked to remind me often.

"I did but Sammy is different." I didn't know how to explain it. For one, Sammy wasn't selfish. He didn't get mad at me if I had an orgasm and he didn't. Yes, he was rough with me, but it was like he read my body and when it gave him the sign he was looking for, he continued. I could still feel his fingers roughly fucking me as his free hand tightened around my throat. The orgasm it caused made me realize that as long as you were safe, darker sex was okay. In the short time I had known him, he had already done way more than Aaron ever did. He actually listened to my body, instead of only taking what he wanted.

"Just be careful," Shawnee said gently. "I don't want you to get hurt." *Again*, going unsaid.

"I know. I appreciate that." I stood from the stool when the hairs on the back of my neck tingled. I looked to my right, finding some of the Hell's Harlem Crew rolling in. I saw a few that I recognized and some I didn't. I also saw Cyrus but didn't see his brother anywhere. My stomach dropped. Maybe he was going to avoid me now that we'd slept together.

My phone suddenly buzzed, startling me from my pity party for one.

Sammy: Spend the night with me.

My heart jumped to my throat. I looked around the room but he was still nowhere to be found, so I glanced back down at my phone.

Me: Where are you?

Sammy: Babysitting for friends.

My chest warmed and if my ovaries could have exploded, I was sure they would.

Me: That's nice of you. I get off at 1am.

Sammy: Trust me, Red, you'll be getting off long after that too. I'll pick you up at 1.

I shook my head at his innuendo.

Me: See you then.

I was going to respond and tell him that he didn't have to pick me up and I could take a cab home, but to have a chance at being alone with him? There was no way I would turn that shit down.

The rest of the night ended up in a blur. I couldn't overly concentrate, knowing full well how the time after my shift was going to be spent.

By the time one in the morning rolled around, I quickly said bye to Shawnee and made my way out of the club, knowing she would ask questions if I stayed.

When I left the building, I was met by a man who had invaded my body a few days ago. Sammy was standing by his bike, puffing on a smoke. He wore his leather cut with a black hoodie and ripped blue jeans. The granite lines of his face seemed to be softer tonight for whatever reason.

As I approached him, I was thankful that I didn't drive my car tonight. It was like fate had a way of pushing Sammy and me together, since I'd already decided to take a cab so I could have a drink after my shift ended.

When Sammy caught me approaching, he stood up taller and threw his smoke to the ground.

"Hi," I said, closing that last little distance between us.

He hooked an arm around my middle and pulled me against him in a rough move.

I gasped, slapping my hands against his hard chest.

His eyes dropped to my mouth and just when I thought he was going to kiss me like I had wanted all along, he lowered his lips to my ear instead.

"Miss me?"

A breathless laugh left me as his beard tickled my ear. "Yeah. You?"

"Oh yeah." His hand reached under my skirt, grabbing a fistful of my rear and lifting me onto the seat of his bike. He pushed his way between my knees, his mouth finding the spot at the base of my throat. A low moan left him. It rumbled through me to the point it sounded like a purr. "I like this look," he mumbled against my skin. "This shirt does wonders for your tits."

A breathless laugh left me. The black pleated skirt was short, and I had settled for a white V-neck t-shirt. It was comfortable but apparently sexy.

"Sam," I whispered, running my fingers through his hair.

He lifted his head just enough that he could look into my eyes.

"Kiss me." It was a plea for more. From him. From life. I wasn't sure. But I wanted something. We had a connection, that part was true, and we definitely couldn't deny the attraction between us. But I wanted to feel his lips on mine. His tongue deep in my mouth as he roamed his hands over my body.

He lowered his mouth to my throat. His teeth nipped, his lips sucked, and his tongue licked. The movements caused this undying want to brew from somewhere deep inside of me.

"Sam." I tilted my head to the side, giving him better access. "Please."

"No." He grabbed a handful of my hair and tugged my head back. "No kissing."

"But—" When a throat cleared close by, I jumped. I expected Sammy to move away from me but instead, he turned to look at whoever interrupted us and stepped between my knees.

"What the fuck do you want?" he demanded.

"Am I interrupting?" Will. *Shit.*

"Yes, you are actually." Sammy turned his back to me, so if I wanted to see Will, I would actually have to look around Sam to do so. It felt like maybe he was trying to protect me. Will had his hands on me not too long ago without my permission and that bothered Sam. I wondered if there was another reason for that or if he had seen it in others he knew.

"You see Red anywhere? She usually works until one and Shawnee said she left already."

"Yes, I've seen Red." Sammy reached behind him.

I took his hand, linking my fingers between his. I wasn't sure why, but that action alone forced a lump to my throat. But setting those feelings aside, I had to focus on the here and now. I didn't know what Will wanted. Not completely anyway.

"Is that her behind you?" Will asked.

Sammy shifted to the right but wasn't quick enough when Will caught me sitting there.

He chuckled. "Moving fast, aren't we, Red?"

I glared at him. "Aaron has been dead for four years." And a piece of my soul died along with him.

"I wasn't talking about him," Will said, staring at me.

My stomach clenched. I looked away, needing Sammy to take me away from here.

"Well, it's been a slice. We have to go." Sammy turned and helped me off the bike. He handed me a helmet and did it up for me, but wouldn't look at me.

I swallowed hard, knowing I would have to explain who exactly Will was to me besides being my late husband's brother.

"I'll see you later..." He winked. "Princess."

"Don't call me that," I snapped. "I am not your Princess."

"You are," he growled. "You will always be *our* Princess."

A dark shadow came up behind me, looming over my head.

"You got this, Red?" Sammy asked, placing a hand on my hip.

Will caught the movement, a slow grin spreading on his face. "Just wait until you tell Sammy how many guys you've actually been with. He won't want your dirty pussy after that."

A harsh scream left me as I charged for him. Arms suddenly wrapped around my middle, stopping me from going after the fucker.

Will chuckled, walking away and heading into the club.

I struggled against Sammy. "To answer your question, yes I had it." I stomped away from him and took off the helmet.

"Red." He took a step toward me.

I lifted my hand. "I need a moment."

He stayed back, keeping his distance but leaving his eyes on me.

I took a breath and then another. "I haven't been with as many guys as Will implied. But I've been with enough. I went through a few of the men in his crew after Aaron died because I was hurting. I was also mad at myself that I never got out of that marriage ahead of time. I feel...I just..." Before I could finish, Sam had me in his arms.

Without even saying anything, he guided me back to his bike and took the helmet from me. He placed it back on my head, did it up, and straddled the beautiful machine before slipping his own helmet on. When the engine rumbled to life, he looked at me over his shoulder.

I took the hint, cupped his shoulder, and swung my leg over the seat behind him. When I was safe and secure, I wrapped my arms around his hard middle.

He cupped my hands, gave them a squeeze, and drove us out of the parking lot.

I wasn't sure where we were going but I found that I didn't overly care. We could go back to my place. His place. Out of town. It didn't matter.

When I saw Will originally, Sammy distracted me from him, but now seeing him again conjured up other memories I didn't like.

As the world whipped past us, I saw the sign to our town, wishing us a good day. I didn't know where we were going but I did know that I wanted to go with Sammy.

Wherever it may be.

(Sammy)

I didn't know her story. Maybe one day she would tell me, but I knew that Will was bad for her. Whatever history they had; it was clearly only one-sided on his part. But it didn't matter. Her past didn't matter. Not to me. I had enough when it came to this woman and how she unraveled me. I wanted her. All of her. Every inch. Her submission. Her sass. The fierce and passionate sides to her. I wanted to show her that the dark side of sex could be beautiful and perfect if it was with the right person. I wanted her at my feet but most of all, I just wanted her.

After leaving Rouge, I had every intention of heading back to her place, but I got a better idea and drove us out of the city instead.

It wouldn't be too far outside of it, but I found that I needed her. Just her. Nothing that would remind her of herself like her apartment would. And the same went with my place. I didn't want any distractions.

When she begged for me to kiss her, I almost broke my own rule and did. Kissing had never been on the table. And I found that I never wanted to actually kiss anyone until I met her.

Kissing was intimate. It brought out feelings that I wasn't ready for. Maybe I never would be. It wasn't fair to Amber. I knew that. But I had hoped going in, that the way I used her body, would distract her from my mouth not being on hers. It was stupid of me to think that way the closer we became.

Amber's hold on my waist tightened, pulling me from my thoughts. Her hands slipped beneath my hoodie, coming into contact with my skin.

A shiver trembled through me, never realizing until that very moment how much I needed her hands on me. The other night, it was just me touching her. Same went with the following morning. My hands had been all over her. But she never touched me. She never even hinted. Maybe she was more submissive than I thought she was.

Her hands moved over my stomach, up to my chest and back down again. They weren't anywhere near my crotch and yet, I was hard as a fucking rock.

When I saw a side road that led into a group of trees, I turned down it. Slowing the bike, I pulled us off to the side and killed the engine. Kicking out the kickstand, I sat there and waited.

As if she could read the way my body reacted to hers, Amber slid off the back of the bike and took off the helmet. She placed it gently on the ground and helped me with my own. I wasn't used to a woman doing things for me. I had been doing it all on my own for so long, that I never even noticed my hand grabbing her wrist.

Her breath caught and even though it was late at night and I couldn't see her except for where the moonlight kissed her skin, I sensed the nerves in her eyes. The fear tickling her skin. The unknown of what we were doing or were about to do.

She pulled her wrist from my hand and undid the straps beneath my chin. Placing the helmet on the ground beside the other one, she waited.

I slid my ass back further on the seat and reached for her.

She came into my arms willingly.

Pulling her onto the seat in front of me, I captured her hair in my fist and tugged her head back. Her breath caught, that single sound, shooting through every cell and nerve in my body.

"I don't kiss." I lowered my teeth to her throat, scraping them along the length of her neck. "Kissing is intimate. Kissing can mean different things for people even if you talk about it beforehand."

"I knew you were scared you'd fall in love with me," she breathed, her chest rising and falling. She had asked me that question the first time we fucked when I told her I didn't kiss.

"No." I licked and sucked at her skin, knowing full well it was going to leave a mark, but the Dom in me didn't care. I wanted everyone to know that she belonged to me. Especially that Will fucker. "It'll be the other way around. When you feel my lips on yours. When you taste my tongue dancing along yours. When I swallow your moans and screams for more. *You* will fall in love with *me*, Red."

A husky laugh escaped her. "Unlikely."

I chuckled against her throat. This woman was different than the others. She pushed and shoved me away one moment and then welcomed me into her life the next. She was confusing, passionate, my complete undoing. We may have only just started finally sleeping together but I knew that I could easily fall in love with her. And I knew damn well that I could make her fall in love with me.

Instead of dwelling on that little matter, I inched a hand up her inner thigh. Thankfully, she was wearing a skirt because I needed her orgasm before we made it to where I was taking her.

"You're going to come for me," I murmured against her throat just below her ear. "And then I'm going to take you to a motel and spend the night fucking every inch of you, pet. And I do mean every inch. Your mouth." I brushed my finger along the crotch of her panties. "Your cunt." I slipped a finger beneath the fabric, a low grunt leaving me at how wet she already was. "Your ass." I shoved two fingers into her, forcing a cry from her lips. "Nice and juicy, baby." I pumped my hand against her, hooking my fingers inside of her and rubbing them against her G-spot.

"God." She shook against me, cupping my knees and digging her fingers into them.

"Do you want all of that?" I knew she did, but I needed to hear her say it. No matter what the rumors were that went around about me, I wasn't a selfish man. I gave as much as I took. More so when it came to Red. I wanted her exhausted from pleasure. I wanted to break her down, beat her ass, and make her fucking cry, but hold her and care for her at the same time. I wanted it all.

"Yes," she whimpered. "I do. God, I want that. All of it. I want to hurt."

"Lucky for you I like inflicting a little pain." I nipped her throat for added effect, licking the spot soon after.

She laughed lightly, rocking her hips against my hand. "Please."

"Lay back and take off your panties." I released her so she could do as she was told.

She hesitated.

"You won't fall." I pulled out my phone, turned the light on low, and held it where I could see the area between her legs.

Amber laid back and reached beneath her skirt, tugging off her panties. When she was finally bare, she sat up and held them to my nose. "Do I smell good, Sam?"

I inhaled, a low growl leaving me as the scent of her body wafted into my nose. I took the panties from her and shoved them into my pocket. "Lay the fuck back."

She did as she was told, and I had a wonderful view of her pussy. Now it was my chance to give her the orgasm she deserved.

(Amber)

When I laid back, I placed my feet on Sammy's knees and waited.

He had the light from his phone aimed directly at my center. The cool night air washed over every inch of me. I shook, trembling with need for him.

Before I could beg for him to hurry up, he reached between my legs and brushed the back of his knuckles over my clit.

The spark of pleasure erupting through me, forced a soft gasp from my lips.

He repeated the movement, rubbing his knuckle back and forth over the swollen nub. "You ever been fucked to the point you have to tap out because you just can't come anymore and your body hurts?"

"Almost." I locked eyes with him, waiting for him to ask me. "When?"

A sly grin spread on my face. "The other night. With you."

He smirked, shoving his fingers into me.

I jumped, the slight burn from being stretched sending every nerve on high alert. Hooking my hands under my knees, I brought them up to my chest.

"My little slut wants to come," Sammy said, pumping his fingers into me in rough, jerky moves.

"Yes," I whimpered, enjoying the name-calling more than I ever thought I would.

"Think this sweet pussy deserves it?" he asked, removing his fingers from my body and giving my center a light slap.

"Yes," I cried out.

"You like it when I slap you," he said, sliding off the bike.

"God, you have no idea," I told him, watching him.

"I think I have an idea." He winked. "I can read your body, babe. But if I do something that you don't actually like, you have to tell me."

I nodded. "I will but that hasn't happened yet."

"I know."

Before I could ask what he was doing, he pulled me off the bike and shoved me to the ground. "Remember your safeword, Red."

I shivered at how deep his voice had become. "Tyler," I whispered.

"Good girl." Sammy grabbed my hips, lifting me to all fours. The sound of a tinfoil wrapper sent a wave of pleasure through my body. "Bend over and keep your ass up," he demanded, his voice smooth as silk.

I pressed my face to the ground, digging my fingers into the cool earth beneath me.

Something heavy suddenly rested on the back of my head and I realized that he was stepping on me. It wasn't hard enough where it hurt but just enough where I knew who was in control. He was showing me his dominance, his power, but at the same time, he was showing me that by using that single word, it would stop. So really, I was the one in control.

"If you haven't figured it out already," he shoved his cock into me, forcing a shattered whimper from my lips. "I like it rough. The other night was nothing compared to how my tastes usually are, Red."

The scent of the earth wafted into my nose as he pressed my head harder against it.

"If you want to stop, we will, but if you don't, I will eventually show you just how sick and depraved I can be, my Little Red." Sammy pushed into me as deep as my body would allow. "You say the word. If you don't, we will explore this together and I will show you. All of me."

"I want that," I cried out as a fast release slammed into me.

Sammy removed his boot from my head and grabbed fistfuls of my hair. He pulled me upright, picked up speed with his hips, and fucked me on the ground like the slut I wanted to be for him.

SEVEN

Amber

MY LEGS TREMBLED, MY thighs shook, and my body tensed as another release slid through every inch of me. We were now at a motel, in a bed. Once we had entered the room, I never got very far before Sammy grabbed me, picked me up off my feet, and threw me down on top of the mattress. The first night with him had been nothing short of amazing but this, this was on a whole other level. Something I had always wanted and tried getting from Aaron but couldn't. I wanted to be used and degraded. I thought I had trusted my late husband enough that I could get it from him and ask about making our sex life spicier, but he didn't take it well and felt it more of an insult than a suggestion.

With Sammy, he read my body like a book. Each breath and moan I took, were words telling him that what he was doing was right. Everything was just…right.

It was like as soon as he fucked me in the woods, a part of him had been unleashed. A part I knew was there but was nervous to meet at the same time.

"That's it you fucking slut, come for me." His hands were wrapped around my throat, his cock deep inside of me, and his eyes locked with mine. "Such a needy little whore."

"God." I shivered at his words. Although they were rude and vulgar, something deep inside of me trusted that he didn't actually mean them. "More, please more."

A sly grin spread on his face as his hands tightened around my throat.

My pussy contracted, squeezing around his cock as my thighs shook. My body tensed, my arms pulling on the belt wrapped around my wrists as every inch of me burned with pleasure.

It had been the first time he hadn't taken me from behind and while my hands were bound above my head and I couldn't actually touch him, I liked seeing him in all his naked glory. He had wrapped his belt around my wrists and a bedpost, so the only way I could get out of my restraints was if I used my safeword. It was exhilarating to say the least, both of us knowing I wouldn't utter that word no matter how far and twisted Sammy took the sex.

He had a tattoo on his ribs that said Mom and Dad in fancy script along with two dates. Other than that, he was completely bare of ink and piercings, but he was hard, everywhere. He had a few scars, from fighting I imagined, but he was still a masterpiece. Beautiful in the way he moved. His hips thrust forward, his brow furrowed, determined to get his orgasm and give me another in return. His grunts and groans made me wetter. His hold on my throat made me moan. His rough touch made me weak.

His dominance had been what I had been looking for all of these years. Before I could think on that further and how it must have been fate, an orgasm ripped through my very soul. It had been so hard, spots danced in my vision. A scream locked in my throat, unable to get out as the release took all of the air from my lungs.

Sammy tensed, his cock swelling and pulsing inside of me. His own release forced a moan from his lips, his eyes fluttering closed. "Fuck me, pet. So good."

A breathless laugh left me.

He opened his eyes, a cheeky grin spreading on his handsome face. He loosened his grip on my throat and unbuckled the belt wrapped around my wrists. Before I could touch him, he linked his fingers in mine and lowered his mouth to my neck. He licked and sucked along the area where his hands had been a few seconds ago.

Tilting my head back to give him better access, I reveled in the way his cock twitched inside of me.

"You good?" he murmured against my skin.

"Yeah." I sighed. "Very good."

He lifted his head, staring down at me. "How are your wrists?" he asked, running his thumbs back and forth over the red marks the belt had caused.

"Fine." I circled my wrists, showing him that I was, in fact, fine. "Promise."

I didn't ask him to kiss me. I knew he would, in time. Because I also wasn't stupid. What we had, what we were doing, was far from being over.

"If you won't let me kiss you, can I at least touch you?" I would get him to kiss me, eventually, but for now, I knew when to not cross that line. Especially when I didn't want to do something to fuck this up between us.

Sammy released my hands and sat back on his heels, pulling me up and into his arms. His hands roamed down my back, his fingers dancing along my skin sent a wave of goosebumps along my flesh.

Brushing my thumb along his bottom lip, I ran my other hand through his hair.

His eyes never strayed from mine. It was unnerving in the way he looked at me. It was almost like he was looking deep into my soul for an answer to a question I didn't know.

As his hands roamed over my ass, his fingers slid between the cheeks of my rear.

I shivered, pushing my ass into his touch.

He grunted, kissing the side of my throat. "Are you on the pill?"

"Yes." I moaned as his finger brushed over the tight rim.

"Good." He bit my jaw, the slight tinge of pain sending a flush of heat over my skin. "Because we're about to break the condom, pet."

Several hours later and Sammy was still inside of me. He had meant what he said when he told me we were going to go all night. He had stamina I never experienced before. We only stopped to have a glass of water and that was it.

"It's been hours, pet," Sammy murmured in my ear.

I was on my stomach with him towering over me. I couldn't even remember how many orgasms he had given me, but I did know that I was tired and hungry. My stomach growled, earning me a deep chuckle.

"We'll finish and then I'll feed you." He kissed my shoulder and made good on his promise. He fucked me fast which resulted in both of us having our releases at the same time. I didn't even think I had it in me to come again, but I did.

Sammy had also been right. We broke the original condom and never used another one. He promised me he was clean after someone he knew had a scare that forced him to get checked out each month as a precaution.

"I don't think I've ever gone that long before," I told him as he slid off the bed.

"We were in the woods for about an hour before I brought you back here too," Sammy reminded me.

I lifted onto my elbows, every muscle in my body protesting at the movements. "I need a shower but I'm tired."

"Come." Sammy pulled me off the bed. "I'll wash you."

"Wash me?" Was he serious?

"Yes." He paused. "Why are you looking at me like that?"

Memories I didn't want to think about tried sneaking their way in, but I stopped them. I had to because in the short time I had known Sammy, I already knew that he was nothing like Aaron.

I went to walk past Sammy when he caught my upper arm.

"Talk to me," he demanded gently.

We were standing there in the doorway to the bathroom. Naked, covered in the scent and aftermath of the sex we shared. I was sure I had marks on my body from his rough touch and I knew for a fact he had scratches on his back.

"Red." Sammy released my arm and gave my ass a light swat. It wasn't hard enough to cause any pain, but it was just firm enough that it got my intention. Which, I was sure, was the point. "I have no intention of hurting you. Should I have manned up and approached you sooner? Maybe. But I also know that you've been hurt. By Aaron. Someone else. Several people maybe. I don't know. You'll tell me when you're ready. But hurting you is not my intention. At all."

"Why didn't you approach me sooner? There has to be another reason besides you thinking that I was hurt by someone." I didn't like the fact that he could read me so well already.

"I wanted you to make the first move. I needed you to be ready because I knew that once I had you, I was never letting you go."

I laughed lightly.

He raised an eyebrow. "You think I'm kidding?"

"No." I pulled from his grip and stomped past him. "Maybe? I don't know, Sammy. I hardly know you and I don't have a good track record with guys. Especially bikers, so forgive me for being leery of what it is we're doing."

"We're fucking, Red. Do I have feelings for you? Yes, but I'm also confused because I don't know what those feelings are. So I'd rather us just take it one day at a time." Sammy came toward me, backing me into the corner of the bathroom. He leaned his hands against the wall on either side of my head, caging me in. "Anything else that happens will be when we're both ready."

I had never met someone who was as honest as him. Most, especially the men I had been with, never told me how they felt.

But the fact that Sam said he was confused about his feelings for me, proved that not all men were the same.

"Why, Sammy, are you wanting more out of this? Are you wanting to fall in love with me? Get married and have babies with me? Are you going to do all of that and still fuck other women?" I knew it wasn't fair to accuse him of things he hadn't done but I blamed Aaron. I blamed him for everything. And what hurt the most was that I couldn't confront him about it.

"Don't blame me for shit I haven't done, Red." Sammy crouched until we were at eye level. "I haven't given you any reason not to trust me. Have I?"

My jaw clenched. "No. Not really."

"Didn't think so. Now, tell me what your issue is. I don't expect you to reveal everything but you gotta give me something here, pet."

"I just..." God, what could I even tell him? That I was scared? I *was* scared but of what exactly? It wasn't like I hadn't dated since Aaron died but even in those cases, I was never fully committed to them. I took a deep breath and let the words flow. "The higher Aaron got within the club, the less important I became. I'm not expecting you to put me first. Especially not when this is so new for us. But I refuse to stand by and let you use me, take whatever it is you want from me, only to fuck other women when I'm not with you. I can't handle that. Not again." Especially not from him. While what we had was new, I knew that Sammy could break me. And not in the sexy dark way we both liked either.

"What history do you have with Will?" Sammy asked, instead of commenting on what I just told him.

I sighed, pushing away from him and went to the shower. I turned on the water before I looked back at Sammy. "I grew up with Aaron, Will, and Shawnee. She was the smarter one and never wanted anything to do with either of them. I always liked Aaron. Will, on the other hand, liked me first I guess, and I think that's what sparked this interest for me in Aaron. He never showed any hint that he wanted to take our friendship to the next level until Will told him he wanted me. Anyway." I swallowed hard. "We had a few threesomes. It was Aaron's idea. But I think he was trying to show his brother up or something. I don't know. I guess I never will. But after he died, Will forced his way into my life even more. He tried consoling me, making sure I was okay and all that shit. He had an ulterior motive, but I was hurt, heartbroken over what had happened with Aaron. So, Will took advantage of that." I looked down at my feet, wishing I had clothes on instead of standing there naked, revealing one of my many truths to Sammy.

"He's an ass," Sam muttered.

I scoffed. "You have no idea."

"I don't judge you."

I looked up then.

"I don't judge you for the mistakes you made, for the men you've been with, for anything you've done," Sam continued. "I'm not perfect. At all. But I promise that I don't judge you for your sexual history. If men can do it, so can women. I just want you to know that while we're fucking, it's just us. No one else. Understand me?"

I nodded, a breath I didn't realize I had been holding, left me on a slow exhale.

"What do you want out of this?" He closed the distance between us and cupped my jaw. "Just sex? Something more?"

"Something more," I whispered.

"Good." He grabbed my hand and led me into the shower. "I want more too. But we don't have to put a label on it. We don't need specifics but I promise you that I won't hurt you and I can reassure you that while we're sleeping together, it's just you and me. Okay?"

"Okay," I replied, running my hands down his chest to his hard abs.

"Good," he repeated, pushing me under the water. "Glad we agree on that because what I did to those bastards before we started fucking, is nothing compared to what I'll do now that we are."

"Tell me more."

A low, sinister chuckle left him as his mouth found my throat. "You want to know what I'll do when another man hits on you, Red? Because you're beautiful as hell, so we both know it's going to happen."

"There's other women at the club. They can have their pick of them," I said, running my hands up Sammy's strong arms. The only arms I had ever truly felt safe in.

"True." He brushed his mouth up to my ear. "But they aren't you. I've seen the way the men look at you, pet, and I don't like it. Not one fucking bit. So the next time someone hits on you, just remember whose cock had you begging for more. Whose mouth had you screaming in a matter of seconds. Whose fingers had you wet as they slipped into your tight cunt. Whose words had you clenching your thighs in anticipation."

"I'm not sure who that is but he sounds delicious."

"You're a brat, babe," he murmured against my skin, running his hands down my sides, over my hips, and to the seat of my ass.

I sighed, wrapping my arms around his shoulders.

"Fuck." He bit my throat, licking the spot after to take away the sting. He cupped my ass, pulling me against his hard body. "You're so fucking incredible."

My chest rose and fell with ragged breaths. Even though he wasn't inside me or even touching me where I wanted him most, my body still burned for him. Every time his hands slid over my skin, I couldn't help the ache that formed between my legs. I had never experienced this before. Not for anyone. It was like now that Sam and I were finally sleeping together, we couldn't get enough. If last night was any example of how it would be with him, I would have to take up yoga just so I wouldn't hurt so much after.

Sammy kept one arm locked around me while reaching for the shampoo bottle.

"When did you have time to buy shampoo?" I asked, turning around in his arms.

"You passed out, so I let you sleep for a bit and went to the store grab some stuff for us." He squeezed some shampoo into his palm, placed the bottle back on the ledge of the tub, and began washing my hair.

I sighed, leaning into him.

"I'm finding that I'm liking this," he told me, his voice low.

"What?" I whispered.

"The aftercare."

"Aftercare?" A moan slipped from my lips as his fingers pushed into my head.

"Yeah, taking care of you after we fuck." He tugged my head back, placing a soft peck on my forehead. "I like this a lot actually."

A husky laugh escaped me. "I like this too, Sammy." And I did. Maybe more so than he did. I had never been taken care of before. Not by a guy. And definitely not by someone like him. While Sammy may have been grumpy and moody as hell, I liked that I got a side of him he didn't share with most. If anyone at all. It made me feel special, almost like he was saving those little bits for me and me alone.

We spent the next little while washing each other in silence. He let me run my hands over him, washing away the remnants of what we had spent the night before doing. While the evidence of our desire for each other slid down the drain, no matter how many times we washed the sex off our skin, I knew that it would forever be embedded on our souls.

EIGHT

SAMMY

AFTER OUR SHOWER, WE got dressed and headed to a restaurant that was attached to the motel so I could feed Amber. Her stomach rumbled as we sat in the booth, making both of us laugh. Her cheeks had turned pink, and the waitress only smiled.

I never thought I could be this comfortable with a woman before. She wasn't all over me on a constant basis. Not that I would complain. But I found for the first time in my adult life, that I wanted to spend time with a woman. Get to know her. Find out what other kinks she was into. I wanted to know what made her tick and what her hobbies were. I wanted to know what made her sad and put a smile on her face. I wanted to know it all. Every single thing that made up Amber.

While she perused the menu, I couldn't help but look at her. She had a glow in her skin that was there because of me. Her red hair was a mess on top of her head with ringlets falling down around her face. She told me earlier while she was towel-drying her hair after our shower, that she always straightened it for work but that it was naturally curly. I preferred the natural look. It made her almost look innocent in a way. Besides the outfit she was wearing, which was her work attire from the night before, she appeared younger.

Letting my eyes roam down the length of her, they stopped at the hem of her black skirt that had ridden up her thighs. Any higher and I would be able to see her. Knowing she was completely bare beneath the fabric, my mouth watered. It was as if her panties were burning a hole in my pocket.

"Everything looks wonderful," she said, interrupting my eye-fucking her. "I want one of each." She laughed at her own joke, chewing her bottom lip. "Hmm...I think I'll get an omelet. And coffee. Definitely coffee."

As if the waitress read her mind, she brought over a mug and poured coffee into it for Amber.

"My hero." Amber took the mug and brought it to her lips, letting out a soft sigh after. As she took a few more sips, her eyes met mine from over the rim. "What?"

"You're beautiful," I told her.

"Oh." She placed her mug on the table, giving me a small smile. "Thank you."

I reached a hand out, brushing my fingers over the soft skin at the hem of her skirt.

Her breath caught. "Sammy."

"Do you not like when I touch you?" I asked, knowing she did but still needing to hear her say it.

"Of course, I do." She turned toward me, lifting her knee onto the bench of the booth beneath us. The movement forced my eyes to drop to her center.

"Fucking hell," I groaned, her pretty pink pussy on full display for me.

"See something you like, handsome?" Amber purred.

"You have no idea." My cock twitched, hardening with each passing second.

She giggled, grabbed my hand, and placed it on her inner thigh.

If we were anywhere else, I would have shoved as many fingers as I could inside her, making her squirm in pleasure and anticipation over what was to come next. But I wouldn't. Not here. There was a time and a place, and this was not one of them, but I would punish her later for teasing me.

"Just so you know, pet, I don't like being teased." I pinched her inner thigh, squeezing the flesh between my finger and thumb until she squeaked.

"I'm sorry." She squirmed, trying to shove my hand away.

"No," I squeezed the skin harder. "You aren't."

"Fine." She glared at me. "I'm not."

"Good girl." I released the skin, running my thumb along the spot that would eventually bruise. "Thank you for your honesty."

"Ass," she mumbled.

Oh, I was going to have fun with her.

Keeping my hand between her legs, I inched it higher up her thigh and brushed the tips of my fingers over her swollen center as the waitress came to take our order.

Amber ordered her food, her voice trembling and her cheeks becoming an even darker shade of red.

When the waitress was ready for me to order my meal, I did with a calm and even voice. The people around us were none the wiser on where my hand was or what my fingers were doing. I wouldn't take it further either, but I wanted Amber to know where I was. Where I would always be. Even if we fought, I would be there. It didn't matter to me that what we were doing was new. I liked her. I liked her a-fucking-lot.

When the waitress left to put our order in, Amber turned to me. "What are you doing?"

"Just reminding you, pet." My cock twitched as the endearment left my lips. It tasted sweet but I knew that as much as I liked calling her that, there was still a long road ahead of us. We had walls up between us, for many different reasons but I wondered if over time, we could shatter them together.

"You don't need to remind me of anything, Sam." She cupped my hand that was between her legs. "I'm not fucking anyone else."

My hand remained curled around her inner thigh, her words sparking this need inside of me. This need for more. A relationship. A pet. A damn wife.

"Tell me something about yourself," she suggested, pulling me from my internal rampage. "Something that has nothing to do with sex. I seem to know you quite a bit when it comes to that already."

I grunted. "Trust me, Red, you don't know nearly enough yet."

She leaned the side of her head against the back of the booth. "Tell me something then. Anything."

I thought a moment, unsure as to what I could tell her and so soon, when something came to me. "I joined a BDSM club in my early twenties and have been a member ever since."

Her eyes widened, her mouth falling open. "Oh. My. I wasn't expecting that."

I shrugged. "It's not a big deal."

"Where is it?"

I stared at her, expecting her to ask what BDSM was but she didn't. "A couple of hours from here. I didn't want to run into women I've already been with because they weren't worth a second glance. And I know that makes me sound like an asshole, but you've heard the rumors, Red. I *am* a dick. I know I am. I also refuse to apologize for that shit unless I know I fucked up."

"You're not a dick to me. Not always anyway. And I also like it when you are." It was Amber's turn to shrug that time.

"I think the term you're looking for is dominating, degradation, domineering or..." A sly grin spread on my face. "Sadistic."

A notable shiver trembled through her. "God, yes."

I tilted my head, staring at her. "Tell *me* something, Red. You didn't ask what BDSM is. Is it something that you already know about?"

"Uh..." A shaky laugh left her. "I've always been submissive when it comes to sex, but I also like being a brat too. I'll submit to you, but I want you to work for it, kind of thing. I tried getting Aaron to work with me on that, but he was selfish. And a few other guys I'd been with didn't do it for me. Then I met you and

I knew instantly that you could be the Dominant I've been looking for."

"Then why did it take you so long to make your move?"

"I was scared," she said as the waitress came over with our plates of food. We thanked her and once we were alone again, Amber continued, "When I saw you talking to the other girls, I thought you would go home with them. I don't know. I saw you talking to them a lot, so I figured I had no chance."

"Right." I grunted. "You do remember that I never fucked any of them, right?" I found my one-night stands by other means, but it had been a while since I'd had sex. Before Red and I finally started sleeping together. Even though that had been the case, I still didn't want her at my apartment. Too many weird and awkward memories there. She deserved better.

"You said that, and I believe you, but you asked me, so I'm telling you." The bite in her tone, sent a ripple of pleasure down the length of my cock.

"Keep up the attitude, pet." I pinched her inner thigh. "I'm adding it to the list of punishments I'll inflict later."

Amber huffed. "You know..."

When her voice trailed off, she stuck her tongue out at me.

I chuckled, shaking my head. "You're fucking adorable and sexy as hell."

A wide grin spread on her face. "So are you, Sam, so are you."

"You think I'm adorable?" I asked her, raising an eyebrow.

"Well, you are sexy as hell but adorable..." She thought a moment. "I think you're as adorable as a snake."

A laugh boomed through me, another wall shattering between us.

"You know it's true." She nodded. "Yup. Definitely true."

I chuckled, shaking my head. "Adorable as a snake. I'll have to remember that."

She giggled, shoveling a forkful of eggs into her mouth.

When she started eating her breakfast, she shifted in the seat. "Don't you need your hand to eat?" she asked, trying to push it from between her legs.

"Nope." I squeezed her thigh. "I'm left-handed." I scooped up some eggs onto the fork and shoveled them into my mouth, giving her a wink.

"Interesting." She tapped her chin. "It explains a lot."

I frowned, choking down the eggs. "What the hell is that supposed to mean?"

A loud laugh burst through her, making several people look our way.

I glared at them. "You got a problem with someone laughing?" I growled at them.

They went back to their own meals, cowering in their seats.

"Be nice," Amber scolded.

"I am being nice but you laughing, shouldn't earn you stares," I grumbled.

"It's fine." She patted my arm. "And I was only kidding. Being left-handed is different and it just proves how unique you are from the other guys I've been with. That's all."

"I'm the only left-handed person in my family." Her words hit home. It did make me feel special in a way that I was original when it came to the hand I wrote and did things with. "But you still didn't finish answering my original question."

"Oh. What was your question?"

"You're stalling, pet."

"Fine." She sighed. "I did some research when I realized that I wasn't into regular sex. I also read a lot and find that I like the BDSM romance novels the most. I also like the different dynamics the Dom and sub have and how it's not the same thing in every relationship." She pushed her food around on her plate. "I just like being controlled in the bedroom I guess."

"No guessing, babe. You do like being controlled. You also like being choked, slapped around, and fucked within an inch of your life." More heads turned our way. I rolled my eyes.

Amber laughed. "Well, I can't say that going out with you will be boring."

"You want to go out with me?" I asked her, liking the sound of that.

"We're out now, aren't we?"

"You know what I mean." I raised an eyebrow when she didn't answer. "Amber."

"We're not teenagers, Sam," she mumbled.

"No, we aren't but I still want an answer. Do you want to go out with me? Do you want to date me? Do you want to be my girlfriend? Or do you want to just fuck and that be it? You want to sleep with other guys too, is that it, pet?" I went to pull my hand from between her legs when she caught it and kept it against her thigh, her gaze hard and determined.

"I want you. I think I've made that very clear. But yes, and I don't really know why when you're an asshole on good days, but I do want to date you. I want to be wined and dined during the day and fucked so damn hard at night, my soul hurts. Does that answer your question, Sam?"

It did, but I found that I couldn't form the words to respond. The fact she spoke those words and didn't care if anyone around us heard her truths, set my blood on fire and had my dick throbbing for more of her.

"For someone who demands answers from others, you sure don't have a lot to—"

I cupped her jaw, silencing her words, and leaned down to her ear. "I'd be careful if I were you, pet." I pushed my nose against her hairline and took a deep breath. "I don't take kindly to idle threats by a submissive little slut who would do anything and everything to get my cock back inside of her filthy pussy."

Her breath caught at my nasty words, but it only made me want to tell her every sick and twisted fantasy I had because I knew. All of them involved her and her alone.

"We are going to finish our food and then I'll take you home and if you're a good little girl and I think you deserve it, I may just let you do whatever you want to my dick. But until then, shut the fuck up and eat your damn breakfast." I pressed my lips to her ear. "You got me, pet?"

"Yes, Sir," she whispered.

"Hmm...I like that title leaving your mouth." I pinched her chin, forcing her head around to meet my stare. "Now, are you going to behave?"

"Probably not," she murmured, her eyes flashing with a hint of lust and mischief.

A wicked grin spread on my face. "I was hoping you'd say that."

(Amber)

"Have you heard of BDSM, Aaron?" I asked him as I knelt on the bed. I had researched that the standard submissive pose was in a kneeling position with your palms up on your thighs and your head bowed.

"Yeah, why?" he asked, not looking at me and continuing to play on his phone.

"Because I'd like to try it. I think it could be fun and spice up our sex life."

He finally looked at me then, a frown pulling his eyebrows to the center of his forehead. "Our sex life is fine, Amber." He went back to his phone which was his way of saying that the conversation was over. But it wasn't. Not in the least.

I sighed, leaving the bed and heading to the door.

"Can you grab me a beer?"

"Yeah, sure." I left the room, closed the door behind me, and leaned against it. Our sex life was fine. Right. For him maybe but it wasn't even remotely fine for me.

"Amber," he called from the other side of the door. "Hurry the fuck up, woman."

I trudged to the kitchen, grabbed him a beer, and headed back to our room. "Can we at least try something new?"

"Why?" he asked, taking the beer from me, popping the cap off, and finishing half the bottle before putting it on the nightstand. "You bored with me?"

"No, it's not that." Before I could explain, he had me on my back and pinned to the bed. "Aaron."

"You want me to choke you? Beat your ass? You into some sick shit that I don't know about?" His questions came out angry and cold, and I had no idea why.

"That's not it." I tried struggling from beneath him, but he was too heavy. *"Aaron, please. I just wanted to spice things up. That's all."*

"I'll spice them up for you."

Although that had been years ago, I could still feel the pain of Aaron's cock ripping into my unprepared body. Even though I had told him no and begged for him to stop, he hadn't. He had automatically assumed that just because I wanted to try something new, I wanted to be forced into submission. Which wasn't the case at all.

After he raped me, I never brought it up again. I never even hinted for sex and waited for him to instead. From that point on, a piece of my soul had shattered, and it only heightened the need to get out and away from him. But at the same time, I was terrified to because I knew too much of what went on in the club life. That had been how he made me feel. That if I left him, they would come after me and kill me, my mom, Shawnee, and everyone else I knew and cared about. But that wasn't true. At all. I just didn't know it until it was too late.

"You should have come to me," Tiny said, covering my trembling hands that were resting on my lap. *"I could have helped you."*

Tears fell on our joined hands. *"Aaron told me…I didn't think you would protect me, and I thought you would side with him."*

"Do you not know me at all?"

My chest tightened at the hurt in Tiny's voice. For a man who was so damn big, he cared. Hard. You just couldn't tell anyone that.

"Hey." Sammy kissed my temple. "Where did you go?"

I swallowed hard. "Nowhere." I smiled up at him for reassurance, but he probably knew I was lying. Especially when he only stared at me and I shifted uncomfortably beside him. Unable to take any more of it, I stood from the couch and mumbled something about getting drinks for us.

We had come back to my place after breakfast and spent the day together.

When I reached the kitchen, I opened the fridge.

I could do this. I could date Sammy and not compare him to Aaron. I could trust that he wouldn't hurt me. Not unless I asked for it. And it wouldn't be him actually hurting me but mixing some pain in with my pleasure that I knew we would both enjoy.

The night before at the motel had been one of the best nights of my life. Hell, any night with Sammy was the best. It was like each moment with him topped the time before. I didn't know how he did it, but he kept it interesting, exciting and fresh.

It was now late the next night. I didn't have to work because one of the girls wanted to pick up a shift to make some extra money since her car broke down. While I needed the money too, I had agreed since Sammy wanted to hang out anyway. Truth was, he wanted to fuck. Hard. My body still burned from the rough way he was with me as soon as we got back to my apartment. The door hadn't even been closed all the way before he was back inside of me.

I shivered at the memory, thankful it took over and forced the nightmare that was my late husband out of my mind.

"I thought you were grabbing drinks."

I jumped, slamming the fridge door shut and backing up into the corner between it and the wall. "I...I'm sorry. I just...I'm..."

"Amber." Sammy reached out for me, but I cowered into myself.

I hugged my arms around my middle, not used to these feelings rushing through me. They conjured up memories from the past and I didn't know why.

Sammy's brows narrowed but he backed off. "What's going on?"

I took a deep breath and then another before finally meeting his dark eyes. "Talking about BDSM earlier suddenly triggered a memory that I didn't like."

"Shit." He backed up, running his hand over his nape. "I didn't know. I'm sorry."

"No, please." I went up to him and placed my hands on his chest. "I didn't know either. I've read BDSM type stories and have done research. We talked about it earlier today and I was fine but suddenly, for whatever reason, when I came into the kitchen just now, this memory..."

"It wasn't a good one obviously." Sammy covered my hand, bringing it up to his mouth and placing soft pecks on my knuckles.

"No, it wasn't." My heart thumped, my stomach somersaulting as I tried getting the words out. "My husband raped me."

NINE

SAMMY

I WANTED TO KILL the fucker who hurt Amber. No, who raped her. Her husband. Someone she trusted. Someone she gave her life to. As I listened to her tell me part of her story, the rage only grew inside of me. Her soft words broke my heart.

"I mentioned to him how I wanted to spice up our sex life. BDSM has always fascinated me, and I wanted to implement it into our marriage. I thought I trusted him enough to do that, but I was wrong. I asked him about it and it made him mad," she told me, wringing her hands in her lap.

We were sitting back on the couch. She was hugging a pillow and averting my gaze.

As much as I wanted to replace that pillow with me, I didn't. I would console her when she was ready, but until then I would listen to her speak her truths.

"After that, I never mentioned it to him again," she continued. "Then I met you and you and I have talked about it briefly, but you told me right away to choose a safeword. You asked me what I didn't like. There's been more communication between us in the short time we've been sleeping together than all the years I was married to Aaron. But I guess talking about it today made me think of him. I don't know. But that's what happened."

"Can I touch you?" I asked her gently, needing her in my arms. Aftercare was important. Even if it was just after a heavy conversation. You didn't need to have sex in order to be taken care of afterwards.

Her head snapped up, her eyes, sad and vacant, locking with mine. She nodded, probably not expecting me to ask for permission.

I inched closer to her, wrapping my hands in her hair and messing up her ponytail. Placing a soft peck on her forehead, I hoped she could feel what I was feeling. Although I didn't know how I felt, I knew that I liked her and cared for her, and I wanted to burn the mother fucking world down to avenge her. Aaron may have been dead and gone, but there was something else too. Other shit happened to her she wasn't telling me. She would. In time. But I needed to first earn her trust, just like she needed to earn mine. It worked both ways.

"I'm sorry that happened to you, pet." I leaned my forehead against hers. "I can be sadistic. I don't need to inflict pain to get off, but it definitely heightens my pleasure. My favorite kink is degradation. I enjoy when I'm deep inside you with my hands around your throat as I call you names. When you didn't mention anything about not liking it, I took a chance and showed you a bit of what I like." I kissed her nose, taking a moment to just feel her in my arms.

"How did you know that I would like being slapped?" she asked softly.

"I didn't but you also didn't say that it was a hard limit. When I slapped your cheek and you moaned, I knew. Fuck, baby, I knew."

She lifted her head. "What did you know?"

I gave her a small smile. "I met my match."

She chewed her bottom lip.

"But if it had been something you weren't into, I wouldn't have done it again. It's why I made you choose a safeword before I even fucked you the very first time. It's also why I asked if there were things you didn't like. Hard limits that you wouldn't even consider. When you said that you were willing to try anything within reason, I showed you what I like and how I am. Sure, we're still getting to know each other but I want you to know that you are in control."

"I do know that," she said, her voice shaking.

"Me calling you names, slapping and choking you..." I cupped the back of her head, forcing her to look at me once again. "Did that bother you? Your body told me one thing, but I need your words to confirm it."

"No," she said breathily. "I liked it. I liked it all, Sam."

"What your husband did..." I swallowed hard. "It's people like that who give BDSM a bad name. Everyone thinks that it has to do with whips and chains and pain. Sure, sadism and masochism are in the name but that's not all it is. It's so much more." I cupped her neck, pushing her head back with my thumb under her chin. "I promise you it's more. While I love controlling you, dominating and degrading you..." I kissed her forehead. "And fucking you until you squeal like a damn pig, taking care of you after is my favorite part. And we've only just started exploring it together. But I'll teach you. We'll learn what we both like. I'll teach you everything I know, and we'll learn even more together. As a couple."

Her breath hitched, her eyes welling. "You won't be mad if there's something I don't want to try or if there is something that I *do* want to try and I ask you about it...it won't piss you off?"

A sour taste filled my throat over what Aaron had done to her. That fact alone, that she thought it would piss me off if she told me something she wanted to try, made this rage inside of me grow.

"No, it won't piss me off." I released her and stood from the couch. I began pacing, needing to control this urge to drive my fist through the wall.

"Sammy."

"I just need a moment." I rubbed the back of my neck, taking slow deep breaths. "Why didn't you leave him after that?" I didn't want to ask the question when her emotions were still raw and very real, but I needed to know.

"He threatened to kill my mom and Shawnee if I did."

I stopped, staring at her. "Are you fucking serious?"

She nodded. "I knew too much that went on in the club. Or he made it seem that way. After he died, I found out that I did actually have some friends in his crew, and they reassured me that I could leave the city and no one would get hurt. They watch out for my mom, and she's taken them under her wing. She's kind of like the mother figure for them even though a lot of them are her age. I just...a lot of shit went down before and after Aaron died and I needed out of there. Shawnee and I packed up our apartment and we moved here."

"Why don't you two live together?"

"Uh..." Her cheeks turned pink. "Shawnee likes to have company. A lot of company. And I'd rather be by myself. I don't have the confidence she does. I know it doesn't make sense when I used to strip but I had to do a shot or two before each dance just to get the nerve to step foot onto that stage."

I went to her, dropping at her feet. I suddenly needed her hands on me, and I couldn't explain why.

"Hey." She cupped my cheek. "I'm fine. A little broken. But I'm okay."

Before I knew what I was doing, I had my hand wrapped around the back of her neck and my mouth on hers in a hard, bruising kiss.

She gasped, her body stiffening at the unexpected impact.

While I shocked my own self that I was finally kissing her, I reveled in the way she eventually melted into my touch. Our conversation had been heavy as I learned more about her, but the fact that she felt she could talk to me made these feelings I had for her, grow into something I couldn't explain. Not that I wanted to even try at the moment.

I split her lips apart with my tongue, needing to taste every inch of her mouth. I pushed to my feet, wrapped an arm around her middle, and lifted her into my arms. Switching positions, I sat with her straddling my lap.

She broke the kiss, her lips swollen from my rough mouth. Grabbing the hem of her tank top, she lifted it up and over her head. Her naked tits swayed at the movement, her nipples erect and hard.

Running my hands up her back, I took a budding peak into my mouth.

She sighed, pushing into me.

Cupping her other breast, I pinched the nipple, sucking and twirling my tongue around the one in my mouth.

Amber moaned, rocking against me. "Sammy, I need you inside me."

"I don't want to take advantage." I released her nipple with a wet pop, sinking my teeth into the pale flesh.

"Yes," she panted. "You do."

Fucking hell, she knew me well.

Reaching between us, I pulled my cock out of the gray sweatpants I was wearing. I was thankful I had some extra clothes in the storage compartment on my bike.

Kissing up her chest, I covered her mouth with mine as I reached between her legs and pulled the fabric of her loose pajama shorts to the side. "Ride me, baby," I murmured against her lips.

She inched closer, lining her hot pussy up with the tip of my dick. "Fuck."

My cock twitched, the tip butting against her center, teasing us both. "Drop this cunt on it. Now," I barked, fisting her hair in both hands.

She did as she was told, slamming her pelvis down on me, igniting a yell from us both.

Now that I was inside her, I held her head, kissed her mouth, and fucked her.

Hard. Rough.

And *violently*.

TEN

Amber

AFTER THAT INITIAL TRIP To the motel, Sammy and I had spent every chance together that we could. We quickly fell into a routine. I would go to work and he would pick me up when my shift ended, if he wasn't there already. We would go back to my place and spend the night wrapped up in each other.

While we still hadn't put a label on what we were doing, we enjoyed spending time together. I still didn't know much about why he was moody, but I liked that I got the softer side to him. When we were in my bed late at night, he would lightly touch my shoulder or slowly link his fingers with mine. The touch, soft and soothing, nothing like the man I had come to develop feelings for.

A few of his crew noticed how his mood had changed. Not a whole lot but enough where he wasn't at least making the girls cry anymore. He also hadn't beat anyone up since before we started sleeping together either but to be fair, no one had hit on me. Yet.

Sammy Butcher took up all of my time. When I wasn't with him, I was texting him. It became obsessive and I thought something was wrong with me. I didn't want to depend on a man again but after speaking with my mom about it, she reassured me that I was strong and fierce, and that it was okay to give a little.

"Is he anything like Aaron was?" Mom asked me, taking a sip of her wine.

I sighed, adjusting the computer screen so I could see her clearly as I leaned back against my headboard. "No. He's not. I'm just scared to give away that part of myself again."

"I get that, baby girl. How long have you two been…" She waggled her eyebrows. "…hanging out?"

I laughed. "A few weeks. Maybe longer. I don't know really."

"And has he ever given you any reason to doubt whatever this is you two are doing?"

I opened my mouth to respond but hesitated and thought over her words. "No," I answered finally. "He hasn't."

And Sammy hadn't. Even if he was in one of his moods, he still touched me gently and fucked me hard when I needed. He never even had to ask and knew how and when I wanted him.

One night, I was getting ready to finish my shift so I could go home and pack for my trip to my mom's the following day. When a dark shadow loomed over the bar top, I knew before looking up that it wasn't Sammy. I hadn't seen him in a couple of days after finding out that his brother's girlfriend had an accident, and he was spending time with them. My heart swelled that he was there for his family, and I hoped that everything was alright with her.

Knuckles rapped on top of the bar, bringing my attention back to the present.

"What do you want, Will?" I asked, my tone bored.

"A beer," came his deep reply.

I nodded, pouring him one before placing the pint on the bar top in front of him.

When he finished it, he pushed the empty glass toward me. "Where's your little boyfriend?"

I snorted. Sammy was anything but little and just because he wasn't around, didn't mean that others weren't watching and keeping an eye on things for him. We may have not officially said we were boyfriend and girlfriend, but his boys still knew that we were together.

"Amber, these are my brothers, Cheesy and Locke." Sammy cupped my shoulders, pushing me forward a little bit.

I looked up at the two younger guys dressed in leather cuts.

"Guys, this is Amber. Or Red. Either work. When I'm not around, she is to be watched. At all times. If you see someone messing with her, take care of it and report back to me. We clear?"

"What's yours is ours." The guy named Cheesy stuck his hand out. "It's also nice to officially meet you."

"It's nice to meet you too." I returned the handshake, shivering as Sammy's thumb pushed into the spot at the base of my neck. "And you," I told the quieter guy named Locke.

He nodded once. "Jamie. Locke is my last name."

"I've been called Red my whole life because of the color of my hair. Who would have thought right?"

They both laughed, the sudden shift in the air making the conversation lighter.

"They'll protect you, pet," Sammy whispered in my ear. "And one day, I'm hoping I'll be able to introduce you as my old lady."

I smiled at the thought of being his old lady, knowing it was the highest form of respect a woman could get if she were with a biker. It was a nice thought and something I looked forward to.

That little introduction had been almost a week ago and every night since, I saw Cheesy and Locke at the club along with a few other guys I didn't know but recognized. They sat at their usual table, talking amongst themselves and drinking beer, liquor, and whatever else they could get their hands on. It had always amazed me how the Hell's Harlem chapter in this area were nice when Aaron and Will were anything but.

"Hey, I'm talking to you," Will snapped, his voice rough.

"She doesn't want to talk to you, asshole," Shawnee told him, walking up to me and grabbing my hand. "Help me with the inventory. Emma will handle the bar." As soon as she said those words, Emma Morin came behind the bar.

"We need to chat, Red," Will called out, ignoring Shawnee.

"Yeah, I'm good." I went to follow Shawnee when his next words stopped me.

"He won't always want you, Red. He'll get sick of you just like Aaron did. And where will I be?"

I looked back over my shoulder at Will, which I shouldn't have done.

A wicked grin spread on his face. He ran his fingers along his mouth, a mouth I had felt on me more times than I cared to count. His grin widened. "I'll be there to pick up the pieces, baby. Just like I always am."

"Let's go." Shawnee pulled me with her, all but dragging me away from the bar and down the hall toward the stock room.

Once we reached the small room off the hallway, she pushed me inside.

I spun around, ready to go after Will and punch the smug smirk off his face.

"No." Shawnee slammed the door closed. "You are not doing this. Not with him. Not with Sammy. Not with anyone. I refuse to let you do this to yourself again."

"I have no idea what you're talking about," I ground out through clenched teeth.

"Do you remember what happened the last time you went after someone who said nasty things to you? Huh, Amber?"

I looked away, my stomach twisting. I wasn't used to this side of Shawnee. She had always been there for me, even when I didn't deserve it, but now she was pissed.

"Listen." She sighed. "I love you. You are the sister I never had, and your mom is like a mother to me. Both of you are my family. You two and the other girls. If something happened to you again..."

I met her gaze. "I'm fine. Sammy's guys will protect me."

"They won't always be with you. Something needs to be done about Will but not by you."

"I can handle my shit on my own, Shawnee." If what Aaron did to me taught me anything, it was how to be strong.

"Should I remind you what happened the last time you approached one of these bastards on your own? They went after you. They searched you out, beat you, raped you, and left you for dead."

I looked away at the not so gentle reminder of that night.

"I saw you in the hospital. I was there to console your mother when she didn't know if her daughter was going to make it. You were put in a medically induced coma, Amber," her voice shook.

My throat closed over a hard lump.

"Your injuries were so fucking bad."

I hugged my arms around myself, suddenly feeling like I was backed into a corner. "Yes, I know, Shawnee. Thank you for reminding me." I was acting like a bitch but this anxiety resting on my shoulders scratched at my skin, and I didn't like it. "I need Sammy."

"You also need to go home, finish packing, and drive up to see your mom. And you need to stop by the clubhouse and talk to Tiny."

"What's he going to do?" I sounded like a whiny brat, but I just wanted people to leave me alone.

"He can protect you from Will." Shawnee took a step toward me. "I'm not trying to be mean, but I just want you safe."

I slumped onto a pile of crates, dropping my head in my hands. "I moved to get away from him. And now he's here." I lifted my head. "Do you know what he wants?"

"No, but I've been asking around."

I placed my hands in my lap and started picking at a loose string of a hole in the knee of my jeans. "You haven't heard anything?"

"No." She sighed. "I haven't. The guy who came here a few weeks ago…"

I looked up then, meeting my best friend's stare.

"He knows people. Although, he doesn't usually help adults but I'll see what I can find out. If I can find out anything at all." She huffed, blowing a loose strand of hair out of her eyes.

"I just want to be left alone."

"Hey." Shawnee crouched at my feet, covering my hands with hers. "I love you."

"I love you too and I'm sorry for being a bitch."

"I'm used to it." She winked.

I laughed, gently pushing her back onto her ass.

She laughed along with me. "Seriously though, you need to do what I said."

"I know. Sammy is dealing with some family stuff anyway." I huffed. "I just want to live a normal life for once."

She snorted. "Even if you never would have married Aaron, your life was anything but normal."

"What does that mean?" I frowned.

"You're so naïve sometimes." She pulled me to my feet, hooked an arm around my shoulders, and led me from the storage room. "You're beautiful. I don't think you know just how beautiful you are. Even before you hit puberty. I was always jealous of you. But not in a mean vindictive way of course."

As we walked down the hall to the back entrance of the club, I listened to her words, unable to believe what she was telling me. She was jealous of me? *She* was beautiful. I always wanted blond hair growing up. I even tried bleaching my hair once and my hair turned out orange instead. So, I gave up quickly and my mom was none the wiser.

"Why do you think you didn't have to audition for Candace when we applied here? I had to. So did the other girls. But one look at you and Candace knew that the guys would be eating out of the palm of your hand. It's also why she charged extra if they wanted you to get naked."

"I don't do that anymore." My stomach clenched at the memories of me dancing completely nude for guys who threw money at me.

"I know you don't but what I'm saying is that with your looks, both Candace and Ronny knew that you could make them money."

"I guess." I liked the owners. Ronny was a good guy and Candace always treated us well. They had an odd marriage that I could never understand, and they cheated on each other countless times, but I couldn't say much when I, for one, was nowhere near being perfect. But if I were married again, with the right man, I wouldn't be sleeping with anyone else that's for sure.

That was all Aaron. And I bent over and took it because I wasn't strong enough then to do anything about it.

"Just please be careful. That's all I'm saying." Shawnee went into the section that held the costumes, change rooms, and everything else we needed to just get away.

"I will." I went to the lockers and grabbed my purse and sweater. "I'll tell my mom you said hi. You know you can come with me, right?"

"I know, and as much as I want to, I need to make some extra money, and I have some things going on." She gave me a small smile.

"Everything okay?" It wasn't like her to keep secrets from me, but I also knew that she would tell me whenever she was ready.

"Oh of course. It's nothing big. Remember that guy you bumped into a few weeks back? I met him at the library of all places." She laughed. "Before you jump to anything, we're just friends and I haven't fucked him. He's married anyway."

"Oh, well we can always use extra friends."

"True." Her face lit up. "I do think I know him or know of him. I can't figure out how though. He just seems familiar or something about him does anyway. I don't know much about his business and the line of work he's in, but I know he and his partners help people. I think they're bikers, but he's never told me that. He has a friend though who looks like Spencer Reid from *Criminal Minds*." She fanned herself. "Holy fuck balls is he hot."

My eyes widened. "What?"

"He is. He's not usually my type. I like older men with tattoos and piercings but this guy, I would drop to my knees for him, that's for sure. But there's something about him that scares me." She shivered. "I would gladly get over my fear though to have him tell me what to do."

"No." I shook my head. "Wait, back up."

Her face fell. "What's wrong?"

"After...the night Aaron was killed and I was...well, it doesn't matter...anyway, I remember seeing a guy who looked like Spencer, but I was so out of it, I thought I was seeing things."

Shawnee and I had spent weeks binge watching *Criminal Minds* and both fell in love with Spencer. Even though, like she said, she preferred the older guys, there was something about the young doctor we liked. We had also joked that even though he was awkward in public, he was probably dirty as fuck in the bedroom.

"Oh...well...it must have been the same guy. It had to have been." She came toward me and pulled me into a hug. "I'll do some investigating. Don't worry about it. Drive safe to your mama's and text me when you get there. Did you tell Sammy where you're going?"

"I did." I hoped I would see him tonight before I left but I hadn't heard from him, so I wasn't sure if that would happen.

"Good. I don't need him showing up here demanding to know where his girl is." She rolled her eyes but as much as she acted as though she didn't like the idea, I knew that she would love it if a guy did that for her.

I laughed, shaking my head. "I should go. Keep me posted on that guy and please be careful. And...I'm sorry again."

"Stop. You take care of yourself. That's most important. I'll wait for your text tomorrow."

"Love you." I went to the door, opened it, and peeked my head out into the hall to make sure that Will was nowhere nearby, then stepped out into it.

"He won't bother you."

I jumped, spun around, and found Locke leaning against the wall, playing on his phone. "He could be outside, waiting for me."

"True, but he isn't. He had another beer, made some noise about how you're ignoring him, and left. Cheesy and a couple of the other guys are outside." Locke looked my way then. "You're good."

"Thank you." I quickly left the building, needing to get home, have a glass of wine, and just curl up in my bed.

Tucking my head down, I waved to Cheesy as I walked to my car. When I was seated inside it, I locked the doors and checked the back seat. To most, it wouldn't be normal to check but you could never be too safe. Especially with the people I had known once upon a time.

When I was home and finally in my apartment, I let out a breath of relief I never realized I had been holding. My body was tight, my muscles bunched beneath my skin as the night played out in my mind.

An hour later, I was showered, in pajamas, had a glass of red wine in hand, and was about to curl up in bed with a book when my phone buzzed.

Sammy: You home?

Me: I am.

I took a picture of my bare legs stretched out in front of me and sent it to him.

Sammy: Fuck me, I need those legs wrapped around me.

My body heated.

Me: I'm about to drown myself in a glass of wine.

Sammy: Drown in me, pet, and I'll help you fucking breathe.

I sat forward, my stomach flipping. I didn't know what he meant by that, but I didn't care. I liked how it sounded.

Me: Come over. Now.

Sammy: You gotta catch up, babe. I'm already at your door.

My eyes widened.

Quickly leaving the bed, I headed to the door and checked the peephole.

"Let me in," Sammy said from the other side of the door.

Unlocking it, I opened it. At the same time, Sammy pushed his way inside and right into my arms. He kicked the door closed, locked it back up, and scraped his teeth up the length of my throat.

My body burned at the slight tinge of pain his teeth caused. "I wasn't expecting to see you tonight."

"I know."

We never did get a chance to talk about it since his mouth covered mine. I still couldn't get used to the fact that he was now finally kissing me.

"I know you leave tomorrow for your mom's place, but I need you right now." His mouth brushed down the length of my jaw to my ear. "I need you hard, pet."

I shivered at the desperation seeping from him. "Take me, however you want."

"You sure?" He cupped my ass, pulling me flush against his hard body. "I don't want to hurt you but fuck me, do I want to make you remember me."

"Yes, God." I ran my hands through his hair, holding him tight. "I'm sure."

Sammy spun me around. "Safeword."

"Tyler," I whispered, placing my hands against the wall for support.

"Good girl." He lowered to his knees behind me. "Use it if needed."

Before I had a chance to comprehend what he was doing, he had my shorts lowered and his mouth between the cheeks of my ass. I moaned, pushing into him. His tongue penetrated a part of me I never expected could be used for pleasure. All too soon, he was standing behind me. His fingers had replaced his tongue, running back and forth over the tight rim.

"I need you here." He fisted my hair with his other hand. "I need to make you scream." He kissed the side of my neck, pushing a finger into me.

I whimpered, the slight burn making my knees shake.

"Fuck, baby, you're tight. I won't last long but I need it. I need *you*."

"Do it, Sammy." My body vibrated at the desperation seeping from his deep voice. I never thought someone like him would actually beg for me. I stuck my ass out, needing to hurt as badly as he wanted to fuck.

"Sir. Call me *Sir*." He bit the base of my throat, slipping another finger into my ass.

"Sir," I moaned. "Please."

"You want me to fuck this tight little ass, pet?" He cupped the back of my neck, pushing me face first into the wall all the while finger fucking me with his free hand.

"Yes, God yes." I arched into him, needing his wrath, his cock, his pain, and his pleasure.

"Keep your cheek pressed against the wall and open your ass for me," he demanded.

I reached around, grabbed my ass cheeks, and spread myself open.

Sammy pulled his fingers from my body, spat into his palm and stroked his cock. "This is going to hurt." He moved his hand from my neck to my cheek, keeping my face pressed against the wall as he thrust into me.

A harsh scream left me as he tore into me.

"That's it, pet. Scream for your man. Let everyone in this damn apartment building know that you're getting your ass ripped the fuck open."

His words forced a moan from my throat. I couldn't help it. No matter how sick and depraved it could get, I knew where I stood with him. I was always safe. In his arms. And like Sammy said, the aftercare was my favorite too.

"Take my cock, you filthy fucking slut."

"Yes, please. Harder."

Sammy pushed into me as deeply as my body would allow then stopped.

I swallowed a gasp.

"You're going to go to your mom's tomorrow," his lips brushed over my ear, his voice deep and gravely, "maybe even see some old friends, but just remember whose cock has been inside you. Every inch of you. I hope when you breathe, you feel me." He grabbed my hips, pulled me back and pushed my upper body down. I was bent at the waist, my hands almost touching the ground. He took a step forward, my back hitting the wall. "Nowhere to go now, pet."

"Use your little slut, Sir."

"You're fucking incredible." He powered into me, taking out whatever it was that was bothering him, on my body. "You're my cum toy, aren't you?"

"Yes," I whined. A tingle started from my toes, shooting up the backs of my legs. "Please, harder," I cried out.

"Fuck." He bellowed, shoving all of him into me. "Take my cock you fucking whore. Take it."

"Yes. Yes. God, Sir, please make me come."

He grunted, thrusting into me with so much strength, I was sure he was going to rip me in half when a sudden release exploded from the center of my very being.

A scream fell from my lips, my legs shaking at the intense orgasm ripping through every cell in my body.

Sammy pulled out of my body, keeping his hand on my upper back. "Fucking hell."

I could feel hot jets of liquid landing on my ass and pussy as he groaned through his own release.

He removed his hand from my back, helping me stand.

My legs were shaky as I turned to him.

Sammy had already put himself away and had me in his arms before I could ask him to spend the night. My eyes became heavy, so I let him carry me to my room.

"Let me clean you up." He kissed my cheek as he placed me gently on my bed.

"Okay," I whispered, rolling onto my stomach.

He came back a moment later, lying down on the bed beside me and dipping a warm cloth over my rear and lower. "You good, pet?"

"Yeah." I lifted my head and cupped his cheek. "Thank you."

"No, thank you." He kissed me hard on the mouth.

"Spend the night with me?" I asked, laying my head back down on my pillow.

He slipped from the bed, threw the cloth in the laundry hamper, and stripped out of his clothes before joining me. He helped me undress the rest of the way, threw my pajamas over the edge of the bed, and wrapped me up in his arms.

"How's your brother's girlfriend?" I asked, letting out a soft sigh when Sammy covered me with half his body.

"She was stabbed but thankfully, she's going to be fine. It's just been a shitty couple of days." Sam ran his hand up my side, cupping my breast and kissing my shoulder. "Thank you for making me feel better."

"I'm glad she's going to be okay." I yawned, rolling back into him. His knee pressed between my legs, pushing them apart. The hold he had on me, made me feel safe and protected.

"Sleep, pet," Sammy whispered.

Pulling the covers up and over us, I drifted in and out of sleep for the rest of the night. I woke at one point with Sammy running his fingers along the hot swollen flesh between my legs. But I must have fallen back asleep because by the time morning came, I was groggy, alone, and horny as hell. Checking my phone, I saw a text from Sammy.

Sammy: Thank you for last night. Drive safe and let me know when you get there.

Me: I will but you didn't have to leave so early. You got me worked up, Sam.

Sammy: It'll give you something to look forward to the next time you see me.

Me: I have two hands. I can take care of this myself.

Sammy: Take a video and send it to me then, pet.

I could almost hear that dominant tone in his voice as if he were there with me. Sitting up, I leaned against the headboard and turned the camera on. Placing my phone on the bed, in my sleep filled state, I stuck my hand between my legs and gave myself a release. I came quickly, sent the video to Sammy, and waited for his response.

Sammy: Good girl.

I sighed, liking his approval more than I ever thought I would.

Me: You still didn't have to leave though, and you could have helped me take care of this ache.

Sammy: If I would have stayed, you wouldn't have been going anywhere. You looked delicious laying there, naked and smelling like me.

I laughed.

Me: Were you worried you wouldn't be able to control yourself?

Sammy: You have no idea, pet. No idea at all.

I smiled to myself. While I got ready and finished packing, I still had a smile on my face. Sending that video to him was new and exciting for me and I especially loved how I got approval from him.

Even as I was driving to my mom's, I was smiling. And once I pulled up in front of my childhood home several hours later, I was still smiling.

ELEVEN

SAMMY

WHEN I LEFT AMBER in bed, naked and marked by my rough touch, it was one of the hardest things I had ever done. Seeing her completely bare, trusting me enough to fall asleep beside me, broke down another wall I had built around my heart.

I wasn't expecting her to actually listen and send me a video of her fingering herself, but I was happy that she did. Fucking her into exhaustion forced the brat in her to comply and it made my inner Dom fucking growl with approval.

She had texted me when she got to her mom's place, and I was thankful for that, but I was twitching. The fact that she was hours away where I couldn't touch her, see her, hear her screams and cries for more, didn't sit well with me.

But I also understood that mothers, good mothers, were priceless. As cliché as that sounded, it was the truth. I no longer had mine, but it didn't mean I had to take Amber from hers. So, I had kissed her cheek, sent her a text, and left her warmth. But now I had that delicious video on my phone I could watch and jerk off to whenever I wanted.

Once I was satisfied that Amber was safe at her childhood home, I met up with my brother. We had breakfast together and went to see our parents' graves. It was a short visit but one that hadn't happened in a long time. It was needed.

Heading to the clubhouse after, I couldn't help but think back to the night before with Amber. She gave as good as she got. My dick still hurt from the way her ass gripped me tight.

"Sammy."

I jumped, stumbling over my feet as I stepped into the only place I had ever considered home since I was a boy.

Greyson Mercer and his wife, Eve, were sitting at the bar. They both laughed.

"Distracted?" Eve asked, her eyes twinkling.

"Nope." Truth was, I *was* distracted. I was distracted by someone I cared deeply about. Maybe was even falling for. I wasn't sure but I did know that I liked her. A lot.

"Right." Greyson chuckled, glancing at his wife. "Remember how we were in the beginning?"

"Yeah, you were grumpy." She laughed. "Probably even more so than Sammy. And you got me pregnant. How dare you?"

They laughed amongst themselves.

"So, what brings you by?" Eve asked, slipping off the stool she was sitting on and going behind the bar.

"I'm heading out of town and needed to grab some things first. I also didn't want to go to the apartment and figured I could grab my shit from here." As soon as I said those words, I realized they would figure out that I hadn't spent the night at the apartment.

"Is she good to you?" Greyson asked. Although most would say he *was* grumpy as hell and hated everyone but his wife and son, Jaron's father was more than my brother and much more than I could ever ask for in an adoptive parent.

"She is," I told him, figuring there was no point in denying the fact that there was someone.

"That's good." Greyson paused. I wasn't sure what he was waiting for. Although he wasn't a man of many words, he still said what was on his mind for the most part.

"What is it?" I asked, his silence making me itch.

"Cyrus said that you've been hung up on this woman for awhile," Greyson answered.

"My brother needs to mind his own business." I had meant the words to come out more as an insult but really, I appreciated that my brother worried about me.

"Sure. But it's not just him your moods affect you know," Greyson pointed out.

"I haven't been that bad." Had I?

They looked between each other.

"Why didn't you say something?"

"We've tried, Sam." Greyson came toward me. "Listen, I don't give a shit about that. I've been known to be grumpy myself."

Eve scoffed. "No. Not at all."

He shot her a look that only made her laugh.

"Anyway." Greyson met my gaze once again. "What I'm saying is that I get it. Before Eve came into my life, I was unhappy. And even when I met her, I tried fighting those feelings, but it didn't last long. I don't want that for you, and I didn't want it for your brother either."

"He's happy now." And he was and I loved my future sister in-law.

"He is, but are you?" Greyson asked gently.

"I don't give a shit about me." I never had. I had spent so many years focusing on easy pussy that when I met Amber, approached her, and she shot me down, it only made me want her even more. I knew it made me sound like a dick, but I had never been turned down before. It was refreshing.

The redhead quickly left the stage, averting her eyes and avoiding anyone who was looking at her. It made me wonder why she danced if she didn't overly like it. Not that I knew if she did or not, but she definitely seemed uncomfortable about it.

Before I knew what I was doing, I was up and out of my seat. My name was called but I didn't give a shit. I needed to find out this woman's name. She had been announced as Red, but it wasn't enough. I wanted to know her real name so I could moan it when I jerked off later.

"Sammy." Candace Owens stepped in front of me before I could head down the hall that Red had gone. "You can't go down there."

"Yes, I can." I went to push past her when she placed her hand on my chest.

"No, you can't. Whatever you think you're doing or are about to do, forget it. Red doesn't want you. She doesn't want anyone."

"I'd like to hear her say that, Candace." There had been a time where I could have had Candace at my feet. Even though she was married, their relationship was rocky at best. She went through most of us in the Hell's Harlem crew. She had been bored, trying to get her husband's attention and we just wanted pussy. It didn't make any of us look good, but it was the truth. But now that I had Red in my mind's eye, Candace did nothing for me.

"Samso—"

"Finish that word, Candace," I growled. "I dare you." No one called me by my full first name. Samson was used by my late mother and that was it. No one else deserved to even think that name.

"I'm sorry but you—"

Before Candace could finish her sentence, a door down the hall opened. Red stepped out, fully clothed and absolutely breathtaking. She wore an oversized large black hoody, ripped jean shorts that showed off long, tanned, and toned legs. Her red hair was pulled back into a messy ponytail and her face was clear of that caked on makeup she wore earlier.

"Red," I said, pushing past Candace.

Red met my gaze, frowning. "Do I know you?"

"Not yet you don't."

She snorted which was sexy as hell. "Right. So smooth."

"Come home with me." It wasn't a romantic approach, but I wanted to know what her legs felt like wrapped around me. I wanted to know how her mouth tasted, which was something I normally didn't do. Kissing was too much. It opened up feelings I never wanted to explore, and it was usually one-sided. Keeping kissing off the table meant that women wouldn't get attached but I found that I wanted this one to get attached. I wanted her to get attached and latch on. Fucking hard.

"And why the hell would I do that? I don't even know your name."
The bite in her tone sent a shiver throughout every inch of me.

"Sammy." I closed the distance between us, overcrowding her space.
She looked up at me with wide eyes.

"Now that you know my name, tell me yours."

She licked her lips, the small move, although subtle, made my cock
leak. "Amber," she whispered.

"Thank you." I leaned down to her ear. "Amber."

As much as I didn't want to, I walked away from her, but not before I
noticed the shiver that trembled through her body. A body that would
eventually be mine. No matter how long it took.

We had come a long way, Amber and I. Even though we
never made what we were doing official, I could feel the walls we
had up to protect ourselves, slowly crumbling away.

"I heard this woman was a stripper at Rouge," Greyson said,
cupping my nape and leading me back to the bar.

"She was but she stopped and only serves drinks and food
now." And if anyone mentioned how hot she looked naked, I
would kill them.

"You know the guys have seen…"

My eyes snapped to Greyson's. "Yeah, and if they say shit, I
don't give a flying fuck who they are, I'll kill them, their families,
and every single person they ever had an encounter with."

A slow grin spread on Grey's face. "You know, Cyrus may
look more like your father but you, you act like him more."

"I agree." Eve handed us each a beer before sitting back on
the stool by her husband. "Although your mom could handle her
shit. She was a tough little thing."

"Did you ever hear about how your parents finally started
dating?" Greyson asked, pulling back a long swig from the bottle
in his hand.

"Not much. Something about a rumor?" I didn't like talking
about our parents. That was Cyrus. He asked questions and every
time he did, I would leave and go find some random woman to
fuck the pain away. But now, I wanted to find Amber. Not even
for sex. I just wanted us to hold each other and not say a single
thing.

"I know you don't like talking about them, trust me, I get it."
A dark shadow passed over Greyson's face. "Your mom spread a
rumor that she was sleeping with all the guys in our club. It

wasn't true but it got your dad's attention. Your mom was a feisty thing and your dad loved it."

Sounded like my mother was a brat and my father liked it. Guess I am more like my father than I thought.

"I had no idea." And I didn't. Whenever people brought up our parents, I never took it well. My brother on the other hand, wanted to know everything he could about them. Which I appreciated but we were both very different that way.

"Your mom wanted your dad's attention and it worked." Greyson chuckled. "I thought he was going to kill everyone in my fucking crew. He's also the one who helped convince me to…" He looked at Eve.

She smiled at him, the love clearly there. Even though they had been together for years. None of that made the love they had for each other dwindle any less. No matter how much time had passed since they met.

"Your dad basically told me to get my head out of my ass." Greyson looked at me then. "Do I have to do the same for you?"

My chest tightened. "Not anymore." That familiar feeling of suddenly being backed into a corner, washed over me. I didn't like it. Before either of them could say any more, I mumbled something about needing to get a workout in before leaving and made my way to the basement.

As soon as I was safely inside the home gym, I closed the door, and sank to the floor.

(Amber)

"So." Mom placed a glass of wine on the table in front of me. "Tell me about this guy."

Before I could answer, my stomach rolled at the sight of the wine. I pushed it toward her. "I think I'll stick with just water for now."

She raised an eyebrow. "Really?"

"I think I got hit with a bug. I had to pull over on the way here to throw up." It made the drive even longer, but I didn't want to throw up in my car. I wasn't sure what was going on but just the idea of tasting the wine on my tongue, made my stomach churn.

The drive to my mother's took way longer than it should have but I texted Sammy as soon as I pulled into her driveway and put the car in park.

His response hadn't been something I expected but found that I craved just the same.

Sammy: Be a good girl.

Every inch of me vibrated at those words because we both knew that I wasn't a good girl. Not when it was just me and him anyway.

She laughed. "Maybe you're pregnant."

My eyes shot to my mother's. "Right."

"So, tell me about him." She took a sip of her wine. "Please."

"He's good to me. Takes care of me. The first time with him, he went to the pharmacy and bought me pain meds and feminine products the next morning." I almost swooned at the memory of Sammy doing that for me.

"Really?" Mom stared at me. "God, I remember how hard it was for you to get Aaron to do that for you. While you were sick in bed, he wouldn't do shit." She shook her head. "I lost so much respect for him the first time he did that and then after everything else..."

"I know." I took a long swig of my water, needing something to wet my suddenly parched throat.

"This guy is a biker too? That's what Shawnee said."

"Yeah, but he's different than Aaron. I sometimes have to pinch myself that he wants to be with me. Not that we've put a label on this yet but it's nice. It's comfortable with him. I can be myself and not have to worry that he'll blow up if I question him on something or tell him that I don't want to do...stuff." She knew about the rape with Aaron and everything else that had happened to me, but it was still hard to talk about. Especially when I had pushed both her and Shawnee away during my time with my late husband, but I now understood it was an abusive nature in him. He was beyond controlling and I never realized it at the time.

"Does he have any kids or crazy exes?" Meaning, did he come with baggage.

"No, he doesn't." But as I said those words, I had never actually asked him, and he never volunteered the information either.

"Keep talking. I'm going to make us some sandwiches," she said, rising from her chair and heading into the kitchen.

"Okay, what more do you want to know?" I asked, opening up my phone to send Sammy a text.

Me: Do you have any kids or crazy exes? My mom is asking, and I told her no, but I realized that I've never asked you either.

The dots started dancing across the screen almost immediately.

Sammy: No, pet. I don't have either of those things. It's just me and me alone.

Me: Thank God.

Sammy: Do you?

Me: No.

Sammy: What about Will?

My stomach clenched.

Me: He doesn't count.

Sammy: He counts until he's dead and buried.

My heart jumped.

Me: That can't happen. Not by me. Not by you. He knows people.

Sammy: So do I, babe. So do I.

I put my phone away before I said something stupid. Like how I would like it if he did that for me. Will was a problem. And he was one I couldn't figure out how to solve either. No matter how hard I tried, I couldn't shake him off.

"What's wrong?"

My head snapped up, finding my mother standing with a tray of sandwiches in her arms.

"I was talking to you, but you didn't respond."

"I'm sorry."

"Are you sure you're okay?" she asked, a deep frown settling between her brows.

I nodded, helping her with setting the rest of the table. Once everything was in order and we began eating, my thoughts traveled back to Sammy. How he had been with me. How different he was compared to Aaron. How different he was to most of the bikers I had met and come across. While he was rough, aggressive, and outright mean at times, there was a piece of him that was made solely for me. It was like he had never shared it with anyone before and knowing that I could reach it, made him feel vulnerable. I wondered if that was why he seemed angry all the time.

Maybe he was scared of what I would find out or that I would get too close. Maybe he was scared that he would fall in love with me. We had both joked about it but the fact that we weren't sleeping with anyone else, it made me wonder if it could actually happen.

"You like him." Mom smiled. "God, I miss that. Those butterflies. The pitter-patter of your heart. The sweaty palms." She sighed. "It's been a long time since a man made me feel that way."

"I thought you had a new guy," I said, realizing that I never denied that I felt those things with Sammy because there was no sense really. My mom knew me. Between her and Shawnee, I wasn't sure who knew me more.

"Yeah, but he's just..." She waved it off. "It doesn't matter. So, I heard Shawnee met an older guy."

"They're just friends and he's married. She's looking into things for me though. I'm hoping she can help me figure out what Will wants." I had texted her the other night, asking her to keep it on the down low. I didn't need word getting out that she was trying to find out information on Will. He wouldn't think twice about having her killed, so I warned her to keep her safe. I had also learned quickly that with Shawnee, if you wanted something kept a secret, you tell her. She would close that shit up tight until she was told she could reveal said secret. And even then, it wasn't enough. If she said she wouldn't tell anyone, she wouldn't. It was one of the many things I loved about her. Especially when I had told her I was going to divorce Aaron. Even though it was too late and it had never happened, it was nice having a friend by my side when a lot of the time I felt so alone.

My mom and I spent the rest of the afternoon talking about the guy she wasn't overly interested in but every time she brought up Sammy, I turned the conversation back to her. I didn't know what was going on between me and Sammy, but I knew that I liked what we were doing. There was nothing wrong with just having sex. It wasn't like I was ready to settle down and get married again. But if Will had his way, I would end up with him. I grimaced at the thought.

Later that day, my mom had gone out. Only after I insisted that I was fine and didn't mind being alone. I was about to curl up on the couch with a book when my phone rang.

My eyes widened when I saw who was calling me. And not just calling but video calling.

"Aww, Sam, did you miss my pretty face?" I teased, resting the phone against a throw pillow and curling my feet under me.

He chuckled, running a hand through his hair. "Nah but I do miss your pretty pussy."

I grinned, my cheeks heating. "I have to say that I'm surprised you're calling me and a video call no less."

"I'm bored." His eyes burned into me. "You alone?"

"Yeah, my mom went out."

"You didn't want to go with her?" he asked, raising an eyebrow.

"No. Going out means I have to deal with people." I wondered where he was. Looked like he was leaning against a headboard. "You in bed?"

"I am." He smirked. "I hate going to the apartment, so I'm not at home."

"Oh." My stomach fluttered that I was getting a little more insight into the man I was currently fucking. "Why do you hate the apartment?"

"Too many memories. Morning afters. Awkward moments."

"Ah, yeah." I laughed lightly. "I get that."

"Why, Red, do you have a lot of notches on your bedpost?"

I snorted. "Not as much as you, I'm sure."

He rolled his eyes. "Trust me, babe, those notches are no more."

"Sure," I said, drawing out the word. I knew he wasn't sleeping with anyone else because he told me so and I believed him. But it didn't mean that I didn't want to egg him on any less. Getting under his skin was fun. Especially since I wasn't there for him to do anything about it.

"You think I'm fucking other women, Red?" He chuckled. "Trust me, the only notches on my bedpost are the ones your head is going to be hitting."

I tapped my chin, pretending to think over his words. "What if I said that I didn't want to continue this?"

A growl left him. "The fuck?"

I bit back a laugh, knowing that I was getting to him. Sure, I would probably pay for this the next time I saw him, but I didn't care about any of that. I gauged his reactions and found they turned me on.

"Aww, what's wrong, Sammy? My pussy isn't that good. You could have any woman you want. What's so special about me?" The words meant to come out as teasing but in all reality, I found I wanted to know as well. What made me so special?

"You drive me fucking crazy, Red." Sam shifted in his spot. "To answer your question...your pussy *is* that good. I don't want any other women. Just you. And what makes you fucking special is that you push me, defy me, yet you didn't give it up right away. You are submissive and a brat, and everything the dominant part of me needs. No." He shook his head, a sly grin spreading on his face. "That *every* part of me needs. And what makes you special..."

When his words trailed off, I swallowed hard. "What, Sam?"

"You really have no idea, do you?" he asked, his voice gentle and soft, nothing like the man on the other side of the screen. So many hours away but close just the same.

"I don't know what you mean." Shawnee had told me something similar, but she just mentioned my looks and naïvety. I liked to think that after being married to Aaron, I became stronger.

"You're fucking beautiful, Amber," Sammy said, pulling me from my thoughts. "The first time we met, I thought I was going to bust a nut just from you saying my name."

A laugh boomed through me. "God, Sam, I'll never know what you're thinking if you keep things bottled up like that."

He laughed with me.

I picked up the phone and carried it down the hall to my childhood bedroom.

"Where are you taking me?"

I waggled my eyebrows. "To bed, baby."

"Hmm...I like the sound of that."

I shook my head. "My mom never changed my room. It's filled with more angst and darkness than a My Chemical Romance song."

"Interesting."

When I entered my room, I changed the direction of the camera, so I could show him what I meant.

"Wow."

I couldn't help but laugh. "Told you." The walls were black, there was a black shag carpet by my bed, and every poster from every grunge and heavy metal band from the nineties that you could imagine hung on the walls. "I tried dyeing my hair black once. I thought my mom was going to lose her shit." I closed the door behind me and went to my bed.

"What did she do?"

"She gave me a lecture on how dyeing my hair would ruin it and to embrace the red, so I have been. Maybe that's the reason the rest of my life is dark." I looked around the room, letting out a sigh as the memories from my teenage years slid to mind.

"I bet you were a brat as a kid."

"No." I looked back at Sammy, wishing he were there with me but appreciating the video chat anyway. "Most of the guys I've been with, including Aaron, didn't like it. So, I stopped."

"I'll never change you," Sammy said.

"Change is bound to happen, Sam. It's inevitable."

"No."

I slid off the bed and placed the phone on the nightstand, leaning it against the base of my lamp. "You don't think so?"

"Listen." He ran his hand through his hair, which I had come to learn he did whenever he was thinking over his next words. This surprised me just the same because Sammy Butcher never thought about his words before he spoke. He said whatever was on his mind. It was one of his traits that I was attracted to. I liked knowing where I stood with him.

I went to my dresser to get changed. He could still see me from where my phone was resting on the nightstand.

"Pet, eyes on me."

Before I knew what I was doing, I turned, my eyes connecting with his.

From where I stood, even though it was a few feet away, I could still see the sexy as hell smirk spreading on his face. "That right there is one of the reasons this isn't ending."

I opened my mouth to speak when he lifted his hand.

"I don't know what we're doing. I've never been in a relationship. I'm not into the hearts and flowers shit. I don't make love. I fuck. Rough, hard, violent, whatever word you want to use to describe it. But I like you. Even before we met, and I saw you dancing on that damn stage. I liked you then and I like you now. I already told you that I'm not sleeping with anyone else."

"I'm not sleeping with anyone else either, Sammy, but we can't continue this if I say no."

"No? You don't think so?" He chuckled, the sound dark and bordering on evil. It sent a delicious shiver down the length of my spine. "Tell me you don't want to continue this, Amber. Tell me you don't want to see where this goes. Tell me you don't want to submit to me and see just how far I can break you, so I can take care of you after and put you back together again. Say it. Say you don't want this to continue. I fucking dare you."

"And if I say that? What are you going to do?"

"Try me, Red. I don't take kindly to little pets who try to top from the bottom. Doesn't sit well with me and I will put an end to that shit. Real fast."

"Well, you aren't here now, are you? So, I guess there's nothing you can do, is there, Sammy?" I went up to my phone and picked it up off the nightstand. "So..." I licked my lips, his eyes following the swipe of my tongue. "I don't want this to continue. I don't want to see where this goes. I don't want to submit to you and I sure as hell won't touch myself to thoughts of you later either." I disconnected the call but not before I heard a growly *fuck* on the other end.

Placing the phone back on the nightstand, I blew out a slow breath, expecting him to call back, but when he didn't, it only made it more exciting. Because I knew, God did I ever know, he was going to make good on his promise and I couldn't wait.

TWELVE

SAMMY

PACING BACK AND FORTH in my room, I stewed over Amber's words and what I would do and how I would take care of this little issue between us. Add to the fact that she was several hours away in another city.

I had planned on driving up to see her right away, but time got away from me and I also found that teasing her was more exciting. It had been one of the reasons I decided to video chat with her instead of just straight up calling her. But little did I know, she would tease and taunt me instead.

Amber had hung up on me over an hour ago and I had been pacing ever since. Her words pissed me off but at the same time they turned me the fuck on. My palms tingled with thoughts of spanking her ass as she was bent over my knees, begging for me to fuck her. Or my fingers down her throat as she gagged, spittle leaking from the corners of her mouth as tears rolled down her cheeks. She would cry. I would make sure of it. But she would love the fuck out of what I wanted and would do to her.

I had never met a woman who could handle me and didn't run crying to their daddy because the big bad boy was mean. I wasn't mean. I just got off on certain things. The women I had been with had never been blindsided by that fact. It wasn't like I ever hid it from them. They just assumed they could take it, take me, and they couldn't.

But Amber? She took and she gave right back. That had been what I hinted for. Always. She had been the only one who understood because she needed it too. She enjoyed being called names and I enjoyed calling her them. It was a trust I had never experienced before and while that single trust came on fast, there was more we would have to eventually explore.

But for now, I needed to see her. I needed to let her know that her sass hadn't gone unnoticed but fuck me, did I ever crave it.

Finally getting an idea, I went to the one person who I knew would be able to give me the information I was looking for. Amber wouldn't tell me where her mom lived but little did she know that I knew people. I would have to call in a favor but having her in the end would be worth it.

As I left my room, I was greeted by my brother and his girl, no less. "What are you two doing here?" I asked as Ainsley Cloet stood from the couch and came toward me.

"We wanted to get out of the house," Cyrus explained, watching his fiancée step into my open arms.

"We were going to hit up that club," Ainsley said softly, hugging me around the middle.

"Really?" I looked between them, keeping my arms around my future sister in-law a little longer than necessary. If it had bothered my brother, I wouldn't hug her like I did, but it didn't, so I soaked up her warmth a few extra seconds. Truth was, Ainsley gave perfect hugs. Knowing she didn't like being touched by anyone but my brother usually, I never took her hugs for granted. Especially when we hadn't gotten along in the beginning either.

"Yeah, I know." Cyrus nodded toward her. "It was her idea."

She laughed lightly, pulled away from me, and went back up to my brother.

He wrapped his arm around her shoulders, leaning down to her ear and fingering the lock hanging from the collar that was around her throat.

She smiled as he murmured something to her. "I know." She kissed his cheek and stepped away from him. "I'll give you two a moment," she said, heading out of the basement and walking up the stairs.

"How are you doing?" Cyrus asked me, still watching the way Ainsley had gone.

I chuckled, shaking my head. "Just marry her already."

"No. We're waiting for Jaron and Piper to get married and then it's our turn."

"I don't know why you guys just don't have a double wedding." I pulled my phone out of my pocket and searched through Amber's social media posts to see if there were any hints for where she might be, but I came up short.

"As good as an idea that is for other people, it wouldn't work for us," Cyrus said, turning toward me and finally giving me his full attention.

I stared at the man I had shared a womb with so many years ago. Now that we were older, you could tell us apart, especially since he was bigger than I was.

"Why not?" I asked, crossing my arms under my chest.

"Because both Jaron and I are possessive as fuck. Not just of our girls."

I grunted. *He* was possessive. He clearly didn't know what I had done before Amber and I started fucking.

Cyrus tilted his head. "What is it?"

"Nothing." I went to take a step past him when a hand landed on my shoulder. "What?"

"You good?"

"I'm fine." But was I?

"Right," he said slowly.

"Why did you stop here when you could have just kept on driving to the club?" I didn't need the details to know that they were going to a BDSM club that was out of town. I was surprised that Ainsley would want to go, knowing that she preferred staying home and not being around people.

"Because I wanted to see your pretty face," he teased, hooking his arm around my shoulders. "I thought you were heading out of town."

"I am. I got a workout in and was a little distracted. But I'm driving out of town to see Amber." Or I was going to try to anyway, if I could find out where her mother lived. I could ask Shawnee but I had a feeling that she would warn Amber that I was on my way if I did. I could ask someone else but he wasn't always accommodating with information, especially when I fucked a girl he was apparently dating. But it was on her, since neither Rowan Crane nor I knew about each other. Rumor had it that he was seeing someone new anyway.

"You are?" Cyrus pulled away from me, staring intently at me.

I rolled my eyes. "Don't act so surprised. You also never answered my question."

"We wanted to stop in and say hi. Wouldn't feel right to drive past and not make an appearance. Also, the ladies who live in this house would kick my ass if I pulled that shit."

I chuckled. "Oh yeah." I headed out of the basement and up the stairs with Cyrus hot on my heels.

"Sam," he said from behind me.

"Yeah." I pulled a pack of smokes out of my leather cut.

"Be safe."

I turned and started backing up. "You two behave. Don't do anything I would do."

Ainsley laughed. "That won't leave us many options."

"You are correct there, Sis." I gave them a wave goodbye and quickly left the large estate before I was stopped again.

As I neared my bike, I thought back to how I first didn't approve of Ainsley. Not because I didn't like her. In fact, it was quite the opposite. She was perfect for my brother. Having a hard life, she stopped talking for the longest time until he brought the

words out of her once again. I had feared that she would take
him from me. It was lame but it had been how I felt. Now I
referred to her as *Sis* and loved her as much as if she were my
actual blood relative.

Straddling my bike, I pulled my phone from my inner pocket
and sent Amber a text.

Me: I'm coming for you, my Little Red.

The dots danced instantly, indicating an incoming reply.

Red: When? And how the hell do you know where I am?

I chuckled.

Me: I guess you'll never know.

**Red: I swear if Shawnee told you where I am, I'm going
to kill her.**

**Me: She didn't tell me but thank you for letting me
know who I need to get the information from.**

I wouldn't go to her, knowing that Amber's best friend
would refuse to give me the information I needed. My phone
rang then, forcing a laugh to shake through me.

"Miss my pretty face, Red?" I purred.

"You can't come here, Sam," she insisted.

My cock twitched. Fucking hell, I loved when she shortened
my name. "No? Why not?"

"Because, there are...I just...I don't want anything to
happen."

My heart stuttered. "Why, Red, if I didn't know any better, I
would think you actually care about me."

She snorted. "Listen, Sammy, don't go falling in love with
me. I'm not worth it. I just don't want anything to happen to you
or anyone else. The Hell's Harlem members here are...different."

"Trust me, I've run into them before and, Red? The next time you put yourself down and tell me you're not worth it, I will have you so fucking on edge, you won't be able to handle it. Have you ever been denied orgasms as punishment?"

"No," she whispered.

"Doesn't sound pleasant, does it?"

"No, it doesn't."

While I was speaking to the submissive in her, I knew the brat personality wanted to call my bluff and I hoped she would. Orgasm denial wasn't something I liked to do but if the situation called for it, I would. Just to show my sub who was in charge.

"Then don't berate yourself, you got me?" When she didn't say anything, I pulled my phone from my ear, thinking she might have hung up. "Red."

"I just don't want anything to happen to you. That's all."

"I'm a big boy, baby," I told her, my chest tightening that she cared.

"I know you are, but I still don't want any issues," she told me.

"Don't worry about it." No one was stopping me from getting what I wanted. We were good together. I just had to prove that to her.

THIRTEEN

Amber

THE NEXT MORNING, I couldn't help but think back to the conversation I had last night with Sammy. He was driving down. Or he said he was anyway. He was probably bluffing and would wait for me to come home instead. It was the only thing that made sense because it wasn't like anyone would tell him where my mom's place was anyway. Would they? Did he know people who could give him that sort of information? Oh who the hell was I kidding? Of course he knew people. He was a biker. I mentally smacked myself, forgetting for a brief moment exactly who I was sleeping with.

The conversation had finished with me telling him he was lying and there was no way he would drive the several hours just to see me.

He didn't argue and only hung up after.

Ever since, I couldn't get it out of my head and I sure as hell couldn't sleep. Looked like I was going to see Tiny sooner than I wanted to.

Once I was showered and dressed, I was heading down the

hall to the kitchen and putting my hair up into a messy bun when I was stopped short by voices coming from the dining room. A higher pitched one along with a deep vibrato. As I neared, I knew the woman's voice was my mother.

When I rounded the corner, my eyes widened at who was sitting with my mom at the dining room table.

"Hey, Red," Sammy greeted, giving me one of his large smiles. He was dressed in a black long-sleeved shirt that hugged his wide torso in all the right places. His leather cut was strewn over the back of the chair beside him. His beard had grown in some and bags sat under his eyes like he had been driving all night, but even though he looked tired, he was still beautiful as hell. My body heated at seeing him sitting there with my mom.

"What the hell are you doing here?" I demanded, shocked at myself that those words came out so suddenly. I was happy to see him, but I didn't like the fact that he had come here when I had told him not to. It wasn't safe. For either of us.

His smile only widened.

My mom's head whipped around. "I know I taught you to be strong and say whatever's on your mind but that's no way to treat a guest, Amber. I definitely taught you better than that."

My jaw clenched, my face heating. "Fine, forgive me. Sammy, it's so good to see you. Whatever did I do to deserve the pleasure of your company?"

Something flashed behind his dark eyes, and I knew that I was going to pay for my sass, but I didn't care. I didn't like that he was here without me knowing. Sure, it was good to see him because I had to be honest, I missed him, but I didn't like that he showed up out of nowhere.

Much to my surprise, both he and my mom laughed, which made my jaw clench even more.

"How did you find me anyway?" I demanded.

"I ran into your mom at the gas station. With her red hair, I told her it reminded me of someone. She said that her daughter has even redder hair and here we are," he explained like it was no big deal.

"Really? That's how you found me?" It almost seemed too innocent. Especially for someone like him.

"I also contacted someone I know and had them track your phone." And there it was. You would think we were just talking about the weather with how casual Sammy was being over the fact that he basically stalked me to another city.

"It's too early for this shit," I mumbled, heading to the kitchen. I needed coffee and I needed to know why he was here. Of all places.

"I'm going to go get ready for the day. Amber, you be nice and, Sammy, it was so good to finally meet you."

"It was nice to meet you too, Andrea," he told her, his voice smooth as damn silk.

I snorted. He was only smooth when he wanted something.

While I was waiting for my coffee to brew, a dark shadow loomed over me.

"I didn't actually think you'd be pissed if I showed up," Sammy said, his voice deep.

I looked at him over my shoulder, narrowing my eyes. "I don't do well with surprises. Whether they be good or bad. I need to know what's going on. And before you say anything, I'm not talking about sex. I like being surprised when it comes to that but not outside of the bedroom."

"Tell me why," he demanded gently, taking a step toward me. "Tell me you're not happy to see me here. In your home. Tell me you don't wish I would kiss you, touch you, fuck you, even hug you. Tell me, Amber."

I looked away, my teeth grinding together so fucking hard, a sharp pain shot up the side of my face.

"I'm talking to you."

I spun on him. "I don't like surprises because Aaron used to pull that shit and I was always left looking like the bad guy. His surprises hurt."

"What do you mean?" He frowned.

I huffed, turning back around and pouring myself a coffee.

Sammy stepped up behind me, placing his hands on the counter at either side of me. "Talk to me."

"They were never good surprises. It was like he didn't know me at all. I remember one time he got me a puppy and I'm allergic, but I wanted to keep him anyway. I would have taken allergy pills, done something to give him a good home. I reminded Aaron that I'm allergic, so he took the little thing from me and..." My throat closed over a hard lump. "I don't know what happened to the puppy but if I know Aaron at all, I know it wasn't good."

"Shit, babe, I'm sorry." Sammy turned me around and pulled me against him. "But you're comparing me to him again. I am not him. I'm just me. I understand that you've had some trauma and I don't hold it against you. I'll also wait for you trust that I am who I say I am."

"I know. I do know that." I took a deep breath. "I wanted to ask what he did but I couldn't bring myself to do it. It was just little things like that. But I am happy to see you." I placed my hands on Sammy's chest, running them across his pecs to his thick arms. "I am. Please don't think I'm not. I'm just shocked that you drove all this way."

"Why wouldn't I? I told you I was, and you have to know by now that I always mean what I say. If I tell you I'm going to do something, I'm going to do it." He stepped toward me, pushing his pelvis into mine. "I'm also happy to see you. Very happy to see you."

I laughed lightly, every inch of him pressing up against me. He was hard in all of the right places and if my mom weren't home, I would show him just how happy I was to see him.

"I promise not to surprise you anymore outside of the bedroom or I'll at least make sure you have a heads-up." He pinched my chin, tilting my head back. "Okay?"

"Okay," I breathed, licking my lips.

His eyes followed the movement, his hand moving from my chin to wrap around my throat.

The firm contact sent a shiver down my spine.

The corner of his mouth twitched.

"Sam," I whispered.

"Yeah, Red?" He inched closer but it wasn't enough. His mouth was a mere breath away from mine, the air crackling between us.

"God, why do you have this effect on me?" I breathed.

He smirked, lowering his mouth to mine ever so slightly. The contact was gentle, soft. While I enjoyed his rough kisses, this was what I enjoyed more. When Sammy gave me parts of himself he never shared with anyone else. I didn't take them for granted, knowing that there were parts of me I only ever gave him just the same.

Sam reached around me and cupped my ass, pulling me flush against him.

I sighed, licking along his full bottom lip.

A throat clearing from the entrance to the kitchen, made me jump. I actually thought Sammy would step away from me but instead, he placed a soft peck on my mouth and moved to my side. He hooked a finger in a belt loop on my jeans and pulled me closer.

"I was just seeing what your plans are for today," Mom said, a hint of amusement flashing in her eyes.

"I need to stop by the club to see Tiny." As soon as those words left my lips, a sharp pain in the cheek of my ass forced a squeak from my lips. I coughed, elbowing Sammy in the stomach.

He grunted, rubbing the spot I hit. "I'm not having you go to a biker club by yourself."

"He's right." Mom lifted her hand before I could argue. "And I know they aren't strangers to you but one, you haven't been home in a few months and two, Will..." She looked between us both.

"He knows about Will," I mumbled.

"He's causing shit," Mom told me, which was nothing new.

"I need to talk to Tiny and find out if he knows anything while I wait for Shawnee to get back to me," I explained.

"I get that, and I trust Tiny." She closed the distance between us and placed her hands on my shoulders. "But I don't trust the guys in his crew."

A sour taste filled my throat. I didn't trust them either. If it wasn't for Tiny, they would have ripped me apart long ago. That had been one of the many reasons I left this damn city.

"I'll be safe."

Mom sighed, heading back out into the dining room. "You better hope Tiny's there."

"He will be." I looked up at Sammy. "You can come with me but you're not stopping me from going to see him."

"Fine." He leaned down to my ear. "I'll deal with you later." He kissed my cheek, gave the spot beneath my ass cheek another pinch, and pushed away from me to join my mom back in the dining room.

As soon as I was alone, it was like he sucked all of the air out of my lungs.

When Sammy sat at the table, his eyes caught mine. He nodded once.

I shook myself and sent Tiny a text, letting him know that I was in the area. I needed to get this done and over with because I knew that with Sammy's temper and possessive ways, this meeting was not going to go well.

For either of us.

FOURTEEN

Amber

AFTER WE HAD BREAKFAST with my mom, Sammy and I were walking down the driveway. I headed to my car when a throat clearing stopped me. I looked over my shoulder, finding Sammy standing by his bike.

"You can take your bike but I'm driving my car." I didn't wait for a response and continued walking to my vehicle.

"You don't make anything easy, do you?" Sammy asked, catching up with me.

"Listen." I stopped in my tracks and spun on him. "I haven't had a lot of control over things that have happened in my life. Driving my car gives me some of that back, so I can leave whenever I want. I know things could take a turn very quickly. I'm not stupid, but I trust Tiny." Or I trusted him more than the others at least, but Sammy didn't need to know that. Tiny never gave me any reason to believe that he would hurt me. The others? Some of them hinted. Some just liked making me nervous. Tiny told me that the guys I had told off forever ago, while Aaron had done nothing about, had transferred to another club, but I had no idea why. I didn't know how it worked. While I knew some of the club rules, I wasn't privy to the business side of things. I had a feeling that, like Will, the guys had gone rogue or worse.

For the most part, they left me alone, but I had seen the way they looked at me when I was with Aaron. I wasn't exactly small chested, and I had curves and long pullable hair. Their words. It didn't help that I let a few of the guys use me after Aaron had died. I was trying to mask the pain and I thought sex would help, but I wasn't built for a quick fuck. I needed commitment, love. A damn relationship. I just wanted to be with a guy and not have to worry about where he was going to sleep that night. I refused to change for any man. I tried that once and it only made things worse.

"So, what will it be, Sammy? You going to play nice and come with me or be your usual grumpy self and complain the whole time because either way, you aren't stopping me."

"Fine." He searched my face, letting out a hard huff. "I'll go with you because clearly you won't listen to me but one, I will deal with you later like I said and two, you stick close to me. Where you go, I go. You got me?"

"Fine," I said, repeating his word and pulling the driver's side door. As much as I wanted to tell him he was being unreasonable and that everything would be fine, I appreciated that he wanted to protect me just the same. Before I sat in the car, a thought came to me. "What do you want in return?" as soon as that question left my mouth, I regretted it.

Sammy slammed the passenger door closed and stomped to my side of the car. In a quick move, he had his hand locked in my hair and my head ripped back. "I'm going to tell you again and this will be the last fucking time I say it." He leaned down until we were at eye level. "I don't want anything in return. Just because I do something for you, doesn't mean that I expect payment. I don't know what the fuck you've been through, but I am not Aaron. I am not Will. I'm not anyone else but me. Am I rough? Yes. Am I an asshole and grumpy as fuck? Yes and yes. Will I push you because I want to break you? You bet your fucking ass I will, but I'll also put you back together again. I will *not* do anything that you don't want."

"People always want something in return," I threw back at him.

Sam's hand tightened in my hair. "I am not people. I am me. You'll learn to accept that, pet, or do I have to take you back inside, throw you over my knee, and remind you exactly who I am?"

His threat sent a shiver down my spine. My throat closed in on itself, my heart racing so damn hard, I could hear the loud thumping in my ears. "Protect me."

The hard lines of his face softened. "You don't have to ask me to protect you, Amber." He leaned his forehead against mine, his hand in my hair, loosening. "That should be a given."

"It hasn't been." My eyes welled. "Not for me." I had spent years protecting myself since it was all I had but now that Sammy was in the picture, I needed more. I just wanted to curl in his arms and have him hold me.

I took a deep breath, refused to cry, and held back the tears.

"You never have to ask me to protect you." Sam kissed my nose. "You should just assume I will." He leaned back, tilting his head. "Understand?"

I nodded.

"Good. Now let's get this shit done and over with. I'm grumpier than normal and the sooner we do this, the sooner I can have your pussy." When he pulled away from me and headed back around to the passenger side of the car, I almost whimpered at the loss. God, what the hell was wrong with me?

Giving myself a shake, I took a deep breath and then another.

My mom had taught me to take care of myself but sometimes, I just wanted that extra help, no matter how hard I tried pushing Sammy away in the meantime.

Once I was seated behind the wheel, I started the car.

"How long has it been since you've been home?" he asked, cupping my inner thigh. His hand was at the spot between the crease of my center and thigh. It was an intimate touch and one I found that I desperately needed. Especially from him.

"Too long," I mumbled, pulling the car out of the driveway. "The only reason I come home anymore is to see my mom. I really wish she'd move but she won't. I offered for her to stay with me, but she told me she doesn't want to be a freeloader even though I would never think that of her."

"I get it. Your mom is by herself. She probably wants her independence and not have to depend on her daughter to take care of her."

"I wouldn't be taking care of her. I just want her out of this city and away from...people." I huffed. "It doesn't matter though because she won't listen to me, but I swear if something happens to her..."

Sammy squeezed my thigh. "I get it, Red."

That single touch calmed me down, easing some of the anxiety rushing through me.

"Please be nice when we get there. I don't want any issues for either of us. These guys know where my mom lives..." I let my words trail off, passing a glance at Sammy.

His eyes were on me, his hand moving higher up my thigh. His knuckles hit the apex between my legs. It was like he was reminding me who I belonged to, but I didn't need a reminder. I knew. I had known for awhile now.

I belonged to Sammy Butcher. And I wouldn't want it any other way.

"I'll behave unless they start shit with you. If that happens, I won't be held responsible for the things I do or say."

"Well let's hope that doesn't happen then." We drove the next little bit in silence. The Hell's Harlem chapter in this area had a clubhouse on the other side of the city. It amazed me how the guys in Sammy's chapter were far different than the ones I grew up with.

When we went down the street that led to the clubhouse, my heart started racing. "I just want to warn you that they're not going to like that you're with me. Doesn't matter if you're in the same club. And it doesn't matter that Aaron is dead."

"They still think you're his old lady," Sammy said, his voice flat.

It wasn't a question, but I nodded anyway. "I'm not. Sure, there was a time where he referred to me as it, but he never respected me like one."

"A lot of the times, even if you are their old lady, you'll still get cheated on, hit, whatever the fuck they feel like doing." Sammy's hand moved to my other thigh, his fingers sliding beneath my leg. "But I promise you that I would never do that to you. Not saying it doesn't happen in the chapter I'm in, but it's not *my* thing."

"That's good to know because if you want this to continue like you keep saying you do, I won't put up with that shit. Not again. I've already been through it. I refuse to—" A firm hand gripped the back of my neck. My eyes met Sammy's heated stare.

"Trust me when I tell you this." He squeezed the back of my neck, leaned forward, and pressed his mouth against my ear.

Every inch of me came alive at how close he was and if I hadn't been driving, I knew I would have ended up in his arms.

"Your pussy is the only one I want, Red." He kissed my temple. "The only one." He released me roughly, sitting back in his seat.

I pulled the car into the parking lot that led to a place I once considered home. "I hope you still feel that way after this."

"What do you mean?" Sammy asked as I parked the car.

"Because the guys call me their Princess." When I turned off the engine, I just sat there, memories rushing back to when I was there with Aaron.

"You mean, they refer to you as their whore," Sammy bit out, his voice rough. "And not in the sexy way."

"Yup, but it's not true. Yes, I slept around after Aaron died but it wasn't enough to consider me a whore or a slut. It wasn't like I was ever paid for it anyway." I tried making light of the situation even though I knew it was anything but.

"Look at me," Sammy demanded.

I took a deep breath, meeting his gaze.

"You are *my* whore, *my* slut, *my* little submissive. My fucking brat. Whatever you want to be, you are *mine*." He nodded toward the large building sitting in front of us. "I already told you that I don't give a shit what you've done before me but I'll say it again.

I do not give a shit how many guys you slept with. I'm here now, so that ends. You got me?"

I nodded, opening the door and stepping out of the car just as a couple guys filed out of the club. As nervous as I was to be there, I was thankful that Will was not around. For the moment anyway.

"I mean it, Red," Sammy said, leaving the car and coming around to my side. "Just because you slept with a few guys, doesn't make you a whore anyway. I hate that shit. Women can fuck whoever they want, whenever they want, as much as they fucking want, just as much as men can. Doesn't make them a whore or a slut." He scowled. "The guys were probably just jealous that you got more action than them anyway."

I looked up at him. "You are something else, Sammy."

"I could say the same for you, pet." He linked his fingers in mine as the three guys who left the club, started walking toward us.

"Well, this is quite the surprise." One of the members, Jack Sure or Jackie to those close to him, approached me first. His eyes flicked over my head to Sammy. "Sammy Butcher. It's been a while. I see you've settled down. Does Amber know how much action you've had?" Jackie wrapped his arms around me, the movement causing my hand to fall from Sammy's.

I didn't know they knew each other but it was no surprise really, seeing as they were in the same club.

"That shit doesn't matter," Sam bit out. "All that matters now is that she knows that I'm the guy who's going to fuck you up if you don't take your hands off of her."

I winced, waiting for Jackie to say something I would regret. If we were anywhere else, I wouldn't have been worried for Sammy but the fact that this crew, although it was the same club that Sammy was in, considered him an outsider.

I pulled away from Jackie, not liking this one bit. "I need to talk to Tiny," I said before he and the two other guys who were on either side of him, asked me why I was there.

Jackie narrowed his dark brows. He was older, pushing mid to late forties, but you would never know by his wrinkle-free face and hair that was still black as night. He was a good-looking guy, with a European background that no one knew much about.

"You didn't wait long for Aaron's side of the bed to become cold," Jackie accused, pulling a pack of smokes out of his leather cut.

"He's been dead for...no." I knew my mouth was going to get me in trouble, but I was sick of this shit. "You know what? I don't have to explain anything to you or anyone here for that matter. None of you said shit when Aaron was fucking anything that walked while he was married to me."

Jackie frowned, sticking a smoke between his lips. "Careful, Red." He lit it up, taking a deep inhale. "Aaron isn't around to protect you anymore," he said, letting the smoke out through his nose.

"He may not be but I am." Sammy stepped up beside me.

Jackie chuckled. "And what are you going to do exactly, Sam?"

When Sam took a step toward him, I moved in front of him. "Nothing. He's not going to do anything." I looked up at him. "Isn't that right?"

Sammy's jaw clenched.

The guys behind me, laughed. That sound sent every nerve in my body on edge. I glared at them, wishing Tiny would make an appearance. But knowing that I would have to go through these guys first to actually get to him, we had to play nice.

"Guess we know who calls the shots now, don't we?" Jackie asked from behind me.

Sammy smirked, kissed my forehead, and stepped around me.

I knew before even having to look, what Sammy was about to do. As I turned, his fist landed against Jackie's jaw. The impact caught him off guard, forcing him back a couple of steps. He rubbed his jaw, his eyes narrowing into slits before he charged for Sam.

Sammy only chuckled and sidestepped to the right. "You know, for someone who likes to think they're in control, you really aren't. You're a worthless piece of shit for the things you say about Amber and probably every other woman you've been with."

Before Jackie could close in on Sammy, I rushed between them. "Stop." I lifted my hand. "I don't want any trouble. I just want to see Tiny. That's it."

Jackie glared down at me. "You're lucky he's here, Princess."

"You don't scare me." I looked around him at the two other guys who did shit all and only just stood there. "None of you do. You are not Aaron." I took a step back, a sense of relief washing over me as the dark shadow that belonged to Sam, loomed over me.

"Where's your president?" Sammy asked, hooking his fingers into the ass pocket of my jeans.

"He's around," another deep voice said.

I peered around Jackie, finding Kellan Rose or Tiny, coming toward us. He had become bigger than the last time I saw him. He filled out a black long-sleeved shirt that was tucked into dark blue jeans, his torso wide and strong. Every part of him that wasn't covered by clothing, was lined with tattoos, including his bald head. Minus his face, there was some form of ink on his skin.

Before any of the guys could stop me, especially Sammy, I went to walk away from them when his grip on my pocket stopped me. I looked up at him, raising an eyebrow. "Let me go."

Sam peered over my head, looked back down at me, and winked.

That wink meant more than his words ever could. He tugged on my pocket, pulling me back against him and wrapping his other hand around my throat. Before I could shove away from him, because I didn't want to cause a scene, his mouth landed down hard on mine. The impact made me gasp, giving Sam the only invitation he needed as he dipped his tongue into my mouth. That gentle touch pulled a moan from the back of my throat. A moan that should have been for his ears only, but I was learning quickly that he liked causing these little noises to leave me. Especially in front of a guy I used to sleep with.

Sam bit my bottom lip, swiped his tongue along the spot to sooth the pain, and lifted his head. "Okay, now you can go," he said, releasing me altogether.

I shivered, walked away from him, and made my way toward Tiny.

"Did you really have to do that?" Tiny asked him as bodies shifted around us.

"Just stating facts, my man." Sam pulled a pack of smokes out of his leather cut and lit one up before holding the pack out to Jackie. "Want one?"

Jackie scowled and stomped away with the other two guys following behind him.

"You still causing trouble, babe?" Tiny asked, his voice low so only I could hear him.

"It wasn't intentional," I murmured, staring up at the only guy I trusted in this club. And one I definitely hadn't slept with. While Aaron spent most nights with other women, Tiny would let me cry on his shoulder, take care of me while I got drunk, or bring me to his gym and help me work it out. He never once hit on me and I often wondered why when the other guys did. They never cared that I was taken.

"It never is." Tiny held out his arms. "Now, give me a hug before your man cuts off my face and wears it as a mask."

I grimaced. "Well, that's an image." I closed the distance between us and wrapped my arms around his hard middle. "And he's not my man." But I did like the sound of that though.

"Sure." Tiny returned the embrace, curling his big body around mine. "From where I'm standing and with how he's looking at you and how he's looking at me for touching you, he's definitely your man, Red."

"Well, it doesn't matter." I pulled away from him. "I need to talk to you about Will."

A dark shadow passed over Tiny's tanned face. "Fine. Come with me."

I looked over my shoulder at Sammy.

"Just you, Red," Tiny told me.

"Not happening," Sammy interjected before I could comment. "Where she goes, I go."

Tiny chuckled, scratching the graying goatee on his chin. "Maybe I should call your president."

"Go for it." Sammy grunted. "It's been a while since he's tasted blood. I'm sure he's itching for a good fight."

I looked between them both. "If you two are done comparing dick sizes, can we get this done and over with so I can go home?"

"Remember, Red, just because Aaron is dead and gone, doesn't mean you shouldn't show him the respect he deserves," Jackie pointed out.

The two guys standing with him, shifted from foot to foot.

"Oh, just like you showed him respect? How about the many times you hit on me while he was still alive? Or when you propositioned me after I got out of the hospital. None of you came to see me. So don't even begin to say shit to me about respect." I had tried finding out if they knew who had killed Aaron and who had put me in the hospital, but it was club business, so I couldn't find out anything.

Sammy only smirked.

"You need to watch your mouth, little girl," Jackie growled between clenched teeth.

I rolled my eyes. "You're only saying this now because I'm no longer fucking you."

Sammy's smirked widened.

"Maybe you should actually grow a pair and not pine after a dead guy's wife." Before I could say anything more, Tiny grabbed my upper arm and all but dragged me into the clubhouse with Sammy following. "You didn't let me finish my thought." I pulled from Tiny's grip.

"He's only saying that shit to get under your skin, Red." Tiny nodded to one of the prospects. The younger guy quickly rounded up three beers and brought them to us.

"Thank you," I muttered, taking it from him. "But since when do you care what I say?" I asked Tiny as he led us down a hall that I knew would lead to an office. Tiny was the Enforcer for this chapter and was left in charge when the president and vice-president weren't around. Which seemed to be a lot lately.

"You need to retract those claws." Tiny stopped at a door. "She like this with you too?"

"She's worse." Sammy winked, taking a long swig of his beer.

I stared at him. "If you want sex again, I suggest being on my side."

Sammy's smirk fell from his face.

"Women." Tiny chuckled. "Always using the pussy card." He pushed open the door leading to the office and stepped into it, leaving Sammy and I alone out in the hall.

Just when I went to follow Tiny, Sammy wrapped an arm around my middle. "I'd be very careful if I were you, pet." His lips brushed along the shell of my ear, sending a shiver down the length of my body I knew he could feel.

"Or else what?" I asked, not liking this feeling of being backed into a corner. A corner that I had no idea how to get out of.

Sammy fisted my hair, turning my head to meet his dark, hungry stare. "Your mom told you to be careful. How these boys don't play nice and shit." He raised an eyebrow. "But she never warned you against me."

"Should she have?" I asked, my stomach flipping at the deep timber leaving his mouth.

"Nope, she shouldn't. But keep up the fucking attitude and I will do everything in my power to make you use your safeword. That I can promise you. You're also going to tell me about the hospital and all of the other shit later." He placed a hard peck on my mouth before releasing me and joining Tiny in the office.

(Sammy)

Amber could handle herself, that much was clear. But it didn't mean that I wouldn't stand on guard. I would wait and let her do her thing until she said she needed my help.

Jaron, Cyrus, and the guys and I had been to this chapter a few times but I had never been by myself.

I never liked that Jackie fucker. I had seen on more than one occasion how he would throw women around, just because he was twice their size.

I would have to call Jaron and warn him, if he wasn't contacted already. I knew going in that this was a bad idea but there was no way in hell I was letting Amber go to this clubhouse by herself. I didn't give a shit that she knew them for a long time. Add to the fact that she had slept with that Jackie fucker and a few of the other guys, she was just pussy to them. That was it. It was uncalled for, but it was the truth.

They treated her like a club whore even though that had never been true. From what I could see, she didn't just sleep with any and every guy like a lot of them did. Also, to be fair, she had been hurting and probably wanted to forget Aaron and all the shit he had done to her.

While I stood by the closed door, Amber sat on a brown leather couch across the room from me. She placed her beer on the end table beside her and blew out slow even breaths. She was too damn far away but I would give her space. For now.

"So tell me, to what do I owe this pleasant surprise?" Tiny asked, sitting on the edge of the large desk.

"Will is causing problems," Amber told him.

"Well, I know you didn't just drive down to tell me that when you could have called, and I also know that you've had problems with him before—"

"You have?" I blurted.

Both heads turned to me at the same time.

I almost laughed but really, the more I heard about this Will bastard, the more I wanted to mount his head on my wall.

There had also been a time that if a woman came with baggage of any sort, I would drop her quickly and move on. But now, whatever baggage Amber had, I found that I wanted to help her carry it.

"I haven't seen him in a while, but he usually shows up before I come home to see my mom," Amber explained.

"Why?"

Tiny scoffed. "Because he thinks Amber is going to either get information from us for him or give him information that she already knows."

I looked at Amber then. I never realized that she was a walking target. Who the hell was protecting her?

"I am and I also have other people looking out for her and her mom as well." Tiny scowled.

I rubbed the back of my neck, not even realizing I had spoken out loud.

Amber only stared at me. She was probably wondering the same thing I was. What the hell were we doing?

Suddenly, she winced, her face going pale before turning a light shade of green. "I..."

Spotting the garbage can beside the couch she was sitting on, I rushed to it and thrust it toward her at the same time she bent over and threw up everything that was currently in her stomach.

"You sick or eat something bad?" Tiny asked, grimacing.

"Neither. I just like throwing up for fun. It's my new hobby," she mumbled.

"You good?" I asked, sitting beside her on the couch and running my hand in circles along her upper back.

"Yeah. Must have been something from breakfast that's not agreeing with me." As soon as those words left her mouth, she threw up again, letting out a low groan. "I'm so sorry."

"Don't be." Tiny moved in front of her and crouched. "Let it out, you'll feel better."

She nodded, pulling the bag from the bin and tying it off. "I think I'm good now." She made a face, placed the bag back in the bin, and put it back on the floor.

Tiny rose to his full height and went to the door. Opening it, he stuck his head out. "Oscar, grab me a toothbrush, toothpaste and a bottle of Gatorade, will you?" he yelled.

"On it," someone called back.

"Are you sure you're good?" I asked Amber, my voice low enough that only she could hear.

"I am." She placed her hand on my knee. "I promise."

A part of me still didn't believe her but I would take her word for it. For now.

"Here." Tiny came back with a bottle of blue Gatorade and a brand-new toothbrush still in the package. "This will help put some color back in those cheeks."

Amber took it from him and twisted off the cap. She took a couple swigs before letting out a sigh. "Thank you. Why do you have a random toothbrush lying around?"

"Sometimes I sleep here," Tiny explained. "It's better to have these things in stock for when I, or any of the guys, spend the night."

"Oh." Amber took another sip of the Gatorade. "But I didn't come here for you to take care of me."

"No, that's my job," I said the words before I could even process what I was saying.

When they both looked at me, I shrugged.

"What? I said what I said." I rested my arm on the back of the couch behind Amber. "You know it's true anyway."

She huffed. "It doesn't matter. What does matter is that Will won't stop asking me for information and I... I'm here because I came home to see my mom. She didn't even want me to come over."

"Why would she? Look what happened last time." Tiny went to the desk and picked his phone up off the top of it.

"What happened last time?" I asked Amber.

"Aaron offered me up to the guys after they went on a ride." She said it so casually, I almost didn't believe her but the pain behind her eyes at the memory revealed all. Being with her late husband was an agonizing time for her and I couldn't imagine what she had been through. I made a vow right then and there that I would show her that I was *not* Aaron.

I would show her that I could be better for her. That I could be what she deserved and she the same for me. Sure, I only went into this wanting sex, but things changed fast when I realized that Amber was exactly the sub I had spent many years looking for. If my brother could find his, I knew I could find mine. And I had.

"He actually did that?" I asked, taken aback by how she didn't even flinch when those words left her mouth.

"Yup." Amber pulled away from me and stood from the couch. She went up to a door and opened it before turning to

Tiny. "Will you contact your people for me please and let me know when you hear why Will won't leave me the hell alone?" She slipped through the door and closed it behind her. Running water sounded a moment later, forcing Tiny's head up from the phone in his hand. He glanced at the closed door before looking at me.

"You be good to her," was all he said when the door opened.

Amber stepped back out into the office and threw the toothbrush into the garbage can. "Thank you."

"You're welcome." Tiny gave her a hug.

"You never answered my question," she told him, her words muffled by his shirt.

"I'll do what I can, Red, but I really think that Will is the only person who can help you with that." Tiny pulled away from her and continued typing away on his phone.

"Sam," Amber said softly. "Take me out of here."

I jumped to my feet. She didn't have to ask me twice.

"Leave the back way," Tiny instructed, not looking our way. "The guys are hungry. It's been a while."

Amber hugged her arms around her middle, cowering into herself.

Before she could lose herself completely, I went up to her and grabbed her hand before leaning down to her ear. "You're so fucking strong, pet," I murmured, pressing my lips against her. "So damn strong. You need me? You got me. Always. You never have to ask for anything."

She looked up at me then. So many emotions swam behind her eyes but the one single emotion I craved the most at the moment, was lust.

I kissed her cheek before standing to my full height and peering at Tiny who was still playing on that damn phone.

Slipping my hand from Amber's, I went up to Tiny. He never even saw me coming. Slapping the phone out of his hand, I grabbed the collar of his shirt and slammed him up against the wall.

"What the fuck?" he yelled, trying to shove me away.

"I don't like the way you look at her," I told him, stepping close to him until we were toe to toe and nose to nose.

"You going to kiss me, Sammy?" he bit out through clenched teeth.

As soon as the door to the office opened, I knew. "Amber, get over here," I demanded, knowing that we were no longer alone.

"Your president isn't going to like this," Tiny told me.

"Yeah, you see, that's where you're wrong." When I felt Amber come up beside me, I continued. "I'll tell him everything that happened here. Amber was trying to be polite, come see some old friends and also ask for your help when it came to this Will fucker. Clearly, none of you like him either, so why wouldn't you just offer to help her like she asked?"

"It's none of our business," Tiny said, his eyes flicking over my head.

"Look at me." I moved my head in his line of sight. "Not them."

His dark eyes met mine once again. "What do you want?"

"I want you to help Amber. I want you to find out what Will wants. Exactly what he wants. None of this assumption bullshit. I also want you to continue keeping her mother safe. I don't give a shit who you know. I know people too. If there's a single hair out of place on Amber's mother's head, I will make it a personal mission to gut you where you sleep. You'll bleed out as you watch me kill your family and every single person you care about."

"No harm will ever come to Amber's mother," Tiny grit out. "But if you don't get your hands off of me, I will head to your little clubhouse."

"Do it." I chuckled. "I dare you. Greyson may be retired but he's still nasty as fuck. I also know for a fact that you met his son. Greyson's a pussycat compared to Jaron." I patted Tiny's cheek. "It was good seeing you again, Tiny."

I turned, ignored the stares of the guys surrounding Amber, and went up to her. Before she knew what I was doing, hell...before I even knew what I was doing, I crushed my mouth to hers and kissed her in front of her late husband's crew.

LIBERATE US

Again.

FIFTEEN

Amber

I DIDN'T TAKE SAMMY'S kisses for granted, so when he kissed me in front of the crew my late husband belonged to, it made me fall for him even more. The fact that he didn't care and was willing to let anyone and everyone know how he felt, even without saying the words, meant something to me I would forever be thankful for.

Whatever it was that we were doing, didn't have a label on it, but I knew that he was the only one I wanted to do it with.

Sammy slipped his tongue between my lips, pulling a moan from the back of my throat. He circled an arm around me, cupped my ass, and pulled me even closer toward him.

Before the kiss could turn into more, he nipped my bottom lip, lifted his head, and gave me a wink.

"That was uncalled for," Tiny growled from his spot behind the desk.

"You know you would have done the same thing," was all Sammy said back.

I shook myself, not liking all of the eyes suddenly on me. "Let's go." I grabbed Sammy's hand, leading him out of the office and to the back of the club. "You know he's right," I said, once we were finally outside. We walked around the building to where my car was sitting at the front.

"Don't care, babe. I don't like how these fuckers think you still belong to Aaron. The bastard is dead and gone and..."

"What?" I asked when Sammy's voice trailed off.

"Forget it."

"No." I stopped, spinning on him. "You've never not said exactly what's on your mind before, so tell me, Sammy. What were you going to say?"

Sammy's brows narrowed. "He still has control over you."

I flinched, looking away.

Sammy started walking, keeping me at his side until we reached my car.

"Where are you staying?" I asked, pulling my keys from my bag.

"A hotel downtown." He slipped into the passenger seat as I opened the driver's side door.

Just as I was about to lower myself into the car, I caught movement out of the corner of my eye. Looking up, I found Tiny and a couple of the other guys standing at the entrance to the older building. Tiny nodded once and lifted his phone.

I pulled my phone from my bag, finding a text from him.

Tiny: It was good to see you. I'm sorry for being an ass. I never liked you with Aaron. He wasn't a good guy. Sammy is better for you. Not that you need it, but you have my blessing, and I will do everything in my power to keep your mom safe. Tell Shawnee I said hi.

I blew out a slow breath, looked up once again, and found Tiny and the guys nowhere around.

As I sat behind the steering wheel, I thought of what I could respond with. I knew Tiny had a reputation to uphold. I got it. I did. But if he only knew half the shit Aaron and Will put me through, maybe he would have been a little more accommodating.

Me: Next time I come visit, we'll have to go out for drinks.

Tiny: I like that idea. Drive safe, Red.

Putting my phone away, I gripped the steering wheel. "Tell me where you're staying."

Sammy cupped my inner thigh, giving me directions. His hand inched higher, almost like a reminder that no matter what happened, he would always be there.

A part of me was surprised that he got a hotel room. I just assumed that he drove down to get a piece and then he would head home. Clearly, I was wrong.

When we reached the hotel he was staying at, I parked the car, killed the engine, and stared straight ahead. "I need you."

"You have me," he said, his hand tightening on my thigh.

"No." I turned to him. "I need you. That part of you that I know wants to play with me and rip me apart. The part that wants to call me names and degrade me. That wants to push me to my limits. That wants to make me cry and beg for more. That wants to try and make me use my safeword. I need that part."

His eyes darkened, searching my face. "I don't know if you're ready for him."

I snorted, shoving his hand from my thigh and leaving the car.

Sammy did the same and came around to my side. "Tell me what you're feeling right now."

"Backed into a corner." My chest was tight, my heart pounding so damn hard, I was surprised Sammy couldn't hear it himself.

"What else?" He stood a foot away, but I could still feel him. Throughout every inch of me. But it wasn't enough.

"Vulnerable," I whispered.

He nodded once. "That's why I hated kissing. Until you, I never wanted to feel another person's lips on mine. But you, Red.

You fucking unravel me." He took a step toward me, but he was still too damn far away. "Tell me now. If you want this to continue, I will do everything you asked and more. I will force you to use your safeword and if you don't because you're strong as fuck, I'll continue to try each time we're together until I make you use it."

"Will you leave if I say it? Like you threatened the first time?" I didn't know why but the thought of never seeing Sammy again made me sick to my stomach.

He tilted his head, mulling over my words. "No. I don't think I could handle leaving and not seeing you again. My friends and family say I'm grumpy as fuck and I agree with them but not seeing you? That would make it worse."

"Then please give me what I need." I knew I was begging but I didn't care. I just needed to feel something other than this anxiety scraping along my skin.

Sammy finally closed the distance between us. In a move faster than I thought possible, he had his hand wrapped around my throat. He pulled me toward him, that single action sending a flutter of desire rushing through me. He licked his lips, his eyes dropping to my mouth. "I'm going to break you, Little Red. And then I'm going to put you back together again. I will be all you need. The *only* thing."

"Prove it." As soon as those two words left my lips, Sammy crushed his mouth to mine. The kiss was aggressive, rough, and deep. It bordered on being angry as he shoved his tongue between my lips and sucked a moan out of me.

I sighed, wrapping my arms around his shoulders and pulling him even closer.

His hands slid down my back, cupped my ass, and tugged me flush against every inch of him. A low growl left him as his lengthening erection pushed into me.

"Please," I whispered, taking his tongue even deeper into my mouth.

Sammy released me, wrapped his arm around my shoulders, and quickly led me to the entrance of the building.

The closer we got to the room he was staying in, the more my body vibrated with a need I had never felt before. Although

Sammy and I had been sleeping together for several weeks already, tonight would be different. It would be a switch in our relationship and whatever it was we were doing. I was offering him my submission. They weren't just words when I told him I wanted the dominant part of him. They were part of my truths. My need for him. My willingness to give him all of me in ways I had never given someone before.

Once we were in the elevator, Sammy grabbed a handful of my ass and leaned down to my ear. "I'm going to tear you apart, pet."

I shivered, inching closer to him.

The elevator dinged again, stopping at another floor. Sammy grabbed my hand and pulled me from the elevator. "How are you feeling?" he asked, leading me down the hall to his hotel room.

"Hungry."

He chuckled. "I meant from earlier."

"Oh." My heart warmed that he cared. "I'm fine. The Gatorade and brushing my teeth helped."

"I have a spare toothbrush if you need it." Sammy stopped us just outside his room. "Still in the package too."

"Aren't you a gentleman?" I said as he swiped the key card through the slot on the door.

He grabbed my hand and pushed me into his room. "Bathroom is to the right if you need it but hurry the fuck up because I'm hungry too."

"God, you're so demanding." I went into the bathroom and found the brand-new toothbrush still in its package like he had mentioned. I brushed my teeth again and took a little longer than normal because I wanted to make him wait before he did whatever it was that he wanted to do to me.

Peeking my head out of the bathroom, I found Sammy standing by the window. Getting an idea, I quietly closed the door and clicked the lock into place.

And waited.

SIXTEEN

Amber

BACKING AWAY FROM THE door, I waited for Sammy to break it down, but when he didn't, I wondered if he even knew what I had done.

"You're playing a very dangerous game, my Little Red," Sammy suddenly said from the other side of the door.

"Am I?" My heart jumped to my throat. "I don't know. You don't seem that scary to me," I threw back at him.

A deep chuckle sounded, sending a hot shiver racing down my spine. "You do know that I'll have to punish you for this. Right?"

"God, I'm hoping so."

His chuckle sounded again. "It's hard to fucking punish you when you like it."

"Why else do you think I'm a brat?" I laughed.

"Because you enjoy driving me fucking crazy." The doorknob jiggled. "You need to let me in."

"Nope. Not happening."

"Amber," he growled.

"Sam, if you want me, prove it."

"I'll break the fucking door down to get to that cunt of yours, pet. Don't think I won't." His threat was cute, but they were just words. Actions spoke louder and I wanted him to beg. I wasn't a switch by any means, and I was truly a submissive only, but this afternoon was a shit show. I wanted a little fun before Sammy gave me exactly what I needed.

"Amber." The knob jiggled again. "Let me the fuck in."

I went up to the door, stripping along the way. Once I was fully naked, I turned and leaned against the door. "I'm naked, Sammy."

"Fuck." I heard the clank of his belt buckle. "Touch yourself."

"Sorry, baby, you don't get to call the shots this time." But I inched my hand between my legs anyway.

"Amber." The desperation in his deep voice, forced my center to clench with need for him. "Fuck."

A breathless giggle left me. "Stroke your beautiful cock, Sam."

A thump sounded against the door, and I could only assume that he was leaning against it.

"Are you hard?" I asked him, slipping two fingers into my body.

"Yes." He groaned. "Are you wet?"

"Yes. So damn wet." I cupped a breast with my free hand, pinching the nipple between my thumb and finger. "Stroke yourself hard."

"I am." Another groan left him.

My hand picked up speed, pumping my fingers in and out of my body. The fact that there was only the door between us and we were both touching ourselves ignited this newfound desire for him. Riding my hand, a low moan left me.

"Rub that tasty as fuck cream all over your pussy and stomach, pet. I want to lick it off of you."

I shivered at his command. Pulling my fingers from my body, I wiped them over my lower abdomen. Repeating the movement, I did as he said and ran the cream that leaked from me over my stomach, inner thighs, and pussy. All because of the man standing on the other side of the door.

"You finished?" he gritted out.

"I…I think so." My chest rose and fell with ragged breaths.

"Good, now open the fucking door."

"No." I shoved two fingers back into my body, a low whine leaving me.

"Don't you dare come," he barked.

"You can't tell me what to do," I panted. "Not right now."

"No? Are you sure about that?" His voice took on a deadly tone and I knew that once I unlocked the door, I was in for it.

I had never felt pleasure like this from my own hand. Sure, I knew how to get myself off but the fact that I was doing this, and that Sammy could hear, turned me on even more. It was like exhibitionism in a way, but it wasn't around a stranger.

"Amber, unlock the *fucking door*," he demanded, his voice rising.

That was what I wanted. This whole time. I wanted him unravelled, begging, pleading for me. I wanted the passion to be so damn intense that it snapped, breaking between us until we could do the only thing that would make us feel better.

Fuck.

With my fingers still in my body, I turned and unlocked the door, quickly stepping back.

Sammy slammed the door open.

My eyes widened at the sight before me. He was completely naked with his hand wrapped around his thick cock. I had never seen him so hard, so unhinged before. His muscles were tight over his bones. His eyes dark. His forehead was creased with a hard frown.

"On your knees," he demanded. "*Now.*"

I dropped before I could stop myself. It was like he had control over that submissive part of me and the rest of me couldn't do anything but go along with it.

He took a step forward. "Keep fingering yourself but if you come, I won't fuck you."

I whimpered.

Sammy cupped my face, the move had been so gentle, nothing like the man who was about to shove his cock down my throat. In a rough move, he gripped my hair, ripping my head back. The move had forced my mouth open and before I could even take a breath, he shoved all of his inches down the back of my throat.

I gagged around him, my lips burning at being stretched wide. My eyes welled, tears rolling down my cheeks.

"Fuck, you're beautiful when you cry." He grabbed onto my head with both hands, fucking his cock hard between my lips.

Pumping my fingers in and out of me in rough moves, a tingle started brewing in my toes, forcing a loud moan from my lips.

Sammy frowned, ripping his cock from my lips. "What the fuck did I say?"

I gasped, taking deep breaths. "Don't come."

"Exactly. Are you going to listen to me?"

"Probably not." We both knew that even if I didn't listen to him and made myself come like he instructed me not to, he would still fuck me.

A wicked grin spread on his face. "Why not?"

"Because I'm calling your bluff." I pulled my hand from between my legs and stuck my fingers between my lips. "I know you can't control yourself when it comes to my pussy," I said, licking the cum from my fingers.

"You sure you want to do that?" he bit out, pinching my jaw.

A husky laugh left me. "Try me, baby."

He grinned. "Open and stick your tongue out."

I did as I was told, waggling my tongue.

He pursed his lips, slowly letting a drop of saliva drip onto my tongue. Much to my own surprise, a moan left me. I had done lengthy research on different types of kinks and fetishes after Aaron made me feel like something was wrong with me and came across something called drool play. I didn't think it would be my thing, but I found that with Sammy, I was willing to try anything at least once.

Sam gripped tighter under my jaw, lifting me to my feet. With his rough hand on me, he pushed me back until I hit the wall.

A gasp lodged free from my throat. Slipping my fingers back inside of me, a moment of shame washed over me at how much wetter I had become, but then I remembered that Sammy wasn't Aaron. He wouldn't hurt me.

"I'm not him," Sammy bit out, his voice rough. It was like he could hear my thoughts, my fears, and my truths.

Removing my hand from between my legs, I brought my fingers up to his mouth.

His eyes darkened as I brushed the wet tips along his bottom lip. His hand on my jaw tightened as he crushed his mouth to mine.

My desire for this man slid between us, coating our tongues and sending my senses on overdrive. I had never felt this. This want. This need. This inexplicable obsession for another person before.

With Sammy's hand wrapped around my jaw, he devoured my mouth.

Circling my fingers around his cock, I pumped hard and fast.

A deep moan escaped him, the kiss picking up speed.

Before I could guide him to where I wanted him most, he broke the kiss and lowered to his knees in front of me. His teeth sunk into my hip. He sucked and licked a path up to my chest. He cleaned the juices I had coated myself in off of me and it left me aching even more for him. Once he was back to standing in front of me, he spun me around and pushed me face-first up against the wall.

"You like when I degrade you." He kissed my shoulder. "You like when I spit in your mouth and treat you like a fucking whore." He kicked my legs apart. "You like when I hurt you." He landed a palm against my ass.

I gasped, the delicious sting sending a wave of warmth over my skin. "Yes. Yes to all of that."

"Good." Sammy kissed my shoulder again. "Keep your hands against the wall and stay still." He stepped away from me before I could ask what he was doing. He left the bathroom and came back a moment later. "Eyes straight ahead, pet. This is going to hurt but if I know your body any and I think I do, you'll enjoy this."

I swallowed hard, my muscles shaking over my bones with anticipation. "Sammy."

"Shhh..." He came up behind me. "You're safe with me, Amber. All of you is safe. But I told you I would make you use your safeword. I have a feeling you won't use it though just to be a brat. Am I right?"

"I have no idea what you're talking about," I murmured.

"Trust me, Amber. That's all I ask."

I rubbed the back of my neck and nodded.

"Good girl."

Those two words did something funny to my belly. I never realized how much I needed his approval until now. While I needed to be in control outside of the bedroom and I also liked being a brat, this, right here with Sammy, was what I actually needed.

"Safeword," he said, his voice low.

"Tyler."

"Spread your legs more but don't move your hands from the wall," he demanded, brushing a hand over my hip.

I did as I was told, sticking my ass out for him. I wasn't sure what he was about to do but I knew that I couldn't wait just the same.

Just when I was about to tell him to hurry up, something hard slid between my legs and over my swollen center. I chewed my bottom lip, swallowing a gasp. The item moved back and forth over my clit, sliding up to my opening and back down again.

Whatever it was, Sammy pushed it against my center. "Color."

As soon as he said that single word, it was like something had switched inside of my brain. Looked like all of my extensive research on the subject of BDSM, came in handy.

Green meant you keep going.

Yellow meant to slow down.

Red meant to stop altogether, and you talk about it.

"Green," I whispered, remembering the three colors that were different levels of safewords in a way.

"Good." He moved to my side, kissing my temple. "Breathe out when I push in."

"What are you pushing into me?" I asked before I could stop myself.

"Don't worry about it." He winked. "I'll tell you after you come all over it."

I shivered at the thought.

"Now breathe, pet."

I took a deep breath as the item pushed against me. Letting the air out slowly, I could feel whatever this hard thing was sliding past the barrier of my body. A little more and it would be inside of me, whatever it was.

We repeated the movement.

Sammy pushed.

I breathed.

He stared at me.

I moaned.

"Keep breathing," he demanded gently.

As soon as I took another breath, the item slid into my body. A hard groan left me, my pussy burning slightly at being stretched more than normal.

"That's my good girl." Sammy kissed the spot by my ear. "You're doing so well, pet." With his free hand, he inched between my legs, running his fingers over my clit.

I jumped, the sudden surge of pleasure was wanted but at the same time, was almost too much. "Sam."

"Shhh…let me give this to you." He pulled the item almost all the way out before slipping it back inside of me.

I whimpered, my eyes rolling into the back of my head. Bending over at the waist, I needed him to fuck me with whatever it was that was currently inside of me. "Please."

Thankfully he got the hint and wrapped an arm around my waist. He held me while thrusting the item back and forth into me.

Whatever it was, I found that Sammy could fuck me with anything he wanted, as long as I got him after.

(Sammy)

The sounds leaving Amber's mouth, were music to my fucking ears. Literally. I wasn't sure if it would actually work but when I grabbed the small water bottle and came back to her shaking in anticipation, I knew that she would enjoy this.

I much preferred to please a woman with only my body but sometimes toys were needed and they could make things more exciting. But I didn't have any toys with me, so I had to improvise.

Holding her up because I imagined that her knees were about to give out from under her, I pumped the bottle in and out of her. The sounds leaving her mouth were almost animalistic. They mixed with her begging me to fuck her but that wouldn't happen. Not yet.

"Safeword," I demanded roughly.

"Tyler," she cried out, pushing back into the rough thrusts of my hand. The bottle slid in and out of her easily. Her body was fucking soaked. The sounds of her pleasure and juicy cunt making my dick throb. "Sammy," she finally screamed, her body shaking as her eyes rolled into the back of her head.

And there it was. That was what I wanted.

Ripping the bottle free from her body, I tossed it in the trash. Her wide eyes stared back at me, probably wondering what the hell I was doing.

I only winked, before shoving four fingers into her.

She gasped, a hard whine leaving her.

Gripping her jaw with my free hand, I licked along the seam of her mouth. She whimpered, taking my fingers like a good little slut.

Pulling my fingers from her body, I slowly, careful not to hurt her, slipped them back into her followed by my thumb.

Her tongue peeked out, connecting with mine.

I gave it a gentle bite, pushing my hand deeper into her body.

Her breathing picked up, her pupils dilating.

LIBERATE US

Pulling my fingers out and pushing back in slowly, I repeated the movement until my hand was fully inside of her up to my wrist.

"Oh…my God…" She shook, a sheen of sweat coating her skin.

"You wanted to hurt, baby," I reminded her, digging my fingers into her cheeks.

She nodded. "Yes."

"Then take my hand like a filthy little slut." Her pupils dilated even more. "You like that. Your sloppy cunt is taking it all."

Sounds of pleasure left her as I fisted the fuck out of her pussy.

SEVENTEEN

SAMMY

FOR THE FIRST TIME in a very long time, maybe even in forever, I slept through the night without waking up from a nightmare. Cyrus and I had built a routine over the years. We would usually wake up at around the same time during the night after having a nightmare about when I was kidnapped as a kid. Although I was saved rather quickly, it had been the last time I saw our father alive. That fact alone didn't sit well with either of us. So, these damn nightmares fucked us up.

Now my brother had Ainsley to console him back to sleep and I was hoping I had Amber.

She was curled against me, her soft snores sending a wave of peace over me. My arm was under her head, her fingers linked in mine. While my arm was half asleep and tingled with lack of blood flow, this was what I needed. I had never been known to be gentle with my partners. Even when I lost my virginity so many years ago, I knew right away that I liked a different side of sex than a lot of people. Over time I came to understand just how important aftercare was. I just never wanted to partake in it with any woman I had ever been with. Not until Amber.

My brother had tried explaining it to me. He told me in the beginning to get my head out of my ass and make a move. I thought at first that he was just being a dick, but now I got it. Even if Amber and I never became more serious than we were, I realized after the shit that had happened yesterday and spending the night with her, she was the calm to the raging storm inside of me.

I knew the anger in me had been festering over the years. I wasn't stupid. I also noticed how people walked on eggshells around me. Scared that if they said one wrong thing, I would blow up. Maybe I would have. But that rage seemed to simmer some ever since she and I started sleeping together.

It was still early in the morning and while I didn't get a whole lot of sleep, I felt more rested than I had in years.

Amber gave as good as she got. She never once used her safeword even though I had tried my hardest to get that single word to leave her lips.

With my cock deep in her ass and my fist in her cunt, Amber rode me. Hard and fast, giving us both what we wanted.

My back tingled from where her nails had dug into my skin. My cock ached from the many times her teeth had dragged along it as I roughly pounded into her mouth.

A twinge of pain erupted through the shaft of my cock. My eyes locked on hers. "Careful with those teeth, pet," I warned.

She released me with a pop. "It seems to me that you like a little pain with your pleasure."

"No. I like inflicting pain with your pleasure."

"I think you should teach me a lesson."

And I did. My dick ached from how many times she had made me come but it was an ache I could live with, knowing that she got as much pleasure from it as I had.

But as much as I enjoyed the sex with her, I meant what I said. I liked the aftercare even more. Taking care of her was my ultimate task. Besides giving her what she needed when it came to her pleasure, what came after was my favorite.

"I can feel you staring, Sam," Amber murmured, her voice thick with sleep.

I kissed her shoulder. "Just watching you."

"Like a creeper." She sighed, rolling over onto her stomach. She turned her head, her beautiful eyes meeting mine. "Thank you."

"For what?" I asked, running my hand down the length of her back.

"For giving me that part of you I needed but you still didn't break me like you threatened."

"Anticipation, baby." I dipped a finger between the cheeks of her ass. "Besides, by the fucking squeals that left your mouth, I didn't want to get a noise complaint or for us to get kicked out."

She laughed, shaking her head. "I think you bruised my pussy."

I raised an eyebrow, my stomach clenching that I had been too rough.

She laughed. "I'm kidding." She reached a hand out to my cup my cheek. "Trust me, I liked it. Everything we did. I liked it all."

I blew out a breath of relief. "You need to use your safeword if I get to be too rough, pet. You know that."

"I know but you weren't too rough. Nothing I can't handle."

I stared at her. "Who the hell are you?"

She only smiled. "Just me."

"No, Amber, you are fucking perfect." I rolled onto my back and stared up at the ceiling, wondering what I did to deserve someone like her. "I've had women leave my apartment because I was too rough. They couldn't handle it even though I had warned them. A lot of those women had come home with me from the BDSM club, so they knew the rules and to use their safewords. But they never did."

"And then they blamed you for being too rough?"

I looked over at her then. "Yeah."

"I trust you, Sammy. I know you would never hurt me." She gave me another small smile, her shoulders lifting slightly in a shrug. "You're different."

"But I still remind you of him." I noticed how there would be moments were she would get this faraway look in her eyes, like she was remembering a previous life or something she smelled, saw, or heard would trigger a memory.

"No." She lifted onto her elbows. "Not exactly. I think my issue is that I'll say or do something and a part of me expects you to react the same way he did. And for that I'm sorry. It's not fair to you. I know that. But I can't...I can't help it."

"Don't be sorry." I turned onto my side, leaning my temple against my palm. "Were you ever happy with him?" I asked, running my hand in small circles over her back.

"Yeah, when we were dating. But as soon as I said *I do*, it was like a switch went off and he turned into a completely different person. But I thought maybe it was me. It was what he said anyway." She shrugged again. "I don't know. It took me a long time to realize that he was abusive. Even after the initial rape, something in my head tried telling me that maybe I asked for it or that it was a kink that I wasn't used to."

"Anything can be a kink or a fetish, but you and your partner still have to consent to it," I said, not liking the bite in my tone.

She flinched, even though my anger had nothing to do with her. No, I blamed Aaron. I one-hundred-percent blamed that fucker.

Needing to see her in her entirety, I turned on the lamp that sat on the nightstand. When I laid back down on my side, she looked away. She was trying to hide herself but she didn't need to. Not with me. I wanted every dirty layer of her. I wanted her quirks, her truths, and her pain. I wanted her. *All of her.*

"I like you, Amber," I said even though she knew that already.

Her gaze met mine. "I like you too," she whispered.

"I meant what I said when I told you that I want to date you."

Her eyes searched my face. "You want to go steady?" she asked, with a teasing lilt to her voice.

"I'm already committed to you, so why the fuck not?" My words came out harsher than I intended but the truth was, this woman was my undoing. It was like she was peeling away layer by layer of everything that made up me.

Her eyes snapped to mine. "Sam."

"You know it's true, Red." I sat up and left the bed, earning me a gasp. I was comfortable in my skin and worked out hard to get what I had. I wasn't conceited but was proud of the work I put in to get a strong, healthy body.

Leaving Amber in bed, I went to the patio doors and stepped out onto the balcony of the hotel room. I didn't care in the least that I was completely naked since no one would be able to see anything anyway when the walls of the balcony weren't glass.

I could feel her before I saw her. Gentle hands pressed against my back, followed by a hot mouth. Her soft touch sent a shiver racing down my spine.

"I want to date you too," Amber finally said. "I'm also committed to you as well, but I still need slow."

I turned toward her, leaning against the edge of the balcony. She was wearing my hoodie and that was it. Her hair was a mess, pink sat in her cheeks from the previous pleasure I had given her and fuck me, was she ever beautiful.

Without me having to ask, she closed the distance between us.

Wrapping my arms around her, I spun us until she was leaning against the balcony. Pulling her against me, I lifted the hem of the hoodie and pushed my cock between her legs. She gasped, her eyes darkening.

"I'm not hinting for more, I just…I need…" I didn't even know what I needed but I knew that I needed her warmth. My dick was only semi-hard but while it sat snug between her thighs, it forced this sense of calm to wash over me. I had spent years teetering on the edge of my rage. I knew people were concerned that one day it would take control of me completely.

"I know, Sam." She sighed. "I know."

Fisting her hair, I tugged her head back and stared at her. With my cock between her thighs and my grip firmly in her hair, I realized something. I could easily fall in love with her. Maybe I already had. I wasn't sure. But one thing was for certain.

Amber controlled me way more than I controlled her.

(Amber)

I stared up at him. The man who had taken me past the point of just being comfortable with the kinks I was into. He took them, used them, and gave them back to me in ways I could never thank him enough for.

What we had done the night before was something I never experienced. With anyone. My body still burned from the rough use of the bottle and then him fisting me. But God, it was a burn that reminded me of what came after. Him taking care of me. Him making sure I was okay. Him, Sammy Butcher, an asshole to most, but gentle and caring with me. He showed me a side of him he didn't let others see and for that, I would never take him for granted.

Leaning back against the balcony, I lifted a leg and wrapped it around his waist.

Sammy lowered his mouth to mine at the same time as he thrust slowly back into me.

He swallowed my sigh, neither of us caring that we were outside. While it was still early in the morning, anyone who was standing at a window or a balcony at one of the buildings across from where we were would be able to see what we were doing. But I didn't care and neither did he.

EIGHTEEN

Amber

SEVERAL WEEKS PASSED AND Sammy and I spent as much time together as possible. I had come to learn that besides being a biker, he worked at his aunt's auto shop and also did construction at a local center for human trafficking and abuse victims. Maybe I should have searched out the place long ago, but instead I had my mom, Shawnee, and the other girls to help me through my trauma. While my mom and Shawnee were the only ones who knew the exact details, everyone else knew that my late husband was abusive. As soon as that single word was uttered, they never asked anything more.

Sam and I didn't dwell on our relationship status, but I did like the fact that he reminded me every chance he could that I was his girlfriend. He had told me he never had a girlfriend before and was proud of the fact that he finally had one who could handle him and his mood swings. It hinted at the fact that I was a brat and enjoyed challenging him whenever I could.

As I spent one afternoon cleaning my apartment, my thoughts traveled back to that morning. Sammy woke me up with his mouth between my legs. I shivered, wishing I could have spent the day with him, but he had to work and promised to see me later that night at Rouge. A part of me was thankful he left anyway since I had spent the rest of the morning after he left throwing up. I wasn't sure what was wrong with me. Over the past few days, these bouts of nausea would come on at random times of the day. It hadn't happened since we went to see Tiny weeks ago but all of a sudden, it had started up again.

Once I finished sweeping the kitchen, the cleaning distracting me from how I was feeling, I went to the fridge to grab a bottle of water. My eyes landed on the calendar I kept on the freezer door. I frowned, seeing the tiny little star I had drawn on the date I should have started my period. But that date had come and gone, and I still hadn't started. I had been so wrapped up in Sammy that I had never even noticed. He bought me that bag of tampons and pads after our first night together but that was weeks ago. Maybe even longer? Had it been a couple of months already?

I flipped the page to the previous month and then another, my eyes widening when I realized that I couldn't remember the last time I had my period. My thoughts recalled the many times Sammy and I had sex. I bled after one time we had gotten carried away. We tried a new position which resulted in him being even deeper inside me. We had assumed that my period was coming. But it never did.

My hand dropped to my stomach. "Oh…shit."

I couldn't be. I religiously took my birth control. I knew it wasn't fool proof of course but it wasn't possible. It couldn't be.

Either way, I had to find out. I had to know if I was carrying Sammy's baby.

Grabbing my bag, I locked up and left the apartment. I was in a fog as I drove to the pharmacy and bought several pregnancy tests and a large jug of orange juice. I didn't even remember getting back home but here I was, sitting on the edge of the tub, waiting for five tests to do their thing.

LIBERATE US

When the alarm on my phone went off, indicating that it was time to check them, I took a deep breath. Silencing the alarm, I checked the tests spread out on my bathroom counter.

The word *Pregnant* stared up at me from one. A pink plus sign was on another. My eyes roamed over all of them. All five tests. All five came back positive.

Pregnant.

I was pregnant.

I couldn't be and yet I was. Sammy and I hadn't used protection for a while, but I was still on birth control. It just proved it wasn't a sure thing.

Would Sammy be mad? Would he react like Aaron had?

As I sat on the floor at the base of my tub, I couldn't help but think back to the one and only time I *had* been pregnant and how my late husband reacted.

"You're pregnant?" Aaron boomed, his face red with fury.

"I thought you would be happy," I yelled back, shocked by his sudden outburst.

"Why the hell would I be happy? I don't want kids. I told you that before we got married." He was lying. He never told me that shit.

"You said it wasn't something you longed for but if it happened, you would be happy." I threw my hands up in the air. "God, I can't even with you."

"How do I know it's actually mine?"

I stopped, slowly turning toward him. "Did you really just ask me that question?"

"I mean, come on, Amber." He shrugged. "I see you flirting with the other guys in the club. Especially with Tiny."

"Kellan has nothing to do with this." Kellan Rose was the Enforcer for Hell's Harlem at the local chapter and I had been the only one who got away with using his first name. He went by Tiny because he was a beast, but also, nothing but a teddy bear if you were lucky enough to get that side of him.

"Are you sure? You two hang out all the time."

"We're friends, not that I have to explain anything to you." I stomped to our bedroom. Aaron was being an asshole. He had been one for awhile now and I couldn't handle it anymore. My thoughts traveled to the divorce papers I had stuffed away in my bag, wishing I had the strength to go through

with it. I could call up Shawnee like she offered and get her to do it with me. No, I had to be strong. I could do it. I just needed the right moment.

"Not that you have to explain anything to me," Aaron repeated, *following me. "Are you fucking serious right now? You're my wife. You do have to explain shit to me if I demand it."*

I stopped, spinning on him. "Yeah? Or else what? You going to rape me again?"

His face turned even redder. "I apologized for that."

I scoffed. "Right, after you got off, had some more beers, and got drunk. That's when you apologized. While I cried myself to sleep, thinking I did something wrong by wanting to connect with my husband on another level, wishing, praying that you would console me but no, you passed out instead. But please, apologize away, Aaron."

I could never explain where I got that bravery from, but I remembered how saying those words to him made me feel better. He never apologized. Not for anything he had ever done to me. He was nice before he fell in with the wrong people. The wrong parts of Hell's Harlem. He wasn't a good guy. Not like Sammy and the guys he hung out with. I knew no one was perfect and that this chapter was trying to clean up some messes based on what Tiny told me, but even he confirmed that they were good guys and were nowhere near being like Aaron and Will.

It got to the point where I hadn't been sure if the baby was Aaron's or Will's. We had several threesomes, not that I was proud of it, and I got pregnant. I remembered back to when I told Aaron that we should let his brother know as well. Just in case.

My stomach twisted at the awful memories rushing through my mind. Before I could get lost in those nightmares, I took a deep breath and sent up a silent prayer.

Cupping my stomach, I prayed that this baby would survive the wrath and evil of the world. But I knew even before I told Sammy that he would take this news far better than Aaron ever did.

I imagined that he would be happy or maybe he would tell me he loved me or that he was at least falling for me. It was a wild thought but a nice one at least. Did *I* love him? I wasn't sure but I did have feelings for him and now that I was carrying his baby, it only heightened them even more.

The past few months with Sam had been nothing short of amazing. We became closer, stayed committed to each other, and just hung out. He never demanded things of me and in return, I didn't either. We just took what we were doing one day at a time.

Word had gotten around that we were together, and I hadn't been hit on at Rouge. Sammy was nicer to the girls and didn't make any of them cry again. Everyone commented how his mood had changed and how it was because of me that his permanent scowl had softened a bit.

I wasn't sure what the next steps would be, but I knew that I *had* to tell Sammy about the pregnancy and set up a doctor's appointment. So many thoughts ran rampant through my mind. I couldn't help but wonder if my baby was okay. If there was even a baby inside of me. Maybe the tests were wrong. Maybe my cycles were just being weird. I wasn't sure how old you had to be to start going through early menopause. Should I call my mom?

Scrubbing my hands down my face, I let out a harsh sigh. My eyes flicked to the bag. I had bought several tests, maybe I should take them all. Because obviously five tests coming back positive could be wrong. Or that was what I liked to tell myself anyway.

Grabbing the big jug of orange juice, I drank some more and waited. When I had to pee, I took the rest of the tests and waited. Again.

I leaned my hands on the edge of the bathroom counter and once the rest of the tests came back positive, I called the one person who I hoped would know what I should do.

"Hey, sweetheart," my mom answered after the first ring. "How are you?"

"Um…I'm staring at ten pregnancy tests, and they all came positive," I said, my tone flat.

"What? Hold on…wait…what?"

"I'm pregnant, Mummy, and I don't…I just…" I sat on the edge of the tub. "I'm scared."

"Okay. Take a deep breath."

I did as she said, blowing out the air slowly.

"Again."

Repeating the action, I waited to start feeling better, but it didn't work.

"Have you told Sammy?"

"Not yet." I rose to my full height and left the bathroom. "I only just found out and called you first. I don't know what to do."

"First thing, how are you and he doing?"

"Good. I think we're good anyway. We don't fight." Unless we were fucking anyway but I never told her that. I didn't need to scar my mother. She already knew that I used to be a stripper. She didn't need to know that I liked being choked until I was on the verge of passing out. God, I was going to go to hell just from the sex I liked.

"Okay, that's good. I'm glad." She cleared her throat. "Now, secondly, are you going to keep it?"

"Yes. Even if Sammy and I don't make it, I'll raise this baby on my own if I have to and I will try my hardest to be the best mom I can possibly be. But I think Sammy will be there for the baby too, no matter what happens to our relationship."

"That makes me happy. I know Aaron didn't react the way he should have."

"I know. Sammy isn't like him thankfully." I tossed the tests into the trash before heading back to my bedroom. Putting the phone on speaker, I placed it on my bed and began stripping out of my clothes. Once I was completely naked, I went up to the floor-length mirror and let my gaze roam down my body. Did I look pregnant? My breasts were a little tender. I turned, cupping my stomach that was still flat.

"How are you feeling?" my mom asked.

"I've been sick a few times but now I know that it was morning sickness. My boobs are tender but nothing I can't handle." I went back to the bed and picked up the phone, turning off the speaker. "I don't think Sammy will react the way Aaron did but a part of me is scared to tell him."

"I know, honey. The only thing I suggest is to tell him in person and not over the phone."

"I will."

"Did you need me to drive down?"

My heart warmed at the thought. "No. Thank you though. If I do, I'll let you know."

"Okay, I love you."

"I love you too."

"Call me in a few days and let me know how it goes."

"I'll do that." We said our goodbyes and while I felt a little better after talking to her, I was still worried about Sammy's reaction. I just prayed that my baby and I could survive it. Whatever his reaction may be.

When I arrived at Rouge, my stomach roiled. Clearly, morning sickness didn't just happen in the morning.

I quickly parked, opened the door, and threw up everything I had in my stomach. Which wasn't much. I hadn't been able to keep anything down all afternoon.

"Amber?"

I stiffened, my head snapped up, and I saw Shawnee standing a few feet away. I wiped my mouth with a napkin I had brought from home. I made myself a little care package packed with napkins, crackers, a bottle of water, and a toothbrush with toothpaste, since I couldn't call in sick. Especially now that I had to save money to take care of my baby. My stomach tumbled. I still couldn't wrap my head around the fact that I was pregnant. With Sammy's baby.

"Are you okay?" she asked gently.

I grabbed my bags and left the car. "Yeah."

"Are you sure?" She frowned, concern apparent in her voice.

Before I could answer, a loud rumble of engines sounded. Several motorcycles pulled into the parking lot but one stuck out from the bunch. It was a bike that I had been on several times already but the time that I remembered the most was when Sammy first took me on a ride. Especially when it ended in sex.

That specific bike pulled to a stop, the engine silencing. Sammy took off his helmet, his eyes finding mine.

I should have gone up to him like I usually did but instead, I tucked my head and headed toward the entrance of the club. He wouldn't like that I did that, but I needed to collect my bearings first.

"Did you and Sammy have a fight?" Shawnee asked, following me.

"No." My stomach twisted, clenching and rolling as a fresh wave of nausea erupted through me. I picked up my pace, practically running to the bathroom.

I knew Sammy was going to question why I didn't greet him like I always did. I also knew that I needed to tell him that I was pregnant. But first, I needed to not cause a scene by throwing up everywhere.

When I rushed into the bathroom, I was thankful no one else was in there. Bounding into a stall, I dropped to my knees just as my stomach emptied into the toilet.

"Geezus, Amber. What the hell is going on?" Shawnee demanded from behind me.

Once my stomach calmed down, I leaned against the wall of the stall and brought my knees up to my chest.

"You're pregnant." She crouched beside me. "Aren't you?"

I nodded, my eyes suddenly welling. So many emotions slammed into me. I wasn't expecting them and they took my breath away.

"I'm assuming it's Sammy's?" she asked gently.

I nodded again, my throat working over a hard lump.

"Good." She stood. "I'd hate to deal with him if the baby wasn't his."

I stared at her. "What do you mean?"

"Girl, that man is beyond obsessed with you. We all see it."

Rising to my feet, I grabbed my things, flushed the toilet, and went to the sink. "You see what exactly?" I started brushing my teeth, meeting her gaze in the reflection of the mirror. "What?" I asked around a mouthful of toothpaste.

"He's in love with you or if it's not love, it's definitely something bordering on it. He's been here when you're not working. He comes with the guys," she said, not that she had to reassure me. I knew he didn't come to Rouge to see the other dancers. "He's overheard customers asking Candace if you'll ever start dancing again. Candace couldn't even get a word in because Sammy was always in the customer's face before she could answer. I can't tell you how many times Ronny has threatened to kick him out."

I knew Sammy had a violent streak to him back even before we started sleeping together, but I didn't realize it continued.

"Does he get jealous?"

My stomach clenched at her question. I breathed through the fresh wave of nausea. Once I was satisfied that nothing else was going to leave my body, I finished brushing my teeth. "If you're asking if he gets jealous like Aaron did, the answer is no. Yes, he gets jealous, but he never blames me if a guy looks at me or flirts with me like Aaron did."

"Good because I like him, and I wouldn't want to mess up his pretty face if he hurts you."

I laughed.

Shawnee winked, coming up to me and pulling me into a hug. Her hand fell to my lower abdomen. "I've always wanted to be an aunt."

I covered her hand on my stomach. "I'm scared."

"I know but your mom, me, the girls…we're all here."

"I know." I sighed. "I need to tell—"

The door to the bathroom suddenly swung open, revealing Sammy.

"What are you doing?" Shawnee demanded. "This is the ladies' room."

Sammy ignored her and came up to me. "What's wrong?"

I went to look at Shawnee when Sammy caught my jaw in a firm grip.

"Don't look at her, pet," That dominant voice in him did funny things to my belly and I welcomed it every time with open arms. "Look at me. She can't help you if you don't answer the damn question."

"You don't have to be an asshole," Shawnee snapped at him.

"It's fine, Shawn," I told her. "Thank you."

She sighed and left the bathroom.

"Answer my question," he demanded.

My hand cupped my stomach on its own accord. I didn't realize I did it until Sammy stepped in front of me and his gaze followed the movement. Something flashed in his eyes. Something I had never seen before or even knew was in him.

"Something you want to tell me, Red?" he asked, his voice lowering.

I swallowed hard. "I didn't want to tell you here but I…I'm…" I took a deep breath, but I couldn't get the words out.

"You are, aren't you?"

I was unable to voice the words and nodded instead.

"Tell me," he demanded gently. "Say the words, Amber."

My eyes welled, my lungs feeling like they were about to collapse in on themselves.

"Say the words." He gripped my jaw when I didn't answer and forced my head back. "Say them." He captured my mouth in a hard, bruising kiss. "Say *it*," he repeated, biting my bottom lip.

I whimpered, the sharp pain sending a wave of heat over my skin.

"Amber," he growled.

I sniffled. "I'm pregnant."

NINETEEN

Amber

I EXPECTED HIM TO snap. To freak the fuck out and blame me for letting it happen. I knew it wasn't my fault but when my ex reacted that way, it was hard not to expect the same from Sammy.

Aaron came around eventually and grew to get excited over the fact that I was carrying his baby but it had been too late at that point.

"I'm not him, Red." Sammy grabbed my hand and slipped his fingers between mine. "I'm not."

I leaned my forehead against his chest, taking a deep breath and inhaling the scent that made up him. Sammy Butcher. The man who refused to back down in the beginning until he got what he wanted and made me realize that I wanted it too.

Sammy didn't comment or even ask if the baby was his. It was like he heard the news and accepted it instantly. He was an asshole most times but this part of him, I held it close, knowing he didn't show it often.

I brought his hand up to my mouth and kissed the back of his knuckles.

"Look at me."

I took a chance and met his gaze.

"Tell me something. Am I the first to know?"

I frowned, searching his face. "I don't know what you're implying."

"Answer the damn question, Red."

I huffed, rolling my eyes. "If you think I've known this for awhile, I haven't. I found out today and called my mom. So technically, she's the first to know and now Shawnee knows too because she found me throwing up when I got here."

Sammy's face softened. "You threw up?"

"Yeah, morning sickness is no joke," I mumbled.

"How are you feeling now?" he asked gently.

"Better now that you know." I stepped away from him and grabbed my things. "I have to start my shift, but I can try and leave early."

Sammy came toward me and grabbed the bags from my hands.

"I can carry—"

He crushed his mouth against mine, dropping the bags to the floor and circling his arms around me. Before the kiss could turn into anything more, he placed a soft peck on my forehead and ran the back of his hand over my lower stomach.

My eyes welled at the gentle contact.

Much to my surprise, he lowered to his knees and lifted my shirt. He laid gentle kisses along my stomach and muttered soft words that I couldn't hear. But that act alone forced a sob from my lips.

His eyes shot to mine at the sound. Jumping to his feet, he wrapped me up in his arms as I cried against him. I wasn't exactly sure why I was crying. Maybe it was due to fear of how Sammy would react and now that we had gotten it out of the way, I was crying with happiness.

When my cries subsided, I pulled away from him and wiped my face.

"You good?" he asked, his brows furrowed.

"I am." I thought a moment. "I need to make a doctor's appointment."

"I'll be there," he said without me even having to ask. "Every step of the way, Amber. I will be there."

"Thank you," I whispered.

He nodded once and gave me a look, but it was a look I didn't quite understand. I wasn't sure what I was expecting but it definitely wasn't this. He was calm. Maybe too calm.

As we left the bathroom, we walked hand in hand to the change room the dancers and other staff used. Sammy handed me my bags, placed a soft peck on my cheek, and without saying anything, went to join his crew.

I was left standing there, watching him walk away. His calm demeanor made me nervous. It had me wondering if maybe he would eventually blow up once we were alone.

(Sammy)

She was pregnant.

Amber was pregnant.

With my baby.

When I left her standing outside of the change room the staff used, I could see the confusion in her eyes. I got it. I did. Because I really had no idea how the fuck I was feeling.

Scared? Definitely.

Worried? For sure.

Excited? Absolutely.

So many emotions ran through me, I wasn't sure how to deal with them all. But I knew she felt the same way and figured she needed some space.

For the first time, in a very long fucking time, I thought of my parents. I tried not to think about them because it hurt. It hurt too damn much, and I couldn't deal with that pain. Amber had kept me distracted, but now that I knew she was pregnant, memories of my parents slid to the forefront of my mind. I wished they were around so I could ask them for advice. I could go to Greyson and Eve, but it wouldn't be the same.

"Sam?"

I stiffened, finding Cyrus coming toward me.

"Hey, you good?" He signaled Shawnee over, ordering a round of drinks for the guys before turning back to me. "What's wrong?"

I glanced at Shawnee.

She nodded once.

I did the same.

But I still wouldn't tell Cyrus. Not yet and definitely not here.

"I'm good," I finally said.

He stared at me, knowing I was lying.

Amber and I needed to talk and we would do that once she was done her shift, but until then, I would do what I normally did and listen while the guys spoke.

The hairs on the back of my neck tingled, forcing my head around.

Amber walked toward me.

I had been too distracted to notice in the bathroom, but she looked hot as fuck tonight. She wore dark ripped blue jeans with a white tank top tucked into the high waist. Her long red hair was pulled back into a ponytail. The white of the top showed a glow in her skin. The weather had become warmer, so whenever I was with her at her apartment, we would spend as much time as we could on her balcony.

I had helped her set up a little sitting area since the balcony was a decent size. I did it so she had something else that could get her out of her apartment if she didn't want to actually go anywhere, but I also used it as an excuse to fuck her somewhere new.

My thoughts traveled back to the other night. Us out on the balcony. Her at my feet. My cock down the back of her throat.

"You know it's rude to stare," Amber said, pulling me from my dirty thoughts. She came up to my side and lightly brushed her fingers along the back of my hand.

I linked my fingers with hers and leaned down to her ear. "You know it's rude to look that delicious in public when I can't do anything about it."

A husky laugh escaped her, her cheeks turning a nice shade of pink.

At least it wasn't uncomfortable between us, but we still needed to talk.

"I'll be here for your whole shift," I told her, placing a soft peck on her cheek. "You need anything, you let me know." I reached an arm around her, grabbing a handful of her ass and tugging her even closer.

A sharp gasp left her, her hand landing against my chest. "You making a point, Sam?"

"Yes." My mouth brushed along the length of her ear. "Letting every fucker in this building know who you belong to, pet."

She turned her head, her mouth finding mine.

I smirked, cupped the back of her head with my free hand, and pushed my lips against hers.

"That's all I needed, thank you." She kissed me one last time before pulling her hand from mine so she could actually work. Didn't think the owners would pay her for hanging out with me.

"She's happier because of you," Shawnee said when Amber was out of earshot.

"I'm happier because of *her*." But although I said those words, I still wished she was in my arms where she belonged.

I sat on a stool at the bar, turning around to face Amber's friend. I didn't know Shawnee well, but she had been nothing but nice to us and she also never hit on me like most of the other women at the club had.

"You really going to be by her side during this?"

My jaw clenched, not liking the accusatory tone coming from her, but I got it. Amber's late husband, ex, whatever the fuck you wanted to call him, messed her up.

"Yes, I will. No matter what." I turned to watch Amber interact with some of the customers. She would laugh every so often at something they said, the sound sending tingles through my balls.

"Sam."

My head whipped around. "Do *not* call me that."

Shawnee raised an eyebrow.

"*She* calls me Sam. My mother called me Samson. Everyone else calls me Sammy. That includes you. End of."

"Huh…Amber said that you're different, but I guess I never believed it until now." She grinned.

I grunted and turned back around to watch my girl when I realized that she was nowhere in sight. Jumping from the stool, I looked around the room. "Where is she?"

"What do you mean?"

I turned to face Shawnee. "I mean just what I said. Where. Is. She?" I was being a dick, but I didn't really give a shit. When there were people who wanted Amber for themselves, the alpha mixed with the Dom in me, needed to protect her. At all times. And not currently knowing where she was, forced this newfound rage in me.

Instead of waiting for Shawnee to answer, I went down the closest hall. I checked the bathrooms. She wasn't in them. The storage room was locked. The change room was also locked.

Every time I checked a room and came up empty, the rage seemed to only grow inside of me.

I could feel the eyes of my crew watching me, probably wondering what the hell I was doing and who I was looking for.

Security at this place was top notch and only the best of the best worked here, so I knew that they wouldn't have let something happen.

A thought came to me, sending a sour taste to my mouth.

Heading down the hall that led to the private dance rooms, I was met by Corbin Wane. He was head of security and was also friends with all of the dancers. He was a big fucker, a little on the twisted side and easy to set off.

"Sam." He came toward me. "You want to book a room?"

"No." I stopped myself from saying something shitty and how Amber was my girlfriend when I remembered that he hadn't been at the club for awhile. I heard that he had gone home to Africa to be with family, but rumors had gone around that he went home for other reasons too. "I'm looking for Amber."

Corbin frowned. "Good. She's in the last room."

"What?" Before I could stop myself, I shoved him up against the wall.

His eyes widened, clearly as shocked as I was that neither of us saw it coming.

"Tell me she's in there by herself," I said, my voice low. But even though I had a hold of him, I saw the cut in his lip and the bruise starting to form around his eye.

"I didn't have a choice. I may be big as fuck but when a gun is pointed at a coworker's head, I listen." Corbin shoved me off of him, straightening out his white t-shirt. "And you did not just put your hands on me."

"She's my girlfriend," I said, ignoring his last comment.

His eyes widened even more. "Shit, I didn't know." Instead of waiting for me to ask, he walked back down the hall from where he had come from. "His boys were adamant that he wanted her even though she doesn't dance anymore. I don't know what the fuck is going on or why this shit is only just starting now but if you don't kill him, I will for causing me stress."

I followed Corbin, needing to know who the fuck was in that room with her.

Corbin stopped and turned to me. "If you kill him, please just clean up the mess."

"If that happens..." I chuckled. "You'll never know."

(Amber)

I didn't like being in such a small room with Will but when he had come to the club with a couple of friends, I didn't want any issues. I had played nice, agreeing to listen to whatever he had to say but when his guys distracted security, Will grabbed me and dragged me to a room.

"Open the door or I'll kill him," Will demanded, holding a gun to the temple of one of the newer security guards.

Corbin tried fighting two of the guys closest to him but they apparently were prepared. One guy punched Corbin, knocking him back and grabbing the young security guard I knew as Tim.

Tim struggled in the arms of the big fucker but as the gun lifted to his head, he stopped.

My chest constricted. "Will, please. You need to stop this. You can't do this here. There are cameras everywhere."

"Yeah, you see, Princess, I don't give a shit about that." Will nodded once.

The man holding Tim, forced him to his knees.

"You have two seconds, Corbin." Will scratched his chin, waiting.

Corbin didn't even hesitate and unlocked one of the private rooms. He looked at me, mouthed that he was sorry and stepped aside.

I never blamed Corbin though. He was only trying to keep his people safe.

"You look good," Will told me, his eyes roaming down the length of me.

"You need to stop this." I went to walk past him when he caught me around the waist and pulled me against him. "Let go of me," I cried, struggling in his arms.

"I heard you paid a visit to the clubhouse when you went to see your mom."

My back stiffened. "How do you know that?" I didn't like that even though Will was no longer part of the club, he still heard things.

"People chat, Princess. You know that."

"Stop calling me that. I am not your Princess." Aaron called me it. So because he did, Will felt the need to continue it after his brother died. But Will turned it into something more. Something worse. All of the guys started calling me that and Will sat back and acted all damn proud over it. It was fucked. *He* was fucked.

"You are definitely my Princess." Will spun me around and pushed me up against the wall.

Bile rose to my throat at being this close to him.

"I miss you."

I snorted. "Says the man who still fucked other women while also fucking me."

"You fucked other men too," he pointed out.

"He was my husband," I snapped. Placing my hands against his chest, I tried shoving him away, but he was too strong for me. "The only time I fucked you before he died was when we had our threesomes, but I never belonged to you."

Will spun me around and shoved me up against the wall. The move had been hard, making my head ring.

"I've tried being nice, Princess," he growled, sliding a hand up the back of my thigh.

"Stop," I pleaded, frozen in fear.

"I remember the first time I felt your wet pussy." Will's voice slid into my ears, making my stomach churn as the memories he was conjuring up, came to mind. "You felt so fucking good. I couldn't get enough. I tried convincing Aaron to let me have you while he wasn't around, but he refused." His hand shoved between my legs, cupping me in a rough move. "Guess if he didn't want you, no one could."

That seemed to jolt me out of my daze, the fear now turning to fury. With all of the strength I could muster, I slammed my head back against his face.

"Fuck." He stumbled back a couple of steps.

The move hadn't been hard enough, and it only seemed to surprise him. So I had to do what I could to get to the door and out of this room before Will did what I knew he wanted to do.

"You bitch," he yelled. "You could have broken my nose."

When he took a step toward me, I sidestepped around him and ran to the door. My fingers had only grazed the doorknob when heavy arms wrapped around my middle and picked me up off my feet.

The door suddenly banged open, revealing a red-faced Sammy.

Will put me on my feet, lifting his hands as Sam charged for him.

Running out of the room, I found Corbin leaning against the wall by the door, playing on his phone. "Corbin."

"Hey, sweetheart," he said, putting his phone in his back pocket. "You okay?"

"I am now." I blew out slow even breaths, trying to settle my racing heart. "Where are Will's boys?"

"The trash has been taken out thanks to some help," was all Corbin said. He checked his watch, mumbling numbers when I realized he was counting. "Ten." He pushed away from the wall and headed into the room. He came back a moment later with a bloodied Will and no Sammy.

"You're lucky I didn't let him kill you," Corbin told Will, grabbing him by the scruff and ushering him down the hall away from me.

Just when I was about to check on Sammy, he came out of the room. When his eyes connected with mine, something shifted between us.

Holding out my arms, I waited.

He took a step and then another, until his big body was wrapped around me. He fisted my ponytail, pushing his face into the crook of my neck.

"I'm okay," I told him, sliding my arms into his leather cut and around to his back. He shook against me, his muscles jumping over his bones. "Sam."

He released me, grabbed my hand, and all but dragged me out of the hall. When we stopped at the door to the change room, he reached into the back pocket of my jeans and pulled out the key card.

"How did you know that was there?" I asked as he unlocked the door.

"Because I know every inch of your ass, pet, and I know when something is out of place." He gently pushed me into the room. "Grab your things. I'm taking you home."

The brat in me wanted to argue but I didn't. Sammy was unhinged.

Even though Will never got very far, the fact that he touched me when I didn't want him to in the first place, opened up old wounds. Wounds I was able to bandage up thanks to my mom and Shawnee.

I grabbed my things and joined Sammy back out in the hall.

He took the bags from me but looked at one in particular. "What is this?"

"I made myself a care package for when I throw up. I haven't been able to keep anything down, so that's what the crackers are for."

"Have they helped?"

"I haven't tried yet. I was a little distracted. Between worrying about how you would react, then you finding out, and then Will…" I shrugged.

Sammy nodded once. "I'll make you this soup my mom used to make us when we got the stomach flu."

"Okay, thank you." I hugged my arms around myself, looking down the hall both ways, expecting Will to jump out of the shadows.

"He's not here," Sammy told me. "Corbin took him out. My brothers helped with the other fuckers. You're safe. All of you are safe."

"Did he…did Corbin…" I shivered at the thought of Corbin actually killing Will because I knew that even if he was dead, it wouldn't matter, his boys would come after me.

"Kill him?" Sammy grunted. "No. Rough him up a bit? Yes."

"How's Tim?" I asked, needing to make sure the young security guard was okay.

"I'm fine."

I turned, finding Tim coming toward us with Corbin at his side, along with a few of the guys in Sam's club.

"I'm upping security," Corbin said. "With Candace and Ronny's permission, I've made some calls, so things are going to be tight around here until Will lays off." He ran a hand over his bald head and down his face, wincing as he did so.

"Are you okay?" I asked him, noticing the bruise around his eye and the split in his lip.

"Yeah, I am, darling. Nothing a little ice won't cure." Corbin nodded to the few members of Hell's Harlem that had joined us. "Keep my girl safe." And with that, he spun on his heel and left the hallway.

"We still don't know what Will wants," Cyrus told Sammy. "But if I had to take a guess, I imagine it's nothing good."

Sammy glanced at me then, staring into a part of me that only he had ever been able to reach. "Are you okay?"

"I am." But to be fair, I had dealt with Will before. The shit he had done to me was nothing compared to how Aaron treated me and that night, that cold, damp, god-awful night...I swallowed hard, pushing those memories to the back of my mind.

"You're lying to me," Sammy said, pulling me from my thoughts.

"I don't want to talk about it here," I told him.

He nodded. "We're calling it a night," he said to no one specific.

"Be safe." Cyrus pulled his phone from the pocket in his inner cut. "I need to make some calls."

Heading down the hall to the bar, I quickly told Shawnee that I was going home sick. She only nodded and said she would cover for me. She had asked me a question, but I was too in my head and distracted, so I never heard her and left the club instead.

When the air around me suddenly grew cold, I stopped, glancing around me. Sammy was a few feet away, his dark eyes on mine. He was talking to Cheesy.

"Come here," Sammy demanded.

The brat in me was quiet as I walked into his open arms. Looked like she needed to be held too.

"Cheesy is going to drive your car home," Sam told me.

"Okay, thank you," I whispered.

Cheesy nodded once, took my keys from Sammy, and went to my car.

"Let's get you home, baby." He kissed my head and slid his fingers between mine, leading me to his beautiful bike.

Once we arrived at my apartment, Sammy parked the bike.

I slid off the back seat and waited for him to do the same.

He killed the engine, turning his head toward me.

"I never wanted kids," I blurted. "Not at first."

"Let's go inside." Sammy slid off the bike, took our helmets, and locked them up.

He came up to my side, linked his fingers with mine, and led me to the front of the building.

When we were in the elevator, he let go of my hand and leaned against the wall opposite me.

I hugged my arms around myself, not liking the way it felt like he was dissecting me with a mere look.

The elevator doors dinged once we reached my floor. We made our way down the long hall. I almost asked him for the keys when we stopped in front of my door, and he unlocked it himself.

I took a breath and stepped into my home. A place I had felt safe ever since I'd moved in, but now it felt like the walls were closing in around me.

My heart started racing, my skin was clammy and spots danced in my vision. My knees shook, giving out beneath me when arms caught me around the middle.

Before I could stop myself, I turned in Sammy's arms and threw myself around him.

Sammy captured my mouth in a hard, bruising kiss. It was so deep, so powerful, that I could feel him throughout every inch of me and he wasn't even inside of me yet.

Ripping at each other's clothes, I was vaguely aware of him lowering me onto the floor. With his mouth fused to mine, he slowly thrust into me, taking my very breath away.

TWENTY

Amber

"**TELL ME HOW YOU** felt when you first found out." Sammy brushed his thumb along my bare shoulder, his eyes watching the movement.

"Scared," I whispered.

His eyes lifted, locking with mine. "Why?"

"I was scared of how you would react. I still am." I hugged the sheet tighter around my body, hiding my nudity from him. We had moved from the living room to my bedroom, staying connected in a way I had never felt with another person before. I wasn't sure if it was due to the hormones rushing through me or what it was exactly, but I realized something; I wouldn't want to do this, although as scary as it was, with anyone else.

"What do you mean?" His fingers brushed down my arm, sending shivers along with it.

"You haven't given me much here, Sammy. I tell you I'm pregnant and I get nothing from you." I turned toward him. "I'm sorry. Please don't think this is my fault."

Before I could look away, he cupped my face. "I would never think this is your fault." His eyes moved back and forth, searching my face. "It takes two, baby."

"I…" I swallowed hard. "I meant what I said before. I never wanted kids. Not after…" I snapped my mouth shut. Was it too soon to tell him about what happened to me and how Aaron died? Was it too soon to tell him about the men who killed him and attacked me while he was dying, so he could watch until he took his final breath?

Sammy frowned. "Not after what?"

I looked down at my hands resting on my lap and took a deep breath. "I got pregnant while I was with Aaron. He didn't react well and accused me of cheating on him." My voice cracked. "He was furious. He blew up and said it was all my fault and that I purposely didn't take my birth control on the right days." A shuddered breath left me. "He eventually was happy, but it took him a while to warm up to the idea." I waited for Sammy to ask me questions but when he didn't and only covered my hands, I took the strength rolling off of him and continued. "He loved me. I know he did. At one point anyway. But in the end, he had moved up the chain of command pretty quickly and I became less and less important to him." My mind took me back to that night. Back to when my life changed forever. Then I met Sammy and my life changed again.

"There are things I haven't told you. Things I don't like to talk about. The night he died. I moved this way after…after…" I couldn't get the words out.

"Amber." Sammy hugged me from the side, cupping my head and kissing my temple. "Breathe."

I took a deep breath, letting it out slowly. "We had gone to a party and were driving home. It was in another town a couple of hours from where we lived. I didn't want to go but Aaron insisted. So I went, he drank, and I drove us home. But we ended up getting a flat tire. There was a guy at the party, a couple of them in fact who were hitting on me and they wouldn't leave me alone. Aaron didn't do shit about it either." Memories of that night hit me hard. They came on strong and fast, knocking the breath out of my lungs. "While Aaron was changing the tire, an

SUV pulled up. It was the middle of the night, but I thought maybe it was someone Aaron knew, and they saw that we needed help. It was naïve of me. I know that now. It's maybe why I pushed you away in the beginning. I have a hard time trusting people. Especially men."

Sammy ran a hand in circles over my upper back. "You don't have to explain yourself to me."

"But I do. I need you to know. Especially since we're in a relationship and we're going to have a baby. I can't have any secrets." I met his gaze. "I went through that already with Aaron. I can't do it again. Not with you."

Sammy nodded. "I'm an open book, pet."

I inched closer to him, needing his strength to get through this next little bit because if I knew Sammy at all, he wasn't going to react well to what I was about to tell him.

His hand that was resting on top of mine, squeezed.

Blowing out another slow breath, I continued. "The guys knew Aaron. They were in his crew. They were the ones who had hit on me that he did nothing about. They were egging him on, saying shit and Aaron being the man he was, let his temper get in the way. I tried stopping him. I tried preventing it from going further but they were bigger than him and the one had him on the ground and the second guy…he…attacked me."

"Fuck," Sammy growled.

"I never experienced pain like that before. The guys took turns, using every inch of me. They beat me and…" Tears streamed down my cheeks. "They knew I was pregnant because Aaron had been gloating about it. There was a third guy who used me last, but I didn't get a good look at him. They took turns kicking me in the stomach. I don't remember much after that. But I watched Aaron die. He saw the whole thing. He was on the ground, dying, while the men he thought he knew, raped and beat his wife, and killed his unborn baby."

(Sammy)

I had seen shit. I had seen men treat women like they were nothing but mere objects but never once in my life, did I see or hear something as horrible as what Amber was telling me.

Something inside of me snapped. I pulled away from her and slid out from under the covers. Leaving the safety of her warmth, I went to my cut and grabbed my pack of smokes. Sticking one in my mouth, I pulled on my jeans.

"Sam."

"I need a smoke." That much was obvious. Going to the window, I pushed it open and lit up the much-needed therapy between my lips. After a deep inhale, I blew the smoke out the window. Staring outside, I wasn't even sure what I was looking for. Something I could hit. Someone I could beat. Someone I could kill.

A warm body suddenly wrapped around me.

Without even looking down at Amber, I slid my arm around her shoulders, holding her tight. I didn't know what to say after what she told me. I had so many questions, but I knew that my words would come out rough. Accusatory. Not at her. It wasn't her fault. But the shit I wanted to say about her late husband would be far from nice.

"What happened after that?" I heard myself ask.

"Another SUV showed up. I thought it was the same guys and that they wanted to finish me off or take me somewhere, but it wasn't. I vaguely remember crawling to Aaron. He...he said something to me before he died." Amber released me and moved in front of me. She was wearing my hoodie and if it were any other time, I would have slid my hands up her bare legs until I reached what laid beneath it. I would check to see what else she was wearing. But this was not the right time. "He...he told me he was sorry and then I watched the life leave him." Her jaw clenched but much to my surprise, no other emotion displayed on her face.

"You were pissed," I ground out. "Weren't you?"

"Yes." Her eyes shot to mine, hard and determined. "I was pissed because he never gave me a chance to divorce him. I was pissed that he brought on the attack. He knew those men wanted me, but he laughed it off and said they were only playing. But I'm not stupid and it wasn't me being paranoid. It was a feeling. And that feeling was right. I was pissed because Aaron apologized. He wasn't supposed to apologize. He was supposed to die not saying anything at all so I could stay mad at him, but instead he made me feel guilty. Guilty, Sammy. I felt guilty. Even after all the shit he had done to me. I still feel guilty for wanting to leave him." She hugged her arms around herself. "I hate him."

"Come with me." I walked past her and left her bedroom. Making my way out to her balcony, I didn't wait for her to follow because I knew she would. There was something she needed. I was sure alcohol would make her feel better even if it was just for a little bit, but she obviously couldn't have a drink for the next several months. So, we would have to improvise.

"Sammy, what are you doing?" she asked, following me out onto the balcony.

"Who saved you?" I asked instead, walking to the patio set and sitting. I pulled her into my arms and lowered her to my lap.

"There were three guys in that SUV. I think there were three anyway. I can't remember much but I do remember seeing one of them. He looked like Spencer Reid from *Criminal Minds*. Have you seen that show? I remember telling him that before I passed out. The next thing I knew, I woke up in a hospital, surrounded by police and hospital staff. It was awful but I was alive."

As she spoke her truths, I couldn't help but focus on one specific thing she said. "The guy who looked like Spencer from that show..."

She frowned. "Yeah? What about him?"

"Did you happen to get his name?"

"No." Her frown deepened. "I wish I could see them again, so I can thank them."

I didn't know this guy she was talking about who was almost like a twin to that actor, but I remembered Piper mentioning something briefly about it.

"What happened with Aaron's body?" I asked Amber gently, running my hand up and down her arm while I smoked the fuck out of that cigarette. I was careful not to let the smoke hit her directly and finished it fast before butting it out in the ashtray Amber had purchased for me.

"Tiny told me that they called him up and he came to collect Aaron, but with everything that's happened, I don't know what to believe. I haven't really thought about it until now. Especially since Will seems to be trying to get something from me, even though I don't know what exactly he wants."

"He wants to fuck you, Amber. He probably wants more than that too, but he definitely wants sex, your body, your fucking soul." And it pissed me off. No, it left me furious and filled with rage. It was a deep-seated anger I had never felt before.

"He's already had me, why does he want me again?"

It was an innocent question and I knew why she was asking it, but it didn't mean that it still didn't piss me off any less. "Because you keep telling him no."

She sighed, rubbing the back of her neck. "I don't want him. I never have. Yes, I used him after Aaron died to make me feel better and I'm not overly proud of that, but I told him that I didn't want anything more. He's worse than Aaron was. I've seen the way he is with women." She shuddered. "Anyway, it doesn't matter. I just…I want this to work for us."

"I want this to work for us too." I stared at her, searching her face for a sign. Any sign that she was possibly lying or hiding something else, but when I didn't see anything, I let out a sigh of relief. "Thank you for telling me all of that. You didn't have to. I also know that it was hard, so…thank you."

Amber nodded. "I used to hate talking about my feelings. I don't know why really. It wasn't like I had any problems as a kid. I had a good upbringing, even though it was just me and my mom. But I was always shy and insecure. Shawnee has helped bring me out of my shell, but I didn't really start opening up until later on in my marriage. Will used to always say that my good girl act was just a ruse." Her eyes locked with mine. "He said that there's a slut inside of me and he was determined to find her."

LIBERATE US

My jaw clenched. I vowed right then that no matter what happened between me and Amber, I would kill him. Since I couldn't kill Aaron as he was already dead, Will would take the brunt of my wrath for both him and his brother.

"But you found her, Sam," Amber murmured, pulling me from my thoughts. "She belongs to you and only you. When you call me names, it doesn't make me feel any less about myself. It makes me feel quite the opposite. It doesn't offend me or make me feel less important either. It makes me feel connected to you on a level I have never experienced before. Even though I tried."

Cupping her knees, I ran my hands up and down her thighs. "The submissive needs to trust their Dom but the Dom needs to also trust their submissive too. It's a two-way street and a lot of people forget that. I've had...I've had issues. I think it's..." Could I tell her my truth? My absolute truth and why I had been a dick and why this rage was growing inside of me as the days went on? "I'm scared to fall in love only for it to be taken away from me. I saw my dad break after my mom was killed. He wasn't the same. I know he tried to be a father to us but both Cyrus and I knew that we would never get our dad back. It didn't matter that we were young and needed him. He was lost and couldn't find himself. And before we could say anything or tell him how we felt, he was murdered as well." My words came out monotonously. I had never voiced those feelings out loud. "I know I could fall in love with you, Amber. Maybe I already have. I don't know. But that's my truth." I lifted the sweatshirt she was wearing, to below her tits. "And it's not because you're carrying my baby." I cupped her stomach. "It's you. It's always been you."

Amber covered my hand with hers. "I never wanted to fall in love again. I didn't even want to try." Her tears fell onto the back of her hand. "But I want to. I want to try with you."

Before she could say anymore, I wrapped my arms around her and hugged her close. "I want to try too. With you. Only with you."

TWENTY-ONE

Amber

SAMMY AND I SPENT the next couple of days soaking up the fact that I was pregnant with his baby. He ended up making me the soup his mom would make for him and his brother when they were kids and it helped settle my stomach a bit. It was something simple. A chicken type broth with some spices, but the mixture was delicious.

Every chance Sam had, he would run his fingers along my stomach or he would kiss it when he thought I was sleeping. He even muttered words to it. Words that I never heard but was grateful for just the same.

I had called into the club, spoke with Candace, and told her I needed a few days off due to a family emergency. I knew that eventually she would figure out what was going on but until then, I would keep this to myself, knowing Shawnee wouldn't tell anyone anything until I gave her the go-ahead.

Sammy was able to take some time off as well but every now and again his phone would ring. He would look at the screen, hit a button, and put his phone away. I never knew who called him, but I found it didn't overly matter. We would tell people when we were ready to.

One night, he was restless as he laid beside me. A wave of nausea had woken me up and I couldn't get back to sleep. Add to the fact that we had a doctor's appointment later the next morning and I was excited and nervous just the same.

Rolling onto my back, I found the spot beside me empty and cold.

Slipping from bed, I headed out into the living room. Sammy was nowhere to be found. "Sam?"

As I neared the doors leading to the balcony, I saw that the main door was open, while the screen remained closed. When I reached it, I heard Sammy's deep voice. He was on the phone with someone.

"She's sleeping," he mumbled. "Yeah, I think I am. Is there a way of knowing?" He grunted. "They need to make how-to books on this shit."

Opening the door, I stepped out onto the balcony.

Sammy lifted his head, the light from the lantern on the table casting a glow around him. He had bought me that lantern weeks ago, so we would have some light on the balcony after the sun went down.

"I gotta go, brother. Give your girl a hug from me." Sam disconnected the call, placing his phone on the table. "You should be sleeping."

"Yeah, so should you." I went up to him and stepped between his legs. "Everything okay?"

He wrapped his arms around me, lowering me onto his lap. "Nightmare."

"Did you want to talk about it?" I asked, reveling in the feeling of his hard body beneath me.

"Not really." He leaned his forehead against my chest, taking a deep breath. "It's the same dream. Cyrus has it too. I guess it's a twin thing. We have it at around the same time and end up calling each other after. It's been going on like that since we were kids. It changes a little bit, but the idea is still the same. I get kidnapped. Dad can't find me. Mom dies. Same shit. Different night."

"I'm sorry, baby," I whispered, running my fingers through the hair at his nape.

"Not your fault." Sam lifted his head. "Are you looking forward to the appointment?" he asked, changing the subject.

"I am." I cupped my stomach. "I don't know if I've just been eating too much but I feel like I'm showing already. I shouldn't be. Should I?"

Sammy sat back, lifting my tank top up to under my breasts. "Your tits are fuller, and you definitely look like you're starting to show. But I don't think it's from food, pet."

"But if I'm doing the math right, I should only be three months maybe." I ran my fingers along my little bump.

"Maybe you're pregnant with twins. I think that would probably make you show quicker but I'm not an expert on that sort of thing."

My eyes snapped to Sammy's, my stomach dropping. "What did you just say?"

"I'm a twin, baby."

"Yes, I know but doesn't it like skip a generation?" Twins. Oh god. It wasn't possible. Was it?

"Not always." He chuckled. "I don't think there's a rule on it. I wouldn't worry about it though, Red. We'll figure it out."

I nodded. The only thing I cared about was the health of the baby or babies.

"You know. Since you're here." Sammy waggled his eyebrows.

I laughed, sliding off his lap and going to the patio doors. Turning toward him, I let my eyes roam down every inch of him as he stood. "I think you should fuck me."

A cocky smirk spread on his face. "I'm going to do better." He came up to me and grabbed my arm. Leaning down, his lips brushed over the shell of my ear. "I'm going to make you fall in love with me."

A breathless laugh left me. "I think it's going to be you falling in love with me first, Sam." I stepped back into the apartment, walking away from him. "'Cause you know, I am irresistible and all."

He grinned. "You're lucky you're pregnant."

"Oh?" I turned to him, walking backwards toward my bedroom. "Why's that?"

"Because I'd have you thrown over my shoulder by now or have you pressed up against the wall with my cock deep in your ass."

I shivered. "God, you say the sweetest things. But the ass part can still happen, baby."

"Nah, gotta keep up with the anticipation and I don't want to hurt you."

I snorted. "Since when," I threw at him.

He raised an eyebrow. "Really?"

Before I knew what was happening, he charged for me. A squeal escaped me as I ran down the hall toward the bedroom, but I never got very far.

Sammy captured me, pulled me into his arms, and had his mouth on mine before I could utter a single complaint about how he cheated.

He pushed me back onto the bed, kneeling between my legs. Breaking the kiss, he lifted his head and winked.

I smiled up at him, though we joked about who was going to fall in love with who first, I realized that maybe I already had.

"Something you want to tell me, Red?" he asked, pushing my tank top up my stomach and over my breasts. "Something you want to confess?"

"I don't know." I stared up at him and ran my fingers through the light beard on his strong jaw. His eyes were dark and focused. They peered into me, searching for more truths. Truths I never thought I would feel again.

"Tell me." He leaned his elbows on the bed on either side of my head. "I know you feel something."

"Of course I do but I don't know exactly what those feelings are. They need to make a rule book on this or something," I said, using his words that I had heard him say earlier.

"I basically said the same thing to my brother." He kissed my nose. "He asked me if I'm in love with you."

My heart jumped to my throat. "What did you tell him?" So that had been the conversation I walked in on.

"I told him that I think I am." He gave me a small smile.

"I told you that you would fall in love with me first," I teased, but truth was, I was happy. No. I was fucking ecstatic that I found love again and it was a love that went past what Aaron and I ever had.

"Careful." Sammy reached a hand between us, his fingers brushing over the crotch of my panties. "Just because you're pregnant, doesn't mean that I still can't punish you."

I shivered at the light feathery touches.

"Hmm...wet already. Has it been that long?"

I scoffed, rolling my eyes. "It has actually."

Sammy sat back on his heels, pulling my panties over my ass and down my legs.

I slipped a leg out of one of the holes, leaving the panties on one foot only.

He circled his hand around my calf, resting my foot on his shoulder. Placing a soft peck on my shin, he kept his eyes locked with mine.

My body wiggled, tensing under his scrutiny the longer time wore on where neither of us said anything. He thought he was in love with me, but he never actually said that he was.

Pulling my foot from his grip, I rose to my knees and knelt in front of him. "What's a position you've never done?" I asked, pulling the tank top up and over my head.

"I've never had a woman ride me," Sammy answered, his voice low as he watched me strip for him.

My eyes snapped to his. "Really? I've ridden you on the couch before."

"That's different. I've never laid on a bed and had a woman on top."

"Oh..." I tilted my head. "How come?"

"I'm a Dom, babe, and before you say that I can still control someone while they're riding me, I already know this."

"But you never trusted someone enough to let them ride you, so you could see just how in control you can actually be." I waited. "I'm right, aren't I?" When he didn't say anything and only looked at me with those dark eyes of his, I slipped off the bed. "Lay down."

"Red," he growled.

"I'm not going to control you, Sam." I rolled my eyes when he didn't budge. "I don't have a dominant bone in my body when it comes to sex. We both know that. But I want to ride you." I went up to him when he didn't move from his spot on the bed. Cupping his cheek, I grabbed his hand with the other and pulled it between my legs. "I want to know what you feel like beneath me."

His jaw clenched behind my palm, the muscle ticking in tune with the beat of my heart.

"You can use our safeword, Sammy. I just want to ride you and maybe kiss you, touch you..." I let my eyes fall to the bulge he was now sporting in his sweatpants. "Suck you."

"Fuck," he whispered.

"Will you let me take care of you?"

He turned his head, his mouth brushing along my palm. "Will you tell me how you feel?"

"Will you tell me?" I threw back at him.

He grabbed my hand, giving the base of my palm a bite. The sting sent a wave of heat over every inch of me.

"I asked you a question, my little pet." He tugged me closer. "Will you tell me how you feel?" he repeated, slower that time.

I swallowed hard, nodding.

"Words, pet. I need your fucking words." He bit my palm again, pulling a moan from the back of my throat. He grinned.

"Yes, yes I'll tell you."

He released me, laid down on the bed, and waited.

(Sammy)

I had subs try and top from the bottom on more than one occasion. I didn't proclaim to know everything there was to know about BDSM, but I knew myself and what I liked. I also knew Amber, and I knew that as time went on, I would learn more about her.

When she said she wanted to ride me, I expected my body to not react at all, but blood started pumping through my dick, clearly liking the idea of Amber slamming her pussy up and down on it.

When I laid down, the evidence was clear. I liked this idea. A lot.

I wasn't a switch. At all. And I knew that this wouldn't be her dominating me but instead showing me that there were other positions where I could be in control, besides fucking her from behind. Although, I knew that position was her favorite.

Amber hooked her fingers in the waist of my pants and, with some help on my part, lowered them down my legs and off my feet. Her gaze dropped to my cock. "You're hard. Already."

"My dick likes the idea of your body bouncing on it," I said, as she stepped up to my side. Grazing my fingers along her hip, I brushed them to the crack of her ass and lower. She shivered, wrapping her hand around my cock.

"You want to suck it, baby?" I asked, my voice low and guttural.

"Yes." She licked her lips.

"Then be a good girl and bend over." I brushed my fingers over her center, noticing how she became wetter at my gentle demand.

Amber bent at the waist, pushing my dick flat against my stomach. Her eyes locked with mine as her tongue dragged up the length of it.

A hot tremble of need sizzled up my spine.

She repeated the movement, sliding her tongue up and down before closing her mouth around the head and taking me to the back of her throat. When her lips hit the base of my cock, she stopped.

"Fuck, baby." I slid my hands through her hair, trying not to take control but needing to just the same.

She cupped my balls, massaging and kneading, sending tiny little shock waves of pleasure along with it. Slowly pulling off of me, she kissed the crown and locked eyes with mine.

"You need to ride me. *Now.*" I wasn't a man who begged, ever, but this, this was on a whole other level of ecstasy I had never experienced before.

When Amber went to straddle my waist, I stopped her. She frowned, clearly not knowing what the hell I was doing because truth was, I had no idea either.

"No." I took a deep breath. "Not my cock. Not yet."

"But…" Understanding dawned on her. "Oh." She moved up the length of my body, her knees locking around the sides of my head.

"Fuck yes." The scent of her was overwhelming but it was a scent I never wanted to be rid of. Before she could get comfortable, I wrapped my arms around her knees and pulled her down hard onto my mouth.

She cried out, her thighs trembling around my head, but I didn't let up. I could be a selfish bastard when it came to sex but this, with her, was my favorite thing to do. It also meant that I was in full control and until she gave me the many orgasms I wanted from her, this was my time.

"Sammy," she whined, grinding her pussy down hard on my mouth.

Releasing her with a wet smack, I spread her open with my thumbs, revealing her pretty little clit. Closing my mouth around it, I sucked and pulled, earning me a sharp gasp and harsh cries as well as a string of curse words that made me fucking proud to be her man.

"God, baby, I'm gonna come." Her breathing picked up, her chest rising and falling with ragged breaths. Her moans became louder.

Gently biting her clit, I licked it to relieve the sting and repeated the movements. I wanted to be covered in her desire, knowing that I was the only one who could make her feel this way.

Suddenly, her eyes widened, followed by an ear-splitting scream as liquid gushed from her body and coated my tongue, chin, and neck.

Not letting up, I covered her core with my mouth and thrust my tongue inside of her, needing to drink up the rest of her orgasm.

"I can't." Her thighs slammed into the sides of my head forcing a grunt from me. "Sorry."

I chuckled, releasing her and kissing her inner thigh. "Don't be sorry, baby."

She pulled away from me, shivering as the air around us hit her damp skin.

"I need inside you," I said as she straddled my waist. "I need…"

"What, Sam?" she asked, her voice husky. "What do you need?"

"For you to drop that cunt—" I didn't even get a chance to finish my sentence as her body dropped down the length of me, forcing a hard shout from my lips. *"Fuck."*

"Is that what you wanted?" she asked, placing her hands on my chest and moving her hips back and forth. Side to side. Up and down. I was reminded then that she knew how to use her body. She could move it in ways that a lot of women would be envious of. The fact that she now kept that part of herself hidden just for me, made me fall in love with her even more.

"Faster," I demanded, digging my fingers into her upper thighs.

Amber ground her pussy down hard against me, my cock as far as it could be inside of her. "God, so deep." Her nails scratched into my chest, pulling a hard groan from the back of my throat.

My balls drew up into my body, my vision fading in and out as my release suddenly poured into her.

While I was trying to catch my breath, I was vaguely aware of Amber slipping a hand between her legs. She moaned, rubbing that tiny little clit.

"Yes, rub harder." I gripped her thighs, pulling her legs open more so I could watch the show before me.

Her pussy clenched down hard on my now soft cock, but it sent jolts of pleasure throughout every inch of me.

Amber whimpered, her fingers moving faster and faster as she tried chasing the orgasm she was desperate for.

A harsh cry left her, her cunt squeezing my dick like a damn fist as her release ripped through her.

Before she could calm down, I sat up, wrapped myself around her and crushed my mouth to hers. I swallowed the rest of her cries, kissing and sucking at her tongue as she fell apart in my arms.

TWENTY-TWO

Amber

AFTER I RODE SAMMY, he was back between my legs and took it slow. It was the first time for both of us where the feelings we had for each other were out in the open. They were raw and fierce as he made love to me and gave us both what we wanted, and more.

Now, a few hours later, we were in my bed. His hand was on my lower stomach, his hot breath fanning the side of my head and my body burning from the powerful releases he had given me.

"You should be sleeping, pet," he finally murmured, his lips finding my ear.

"I know." He never asked me to tell him how I felt, even though he said he would. "Tell me how you feel," I blurted. Guess there was no time like the present.

"I feel tired, sore, and like my dick is going to fall off from how hard your pussy squeezed it, but I also feel happy. For once in my life…" He cupped my jaw, turning my head to face him.

"I'm happy."

"I'm happy too." I rolled onto my back, grabbing his hand and pulling his arm tighter around me. "So happy."

Sammy kissed my shoulder. "Tell me."

"You're so demanding." I faked a yawn. "Maybe later."

"Amber," he growled, giving my shoulder a gentle bite.

I laughed and sat up before turning toward him.

His gaze roamed down the length of my naked body, his hand finding my inner thigh. The firm hold on me reminded me that he was there. That he would always be there. No matter what. He was my safe place. He would protect me. He wasn't Aaron.

"Shawnee went with me to get the divorce papers," I started, knowing that even though we joked about it, I did need to tell him how I felt. "She made a joke that she would move in with me and help me take care of the baby and we could both be mothers to it but still sleep with other people. We laughed about it at the time, but I know she was serious. This time..." I stared at Sammy, wishing I could put every single thing I felt into words but would try just the same. "I'm in love with you, Sam. Not because you got me pregnant. But because you take care of me. You make me feel things I've never felt before. I've been attracted to you from the first moment I met you and you asked me to go home with you. When I said no, I actually thought you would have moved on to someone else. I'm not an easy person to love because I have a hard time trusting people and yet, I think you love me anyway. Or I hope you do at least."

"I do." He grabbed my hand and pulled me against him. "I'm in love with you, too." His hand ran through my hair, holding my head tight. "I've been in love with you this whole time. I just didn't realize it until recently. I haven't been with anyone else since that first night. Since I saw you dance and leave that stage. Since I made you tell me your name." He held my hand between us, kissed my fingers, and leaned his forehead against mine. "I know you've had it hard. What Aaron did, what those fuckers did and now Will...but I promise, baby, I will not hurt you. I will not break your heart. You know how dark I like my sex to be but if I do something that you don't like, you need to tell me."

"You need to tell me too," I told him. "We need to communicate." I ran my fingers through his beard, pushing my lips against his.

"Yes, we do but I think we've been pretty good at doing that so far." He winked.

I laughed lightly. "I think so too." I leaned back, running my thumb along his mouth. "I told you that I would make you fall in love with me first."

He pushed me onto my back and snarled into the crook of my neck.

A burst of laughter left me at the ticklish feeling of his beard against my skin.

Sammy lifted his head, lying on his side beside me and linking his fingers between mine. "I'd like you to meet my parents. I know that sounds weird since they're both..." He cleared his throat. "Anyway, I just..."

"I'd love to meet them." I brought his hand to my mouth, kissing the back of his knuckles. "Just let me know when."

"I will, thank you." He paused. "We have a few hours before your appointment."

"Are you telling me that I should shut up so we can get some sleep?" I asked, pulling the blankets up and over us.

"If it gets you to shut up." He lightly smacked my ass. "Yes."

I laughed, pushing my ass into his waist. "I love you, Sam."

He wrapped himself around me, kissing the side of my neck. "I love you, Amber."

(Sammy)

As soon as I uttered those words, it was like a weight had been lifted off my shoulders. It was something I never expected to feel. Something I never even wanted to feel if I was being honest with myself. I thought back to my parents. How much they loved each other. How much they needed each other. And when my mom was taken from my dad, even though his heart was still beating, it killed him. He wasn't the same and ever since, I regretted not telling him how I felt. I knew my brother felt the same way. We were pissed at him. It wasn't right. Both of us knew that. But it was the truth.

My phone buzzed, vibrating on the nightstand beside me.

Kissing Amber's temple, I slipped out from her warmth, grabbed my phone, and left her room.

Instead of texting Cyrus back, I called him up.

"Hey, brother," he answered almost instantly.

"Couldn't sleep?" I asked him, making my way out to the balcony. My eyes landed on the pack of smokes and ashtray on the table, remembering when she told me she bought them for me so I would have them when needed. It was one of the things I loved about her. How she didn't judge me for my habit.

"Ainsley woke up from a nightmare and I saw the time. Figured I'd give you a call to see how you are."

"I know," I told him, as if I could read his thoughts.

"You're good?"

"Yeah, Cyrus. I am." I sat on the patio couch, lit up a cigarette, and blew the smoke out slowly. The spicy sustenance sent a wave of peace over me, and I couldn't help but lean back against the couch and let out a heavy sigh. "I really am."

"It's about time huh?"

"You have no idea."

"How's Amber?"

The conversation went on like that for the next little while. He would ask about my relationship. I would ask about his. It was something we never talked about before and just assumed the other was happy. But I was glad we did.

Though we constantly texted back and forth and I saw him and Ainsley at the clubhouse from time to time, it wasn't enough. We decided to change that.

"It's us against the world," he reminded me.

"It is." And it really was.

LIBERATE US

(Amber)

"I'm nervous." I wasn't exactly sure why. I hadn't been nervous. Not once. Not until we arrived at the doctor's office and were now waiting for him to do an ultrasound and whatever else it was he had to do.

"You're healthy and I'm sure the baby is healthy too." Sammy squeezed my hands resting on my lap. "But whatever happens, I'm here. No matter what."

"God." I cupped his face, giving him a soft peck on the lips. "Who are you and what have you done with the asshole I fell in love with?"

He chuckled, the sound delicious but dangerous. "Careful. He's still there." He cupped the back of my head and gave my bottom lip a gentle bite. "He's just being nice until you give birth to his baby. Then all bets are off, Little Red."

I shivered. "Sounds exciting."

He shook his head, his laugh deepening.

Before we could continue this inappropriate flirting that I enjoyed immensely, the doctor took that moment to enter the room.

"Amber Bishop?" The older man dressed in white, greeted us with a wide smile.

"Yes, I'm her." I smiled back, liking him already.

"And you're the father?" he asked Sam.

"Yes, Sir." He stuck his hand out. "Sammy."

"Nice to meet you. I'm Dr. Shaw," he said, returning the handshake. He pulled the ultrasound machine up beside the bed I was lying on and sat on a stool. "Now, usually I would have the tech doing this but we're a little short-staffed today. So, you get my friendly face instead."

I laughed. "Works for me."

"Thank fuck he's old," Sammy muttered.

"What was that?" the doctor asked, raising a gray eyebrow.

"Nothing." I rolled my eyes and laid back on the bed. "Ignore him. He's not a morning person."

"I take it you wouldn't want a young doctor doing this, then?" The doctor lifted my shirt to just under my breasts. "Am I right?"

"You're right," Sammy told him.

"Yeah, I wouldn't want that either." Dr. Shaw winked.

"I like him," Sammy told me.

"Good because he's going to be the one between my legs when these babies are ready to be born." As soon as I said it, I realized my slip.

"Babies?" Dr. Shaw stared at me.

"I'm a twin," Sammy explained. "So, we thought it could be possible. Especially since she's showing already."

"But if I did the math right, I should only be about three months. I think." I realized something then. "Oh god."

"What?" Sammy closed his hand around mine. "What is it?"

"I don't think I've had my period since you and I started sleeping together." We used condoms in the beginning, and I was on birth control. Clearly neither of those things worked where Sammy's boys were concerned.

"Let's take a look." Dr. Shaw squeezed some jelly on my stomach before pressing the wand against my belly. "Well…" He turned the screen toward us. "It looks like you're right. There's baby one." He pointed at the black and white image. "And baby two. Did you want to hear the heartbeats?"

"Yes." Sammy brought my hand up to his mouth, kissing my knuckles. "Please."

Twins.

I was carrying twins.

I was carrying Sammy's twins.

Dr. Shaw pressed a couple more buttons on the machine and I was just about to ask if everything was okay when the most beautiful sound erupted around the room. It sounded like a woosh but there were two of them and they weren't in sync, but they were perfect.

"That's…" My throat closed, working hard over a lump.

"That's the sound of very healthy heartbeats." Dr. Shaw pressed another button on the machine, the sounds disappearing soon after. "Here." He printed two pictures of the ultrasound for us and cleaned the jelly off of my stomach. "Everything looks good. Get some rest. Eat healthy. Take folic acid. No strenuous activity." He went on to list more things I should and shouldn't be doing but I couldn't help but focus on anything but the fact that I was staring at an ultrasound of twin babies that were currently growing inside of me.

"Did you hear him?" Sammy asked a moment later.

"What?" I looked up, finding Sammy and I alone. "Oh, I was distracted."

He gave me a small smile and stood. "You're around four months, Red." He kissed my temple. "That means I got you pregnant the first time I fucked you."

My breath wavered.

"That means that one of my boys, really wanted your egg." His mouth moved from my temple to my ear. "That means that we didn't just break your table, but we also broke the damn condom too."

A husky laugh left me. "Have we really been sleeping together for that long already?"

Sammy cupped my stomach. "Time flies when you're having fun." He helped me off the table, righted my shirt, and kissed me hard on the mouth. "Come. Let's go back to your place and we'll call your mom."

"You still spending the rest of the week with me?" He had made plans to, but I wasn't sure if anything changed.

"Yes." Sammy grabbed my hands, bringing them up to his mouth. "I love you."

My stomach did a flip. "I love you, too."

And I was so damn thankful that I had a second chance at happiness. Sammy and I would have to work for our relationship just like most had to, but I knew right then, with the way he was currently looking at me, that I wouldn't want to do this with anyone else.

TWENTY-THREE

SAMMY

AFTER WE FOUND OUT that Amber was pregnant with twins, I took her out for lunch. We ended up spending a couple of hours at the restaurant, laughing, flirting, and enjoying our time together.

"Could you imagine if it's two girls?" Amber teased, placing her feet on my lap.

I looked down, wrapped a hand around her ankle, and pulled it against my crotch.

Her cheeks turned pink, a knowing glint flashing in her eyes.

"If it's two girls, I'm going to have to invest in a security team for them." I pushed a thumb into the arch of her foot.

Amber sighed, staring at me from across the table. "*I'm happy with whatever gender they are.*"

"*Me too, pet.*"

And I would be. I just wanted both of the babies to be healthy.

The picture of the ultrasound burned in my wallet, and I

couldn't wait to show my brother. I hadn't seen him in awhile and I was excited to share that our family was growing.

I was sitting outside his house that he shared with his fiancée, and I found that I was nervous to tell him. I wasn't sure why exactly. Maybe he would think it was too soon for me and Amber or he would say that I wasn't ready to be a father. It wasn't the fact that I wasn't ready but I was terrified, and I knew that Amber was too. Especially since finding out we were going to have two little humans to take care of. This world was fucked up. We would have to raise our children to be strong enough to handle it.

As I slid off my bike, I sent Amber a text letting her know that I was at Cyrus's place. She hadn't been feeling well, so she stayed home. I left her in bed with the TV on, a box of crackers on her lap, and a bottle of Gatorade on her nightstand.

Red: Have fun. Love you!

Me: Love you too, pet. Send me a picture.

An image came through a minute later, showing me her long, beautiful legs. Every cell in my body stirred.

Me: If you're up to it, I'd like to have those legs wrapped around my face later.

Red: They can be wrapped around your face while I suck your cock. How does that sound?

Me: Fucking hell, I love you.

I could almost hear her laugh from here.

Red: I might head to Rouge to work a few hours. Depends on how I feel later. But that'll give you something to look forward to. Love you, Sammy.

Me: Be safe and I love you too, Red.

I didn't want her to work but I understood that she needed the money, so I never argued with her.

"Hey, we weren't expecting you."

My head snapped up, finding my brother standing on the front patio. "I know. This is a little last minute." I put my phone away and trudged up the path to him. "Can we talk?"

"Of course." He clapped my shoulder. "Everything okay? We were just about to sit down for lunch if you wanted to join us."

I shook my head. "Thank you but I just stopped by to tell you something." I pulled my wallet from my pocket, figuring showing him would be easier. "So…" Taking the ultrasound picture out, I handed it to him. "This happened."

Cyrus took it from me, his eyes widening. They snapped to mine, back down to the picture between his fingers, back to me. "Really?"

I nodded. "Twins."

"Fucking hell." Cyrus pulled me into a hug. "I'm going to be an uncle."

I swallowed hard at the thickness in his voice. "You are."

He leaned back, cupping my nape. "Are you happy?"

"I am. We're still trying to wrap our heads around the fact that she's carrying twins, but we are. Very happy." This had been the first time in a long time where Cyrus and I actually spoke about our feelings. It wasn't something we did often. Not since he and Ainsley started dating. "I told her I love her."

"It's about fucking time." Cyrus pulled away from me and went to the front door of the house. "I know you said you're not staying but come in and see Ainsley. She'll be pissed if you don't at least say hi."

Doing as I was told, I followed him into the house. "She said it back."

Cyrus stopped, looking at me over his shoulder. "Were you concerned she wouldn't?"

"I don't know. Maybe? I'm not an easy person to get along with and I know I've been moody." I shrugged, not liking this sudden anxiety rushing through me. I needed Amber. I needed the comfort of her arms wrapped around me as I tried gathering my thoughts.

"We've been through a lot, Sam. All of us have."

"I know." I thought a moment, shoving my hands into the pockets of my jeans. "I am happy, but I feel like something is going to fuck it up. I don't know how or when but something's going to happen. I'm not being paranoid, but Amber has…baggage to say the least."

"Need me to look into things?" Cyrus asked, the protector in him coming out. "That Will fucker bothering her?"

"He's making noise and I need to know what he wants."

"I heard you had a run-in with him at Rouge," Cyrus said as Ainsley came down the hall.

"Hey guys," she said softly.

I held my arm out, waiting for her hug.

"I did. The bastard wouldn't leave Amber alone. When I charged into the room and found her in his arms but not because she wanted to be there," I explained as Ainsley hugged me from the side.

"Is she okay?" she asked, squeezing me.

"She is, Sis. Thank fuck for that," I said, holding her close. "She's pregnant."

Ainsley leaned back, a slow grin spreading on her face. "It's about time."

I scoffed. "That I got her pregnant? I only wanted to sleep with her. At first anyway." And it made me sound like a dick, but I didn't care. It was the truth. But now, I wouldn't change it for anything.

"I'm glad you're happy and I can't wait to officially meet her," Ainsley said softly.

"What happened after her run-in with him?" Cyrus asked, leaning against the wall opposite us.

"I knocked him around a bit and Corbin kicked him out. I haven't seen or heard from him since and neither has Amber. Things are fucked up, C. I don't know what's going on. We went to the Hell's Harlem Chapter in her hometown." I pulled away from Ainsley. "I need a smoke."

"We'll go to the back." Cyrus led me through the house and out to the backyard. "Tell me what happened."

I explained everything. From meeting up with Tiny, to the run-ins with Will and how he wanted something but neither Amber nor I knew exactly what that was. Will was a problem, but it wasn't going to stop me from being with her.

She loved me. I loved her. That was all that mattered.

(Amber)

"You're pregnant."

I jumped, finding Candace sitting on a stool on the other side of the bar. "Why do you say that?"

She laughed. "One, I'm not stupid. Two, your tits are huge. Three, you have a glow to you that's absolutely beautiful. Four, you can wear loose fitting clothing, but I can still see that sexy little bump."

"I didn't want to make a big deal of it," I told her, looking down at my stomach. It was like I woke up one morning and my bump was suddenly there.

"How far along are you?" Candace asked, reaching over the bar top and grabbed a glass.

"Just over four months," I said, watching her pour herself a beer.

"Can I ask who the father is?"

"Sammy Butcher," I said, bracing myself for her comments.

Candace's eyes snapped to mine. "You're kidding."

"Nope." I mentally patted myself on the back that I was able to get through to him when others had tried and failed.

"Wow." Candace sat back on the stool and took a long sip of her beer. "I had no idea. I know he's asked about you and was determined to meet you in the beginning but that was a long time ago. I just...wow."

"It's not that surprising." I went back to cleaning the counter. "Is it?"

"Girl, you do realize what his role is within this chapter of Hell's Harlem, don't you? Add to the fact that most of the girls here tried getting into his bed and weren't successful. But you did better than that, you're having his fucking kid."

"I know he's a little rough around the edges and I'm actually having two of his kids and I also made him fall in love with me," I added nonchalantly.

A hard laugh left her. "Exactly." Her face fell. "Wait...what? Two of them? You're having twins?"

I shrugged, a light laugh leaving me.

"Wow." She shook her head.

"But what role does he have exactly?" It wasn't like it ever came up in our conversations. Especially now, when most of our talks consisted of when he was going to move in with me and what color we wanted to paint the nursery.

"He's the Enforcer. I don't know what it all consists of, but I do know that he's lethal as fuck. Ronny's seen him fighting at The Ring." She shook her head. "Just be careful."

"I will." I wanted to ask more about The Ring and what Sammy did there. He fought? I had no idea. But before I could ask any more on it, I couldn't help but notice how a few members of Hell's Harlem strolled into the club.

"Speak of the devil," Candace murmured, slipping off the stool. She grabbed her beer and started walking backwards. "Remember what I said."

How could I not? She warned me about the guy I was in love with. The guy who had gotten me pregnant, not with just one baby but two.

While a few of the Hell's Harlem crew rolled in and sat at their typical booth, the man I had been thinking about, started stalking toward me.

Our eyes locked, a slow grin spreading on his face as he neared.

My body heated, watching him walk around the bar. "You shouldn't be back here."

"Don't care." Sammy closed the distance between us, cupped the side of my neck, and placed a hard peck on my mouth while running his other hand over my lower stomach. "How's my family?"

My heart stuttered. "Good." I covered his hand on my belly and looked down. I was almost five months along, but you would think I was more. I couldn't hide the fact that I was pregnant anymore and I knew that Sammy liked that idea. If I could walk around naked all the time, just so he could see my stomach, he would be happy.

"How are *you* doing?" I asked him.

He gave me a final kiss and went around to the other side of the bar before sitting on a stool across from me. "Good." His eyes roamed down the length of me, landing on my stomach and staying there.

"You saw me this morning, Sam." I laughed. "By the way you're looking at me, you'd think you'd never seen a pregnant woman before."

"Not one who's carrying my babies, pet," he said as Cyrus and Jaron came up the bar.

"Amber," Cyrus greeted. "I haven't had a chance to wish you a congratulations. I'm also glad you finally kicked my brother's ass into gear," he teased, punching Sammy in the shoulder.

Jaron chuckled. "I agree." He leaned across the bar. "We haven't officially met. Jaron."

"Amber." I returned the handshake. "I guess you guys will be seeing more of me." I cupped my stomach. "Literally."

They laughed.

"So, twins," Cyrus pointed out. "Our mom would have lost her mind over that fact. You'd already have a nursery set up and everything."

Sammy grunted. "Dad would probably have started a trust fund already too and bought a few dozen shotguns. Especially if they end up being girls."

My heart swelled, my stomach doing a little flip over the fact that Sammy was sitting there with his brother and Jaron. His family. And now I was part of it.

"You're good, Red?" Jaron asked, something else hidden behind his question.

Sammy's head whipped around. "Leave it alone, J."

"I need to know she's safe," Jaron told him.

"Forgive him," Cyrus mumbled. "We've become a little paranoid."

"Oh…well…" I distracted myself by pouring them each a beer. "I haven't heard from Will if that's what you mean."

"Good."

"Thank fuck."

"I'm going to kill him." That was Sammy and I knew that if I gave the go-ahead, he would. But a part of me wondered if he would continue listening to me or if he would take the matter into his own hands and kill him like he threatened on more than one occasion.

"I don't like him either but you…" I sighed. "He's not part of Hell's Harlem anymore but he still knows people. He made a name for himself, and I can't…I can't have anything happening to you." I placed a pint of beer in front of each of them. "I can't."

"Nothing will happen, pet," Sammy said, taking a long sip of his beer.

"You don't know that," I threw at him.

"I'm going to go call Piper." Jaron stood from his stool. "See how she and the kids are." He grabbed his beer and pulled his phone out of his leather cut. "Hey, baby, just wanted to check in," he said, holding the phone up to his ear and walking away.

"I should call Ainsley." Cyrus went to stand when Sammy cupped his shoulder, stopping him. "You two need to talk about this on your own."

"No." I went back to cleaning the bar. "We are not talking about this here."

"Amber."

I looked up, finding both of the brothers looking directly at me. "What? I need to clean. I need to work my shift, so then I can go home and go to bed like a normal pregnant woman. I can't constantly be worrying about what Will wants and doesn't want. I can't stress over it." I threw the rag on the counter. "I need to go get some napkins." I spun on my heel before either of them could stop me and went down the hall to the storage room.

LIBERATE US

As I walked by the staff room, I heard muffled voices coming from inside it. Opening the door, I peeked my head in, finding a few of the girls getting ready.

"Hey, Red," they greeted in unison.

"Hey, I just wanted to see if you girls needed some drinks." I was also stalling because I loved Sammy, I really did, but his overprotective ways were enough to drive me mad.

"Sure."

"Yes please!"

"Oh, I'd love a shot of anything right about now."

I laughed as the girls spoke at the same time. Taking their orders, I noticed that Emma Morin was nowhere around. "Where's Emma?" I asked, once I had their drinks committed to memory.

"I think she's talking to Candace and Ronny," Penelope Caissie said, pulling the elastic out of her long auburn hair. "Something about a group of guys who have been here a few times over the past few weeks."

"Group of guys?" I asked, stepping into the room and closing the door behind me.

"Penny," Shawnee warned her. "Leave it alone."

"What?" Penny looked my way. "They keep asking about you. She needs to know," she told Shawnee before she could get scolded again.

"Great." I pinched the bridge of my nose. "Have they bothered you girls at all?"

"Not me but they've given Emma a hard time," Penny said.

"Penelope Caissie," Shawnee snapped. "Seriously."

"What happened?" I considered these girls family. If Will was causing shit, I needed to know.

"It's not a big deal." Emma huffed from behind me, coming into the room. "They just said some shit about me liking women and how they could get me to convert. It's nothing I've never heard before." Her face softened. "I promise, baby."

"Did they hurt you?" I didn't like how weak my voice sounded but Will did this to me. He made me feel small and worthless, much like his shithead of a brother. I couldn't have my problems constantly following me.

"No." Emma came up to me and pulled me into her arms. "I promise, Red. I'm fine. I'm a big girl."

"Okay." I returned her embrace, the scent of her light floral perfume tingling my nose.

"I do have to say though that you look really good pregnant." She leaned back, cupping my stomach. "If you were carrying my baby…" She waggled her eyebrows when her words trailed off.

I giggled, shaking my head. "And here I thought it was only men who became turned on by that."

"No, not at fucking all. You look good. Really good." Her eyes dropped to my stomach, her hand moving lower.

"Alright." I grabbed her hand, stopping it from going places it shouldn't be going. "You need to get out more."

"Before you hump the poor girl's leg, zip me up," Penny demanded, shaking her head.

"Why can't any of you like women too?" Emma sighed, going back up to Penny and helping her zip up her dress.

"Shawnee has been known to dabble outside of the male territory," I reminded Emma, as a few of the other dancers came into the room.

Shawnee laughed, slipping into a tight neon pink dress.

"Oh yes." Emma's smile widened. "I'm well aware of that." She winked.

Shawnee scowled, throwing a shoe at her. "Shut up. That was one time and I had too many margaritas."

"Doesn't matter." Emma wrapped an arm around Penny's waist. "You still let me eat your—"

"Alright, that's enough." Shawnee glared at her. "Zip me up so I can leave."

"You're leaving wearing that?" Emma released Penny and went up to Shawnee.

"Yes, I'm going to a party if you must know." Shawnee pulled her long blond hair over her shoulder as Emma came up behind her.

"I can give you a party with my face between your legs," Emma said, waggling her eyebrows.

"Is that all you think about?" Shawnee laughed, shaking her head.

Emma looked at me, giving me a wink before turning back to her on again, off again fling. "Yes."

Laughter filled the room and I realized that this was one of the reasons I still worked at the club. Sure, I didn't dance anymore, but Candace kept me on anyway and I was thankful she did.

While the girls continued getting ready and talked amongst themselves, I left the room to grab the napkins and their drinks.

Heading to the storage room across the hall, I was gathering up packages of napkins and putting them in a bag when suddenly, a loud eruption sounded.

I jumped, spinning around. The movement had been so hard, my hip hit the edge of a crate.

"Ow," I mumbled, rubbing the spot to take out the sting.

Another loud bang sounded, forcing my stomach to drop to the floor at my feet. Something was going on. I heard shouting and muffled voices but I couldn't make out what anyone was saying.

Rushing forward, I never made it to the door when a third eruption sounded, knocking me back.

Falling to the floor, I instinctively covered my stomach. I went to push to my feet when the tiered shelving unit to my left, fell toward me.

TWENTY-FOUR

SAMMY

SMOKE FILLED MY LUNGS to the point it hurt to breathe. It wasn't the good smoke either. Not the kind I took into my body on a regular basis. Or the kind I used to curb the edge sometimes. No, this was worse. Every inch of me ached as I tried moving. I did a quick body scan, making sure all of my bits and pieces were still intact but fuck me, I hurt.

There was a constant ringing in my head, pounding throughout every inch of me.

"Sam."

I heard my name being called from somewhere off in the distance, but I couldn't move. Was my back broken?

"Sam, breathe."

There was that same voice again.

Taking a deep inhale, my body relaxed, finally able to move. What the hell happened?

Amber.

I shot to a sitting position, my head swimming at the sudden movement. "Fucking hell." I pinched the bridge of my nose, breathing through the dizziness.

"Sammy." Cyrus's face came into view. He crouched in front of me. "Are you okay?"

"Where's Amber?" I asked, ignoring his question. I didn't give a shit about me. I needed to make sure my girl and our unborn babies were fine.

"I can't find her but there's…" Cyrus's jaw clenched. "There are bodies everywhere, Sammy. Some of our crew…we need to start getting people out of here."

"Jaron." I grabbed his leather cut. "Tell me he's okay."

"I'm fine."

My head whipped around, finding Jaron coming toward us.

He held a hand out. "Can't get rid of me that easily."

I slid my hand in his, letting him help me to my feet. "We need to find Amber," I told them.

"Did you call anyone?" Cyrus asked, pulling his phone out of his inner pocket. "Fuck, my phone is smashed. I must have landed on it when the explosions hit."

"Who the fuck blew up my club?" came Candace's high-pitched voice.

"This is a mess." Jaron checked his phone. "Mine's fine. I called 911. Everyone is on their way. We'll get those who survived out of here and then we'll call our girls."

While they were helping get people to safety and checking in with their old ladies, I went to search for Amber when a scream sounded out of nowhere.

Bile rose to my throat that something happened to her, the mother of my unborn children. The one and only woman who had ever been able to crack down my walls. To get under my skin and stay there. To make me fall in love with her.

"Amber," I yelled, charging for the hallway that led to the change rooms along with the storage rooms. I didn't know where she was, but I remembered her saying something earlier about needing to get some napkins. At that point, I had every intention of going after her but Cyrus had stopped me.

Trust me when I tell you this," he told me. "*Amber went off to be alone. You need to give her some space.*"

But I didn't want to give her space. I wanted to overcrowd her damn life and stay there. Whether she liked it or not.

"Sam, wait!" Cyrus ran after me.

I checked the change rooms, my heart sinking at the mayhem before me.

"Oh, Penny." Emma was holding her friend in her arms, rocking back and forth. Penny's eyes were vacant, staring into nothing as life was no longer in her. Tears streamed down Emma's face, soft sobs wracking through her small body.

"Shit," Cyrus muttered. "We need to get the girls out of here." He barked orders at Cheesy and Locke and a few of the other guys to help get people to safety. "We also need to find out what the hell happened."

"What do you think happened?" I growled. "It was Will. It had to have been."

"That's a big fucking accusation, brother."

I spun on my twin, grabbing the collar of his cut and slamming him up against the wall. "I don't give a shit. If something happened to Amber because of that bastard, my pretty face will be the last thing he ever sees."

"You do remember what happened when Jaron took things into his own hands right?" Cyrus reminded me.

I grunted, releasing him. "That fucker got off too easily if you asked me." A friend of Piper's had attacked her, and Jaron walked in on it. He stopped it from going further but it had gone far enough and Jaron killed him. It was too easy. I would have made him suffer just like I was going to do to Will, even if he had nothing to do with these explosions.

"Guys, we lost one of our security…" Candace's voice trailed off as she stopped in front of the doors leading to the change room. "Penny, oh God." She rushed to Emma, dropping to her knees in front of her and crying with the girls who had not only worked for her but had become part of her family just the same.

My eyes scanned the room. Besides Penny, everyone seemed to be breathing. Shawnee held a towel to her forehead, her eyes meeting mine.

"You good?" I asked her, knowing she and Amber were best friends.

She nodded. "Find Amber."

Cheesy and Locke rushed into the room, helping the girls bring Penny out of the club.

A muffled cry suddenly came from the storage room across the hall followed by a curse. "Amber." I went to the door, trying to open it, but it wouldn't budge. "Amber," I called out. "Are you in there?"

"Sammy," came her muffled response.

"Oh thank fuck." Relief rushed through me that she was alive but even though I could hear her voice, I needed her in my arms to prove that she was in fact fine. I needed to touch her, hold her, and kiss her. "Baby, are you okay?"

"I hit my head and I'm bleeding but that's it."

"We need to get in there," I told Cyrus as both he and Jaron came toward me from down the hall.

"There's something blocking the door," Amber said. "I can't move it."

I tried the door, opening it slightly, but she was right. There looked to be a beam from the ceiling that had barricaded her into the small room. "Come to the door, pet. I need to see you."

When she came into view, all my breath I didn't realize I had been holding left me on a whoosh.

"Hi," she whispered, reaching her fingers through the small space.

"Hi." I hooked my fingers around hers and kissed them, my gaze moving over every inch of her that I could see. I frowned when I noticed the gash on her head. "We need to get that cut taken care of." I knew that head wounds bled quite a bit, but it didn't make me feel better. Not where she was concerned. "Move out of the way as best you can."

She nodded, moving out of my line of sight.

"Sam, police, ambulance, and fire are here," Cyrus told me.

"I got this," I said. "Go help the others."

"Sammy." Jaron looked between me and my brother. "This isn't good. None of this shit is."

"Get Amber out of there and then we'll have a meeting once the police let us leave." Cyrus ran a hand through his hair. "We need...fuck, I don't know what we need."

"You guys okay?" Corbin Wane stomped toward us, a deep scowl set on his face. "This is a shit show. Whoever set off these bombs, only wanted to do enough damage to make a point. Fucking fuckers. I don't know much about explosives, but these were tiny apparently." He scowled. "It's like they were messing with us."

"Amber's stuck in the storage room," I told him, interrupting his rant.

"I'll help you." Corbin nodded toward Jaron. "Call your people. Candace and Ronny are outside and about to burn the fucking world down to try and figure out what the hell happened."

"Let's go. I'll call my dad." Jaron clapped Cyrus's shoulder. "Sam, you need us, you fucking yell."

"Sammy."

Amber's voice pulled my attention back to her. I needed to get this shit taken care of. I needed her in my arms and to take her out of here. If Will set this up, there was more to this than Amber and I understood. It just proved that he was willing to do anything and everything to get to her.

I just didn't know why.

TWENTY-FIVE

Amber

I MOVED OUT OF the way so I wouldn't get hit by the door if Sammy was able to break it down like I assumed he was going to try and do. My head hurt; a pounding sounded in my ears from whatever it was that had hit me. I needed out of that room, suddenly feeling claustrophobic. But most of all, I needed Sammy's arms around me.

"Alright, baby," he said, his voice giving me hope that he would help me out of this room. "We're going to try and break down the door."

Sammy stepped out of the way.

"We'll get you out of there," a new voice told me.

"Corbin?" My voice shook, my head continuing to throb.

"Yeah, sweetheart. Let's get you free before Sammy tears the walls down." As soon as those words left Corbin's mouth, a bang sounded against the door. It continued, the door opening a little more each time. It slowly pushed the beam out of the way, but it seemed to take forever.

As the guys tried with everything they had to get me out of that room, I prayed that whatever happened hadn't take any lives.

When they were finally able to get the door open and the beam pushed back enough that I could get out, I took a step forward as Sammy slipped into the room with me.

I stopped suddenly, staring at the man who was the beginning to a future I never knew I needed.

"My arms," he demanded. "*Now*."

Rushing to him, I threw myself around him.

He didn't even give me a chance to enjoy the feeling of hugging him when he tugged my head back and captured my mouth in a rough kiss.

"Sam," I breathed, a whimper escaping me as his teeth sunk into my bottom lip.

Before I could say any more, he scooped me up into his arms, shoved my head into the crook of his neck, and rushed me out of the room.

"How's my family?" he asked as he carried me. It was something he always asked whenever he greeted me.

When we reached the main area where the bar, booths, tables, chairs, and stage were, it was like walking into another world. The room was unrecognizable from the destruction.

"God, Sammy. Who could survive this?" I said more to myself.

"We did, pet." His hold in my hand was firm.

"We're good," I murmured. "You can put me down."

"Not happening." Once we reached outside, he held me even tighter against him. "There's something I need to tell you."

"What is it?" I asked, my heart jumping to my throat.

"There's been some casualties, baby," Sammy said gently. "Penelope was one of them."

My eyes welled. "Oh God. Is Emma...where is she? Where's Shawnee?"

"Emma and Candace were with her. So was Shawnee. I'm sorry, Amber." Sammy hugged me to his chest, kissing the top of my head. "I'm so fucking sorry."

"Will." I tried shoving out of Sam's grip but his hold only tightened. "He did this. It's the only thing that makes sense. It's my fault. Because of me, Penny and... I don't..."

"It's not your fault." Sam set me on my feet once we were out of harm's way. "You didn't know that Will would do this shit."

"But I should have known," I cried, shoving away from him.

"No, you will not pull away from me." Sammy wrapped his arms around me before I could get away and held me against him. "We're going to get you looked at and then I'm taking you out of here." His tone left no room for argument. I was too damn tired to argue anyway, so I only nodded and let him lead me further away from the club.

I looked around us and saw Candace huddled with Emma and Shawnee and a few of the other girls.

"Shawnee," I said, attempting to pull my grip from Sammy. Turning back to him when his hold on me only tightened, I closed the distance between us. "I need to see my girls."

"And I need to keep you safe," he reminded me.

"I am safe. The police are here, you're here, some of your guys are here." I slid my hand beneath his hoodie, my fingers coming into contact with his hot skin. "I'm safe." But although I said the words, a part of me wondered just how safe I actually was. Especially if this was Will's way of saying that he was coming for me.

"I'll take you to your girls, Amber, but I'm not leaving your side. You hit your head." He kissed my cheek. "It's my job to protect you. It's my job to keep you and our babies safe. I don't need your mom hunting me down if something were to happen to you."

"Oh God, I need to call her." She was going to be so damn upset and demand for me to go home.

"I'll call her. But I'm still not letting you out of my sight." Sammy wrapped his arm around my shoulders. "Come."

When we reached the girls huddled together by one of the ambulances, Candace rushed to me before I even had a chance to ask if she was okay.

"She's pregnant with twins." Candace pushed me toward an EMT. "Please check to make sure her and the babies are okay. I don't need Sammy burning the rest of my business down if something happened to you," she told me.

"What's with everyone threatening everyone? I'm fine." But even though I said those words, the EMT put me in the back of the ambulance and did what they could to check to make sure that I was in fact fine. They cleaned the wound on my head and bandaged me up, but as they were checking my blood pressure, they advised that it was high.

"Of course it's high." I snorted. "I lost a friend, my boyfriend is ready to hunt the bastards down who did this to find out what happened and why, my boss is looking at me like I have a penis sticking out of my forehead, and I really need out of this ambulance."

Before the EMT could say anything, Shawnee came into the back and sat on the bench beside me.

"Why are you here? I thought you were leaving." I didn't like that she was here. It meant that she could be in harm's way.

"I wasn't able to. Everything happened so quickly." She shook her head. "I can't believe Penny…" she sniffed, grabbing my hand and holding it tight in hers. "I'm glad you're okay."

"I'm glad you're okay too," I told her, sitting up. "But I need to go home. I need to know what happened tonight. I need—"

"Amber." The barked use of my name, sent a hot shiver down my spine. "You know that's not fucking happening."

I looked up, finding a scowling Sammy standing a few feet away.

Before I could argue, Sammy joined us in the back of the ambulance.

"You need to stop being an asshole," Shawnee threw at him.

"And you need to mind your own business," Sammy snapped at her.

"Really?" She raised an eyebrow. "Amber is—"

"Stop. Please. Now's not the time," I told her. "I was stuck in the storage room, so he's freaked out a bit."

"Stop making excuses for him," she said, her voice shrill. She laughed but the amusement wasn't there. "God, Amber. He's a domineering—"

"I love you and I know everyone is stressed right now but Sammy is not Aaron." She didn't have to even say the words and I knew she was comparing the two of them. "Will you give us a moment?" I asked the EMT. "Please."

He looked between all of us. "I wouldn't normally leave you alone but the club he's with helped my sister's place of work." He stepped out of the ambulance and stopped beside Sammy. "You have ten minutes."

"What's with you?" I asked Shawnee.

"It's because Will is causing shit," Sam answered. "Putting noise in her ear about me."

"What? What the hell does that even mean and how would you know that?" I huffed when no one spoke. "Someone, answer me."

"I went up to see your mom," Shawnee finally answered. "Sammy's right. But how would you know that?"

"Because Tiny contacted me." Sam only shrugged.

"Wait. What?" My head whipped around. "He did? When?"

"A few nights ago." Sammy reached for my hand. "I'm sorry I didn't tell you, but you've had enough issues when it comes to knowing things within the club. I'm trying to keep you safe. I also figured that the less you knew, the better."

"This is fucked up." I sighed. "What happened when you went to see my mom?" I asked Shawnee.

"I stopped by the clubhouse, and everyone was in a mood. Will was there. He was asking about you. He wanted to know how you were doing and he said that he hoped you were well, which was weird by the way. I waited to see if he would say anything about your pregnancy, but he didn't mention it. I didn't tell him but..."

"What?" I cupped her hands that were resting on her lap. "Shawnee."

"He knows," she told me, reaching over and placing a hand on my stomach. "He knows you're carrying twins. That's why tonight happened."

"Fuck," Sammy muttered.

My heart started racing, my palms became sweaty. "I... you can't be serious. He wouldn't go to all this trouble just because I'm pregnant."

"You're right. He wouldn't." She paused. "If you were carrying his baby."

"Fucking hell," Sammy growled. "So, you're saying that because the babies aren't Will's, he's throwing a damn tantrum?"

I swallowed hard at the thought.

"Yes, that's what I'm saying. If the babies were Will's, which I know is impossible, then he would do everything he could to keep Amber safe. But because they aren't, he doesn't care who he has to go through to get his point across." Shawnee grabbed my hands, holding them tight. "I'm sorry. Will is unhinged and deeply disturbed. It's like because he can't have you, no one can."

"But I've never hinted for more with him. Even after Aaron died, I told Will exactly what I wanted from him." I pulled from her and dropped my head in my hands. "God, this can't be happening."

Sammy wrapped his arm around my shoulders, kissing my temple. "He's sick, pet."

"You need to keep my girl safe," Shawnee said. "And I'm sorry for jumping down your throat."

He shook his head. "Don't worry about it."

"But I do," she said, covering my hands with hers. "I worry about her. I saw Amber after that accident. I saw how she was, the beating she took and the..."

I glanced at Sammy.

"I was there with her for all of the recovery," Shawnee continued.

"I'll take care of her," Sammy told her, looking directly at me.

"He will," I reassured her.

"I know." Shawnee gave me a hug. "I love you. Sammy's good for you. I see it. I'm going to spend a few days with Emma. She's taking Penny's death hard."

"Be safe." I gave her a hug. "I love you."

"I love you, too." She squeezed me one last time before pulling away and leaving the ambulance.

The EMT took that moment to join us once again. "We good now?"

"Yes." I pulled the blood pressure cuff off my arm and slid off the bed. "I need to go home."

"You need to go to the hospital," the EMT corrected.

"Come." Sammy held his hand out. "I'll take you and then we'll stop by your place and grab some of your things."

I let him help me from the ambulance. As soon as I stepped foot onto the ground, we were met with a few police officers.

A woman dressed in a suit came toward us. She was younger. Maybe mid to late thirties. She had a scowl etched on her face that could give Sammy a run for his money.

When she opened her mouth to speak to me, Sammy stepped in front of me. "She's pregnant with twins and needs to go to the hospital," he told her.

"Fine." The woman spun on her heel and started walking away. "We're following," she called out.

Sammy turned to face me. "We're going to go to the hospital, get our babies and you looked at, then we'll go to your apartment and grab some things. Or we can do that later. A week from now. I don't give a shit. I just need you with me. Okay?"

"Where am I going after that?" I asked, not wanting to be alone.

He wrapped his arms around me, pulling me close. "We're going to the clubhouse," he murmured in my ear. "You keep that between us though, alright?"

I nodded. "Take me home, Sam," I whispered, needing a shower and to get out of here. I needed him.

"Sam, where are you going?"

Both of us turned to Cyrus coming toward us with Jaron following behind him.

"I need to take Amber out of here," Sammy explained, keeping his arm around me. He hooked his other arm around Cyrus, muttering something in his ear that I couldn't hear but could guess just the same. It had to do with what Shawnee had told us.

I knew Will used to have a crush on me, but I never realized it had gone further than that. Especially now that he knew I was pregnant.

"Let me round everyone up," Jaron finally said, walking away.

"Who did we lose?" Sam asked.

"Psycho and one of the new prospects." Cyrus huffed, scrubbing a hand down his face. "I'll call their families."

"I'm sorry," I finally said.

The brothers looked my way.

"It's not your fault, little one." Cyrus let out a harsh sigh. "I'll help Jaron with this shit. Go get her checked out."

While Sam and I headed to my car, I couldn't help but wonder if Cyrus only said those words because of his brother. Whatever was going on with Will needed to end but something inside of me told me that it was far from being over.

TWENTY-SIX

Amber

"WE'RE HEADING TO THE clubhouse now," Sammy said, squeezing my inner thigh.

"Good. Jaron and I are here, along with everyone else," Cyrus said from the cell I was holding. He was on speaker since Sam was driving.

While they talked, I looked out the window. It was the morning of the following day. We were tired, exhausted even, but I was safe and so were our babies. I was able to get checked rather quickly once we got to the hospital. Our babies were strong, but I was advised to get some rest as my blood pressure was still high. Any higher and I would have to go on bed rest, which was something I didn't want but would, of course, if it came down to it.

After it was determined that me and the babies were fine, the police started badgering us with questions.

We met a Detective Baldwin who seemed nice enough but neither Sammy nor I had any information for her. She told us not to leave the country anytime soon and we were now finally on our way to the clubhouse.

"We're here, Red."

My head turned, finding a large house sitting in front of us and the car no longer moving. "Oh, I must have been in my head. Sorry."

Sammy gave my thigh a squeeze. "You're probably tired too, which doesn't help. Let's go and get you to bed."

"Are you going to join me?" I asked, hopeful that he would.

"As much as I want to dive into your tight as fuck body, you need your rest," he said and left the car.

I sighed, doing the same.

"We'll stop by your apartment later and grab some of your things." Sammy came around to my side of the car, pulling me into his arms. "Okay?" he murmured, pushing his face into the crook of my neck.

"Okay," I breathed.

"I was worried I lost you, pet." His mouth found the side of my throat, his body shaking as he took a deep inhale. "I was worried I lost all of you."

"I'm here." I brought his hand to my stomach. "We're here and safe."

"I know." A shuddered breath left him. He stepped away from me, holding out his hand. "Let me introduce you to my bed, baby."

(Sammy)

She was safe. I saw that she was safe. I even heard it from the doctors and nurses at the hospital. But even though that was the case, it didn't stop me from wanting to tear Will apart.

It didn't help that Will was now nowhere to be found. It was like he was teasing us. Making us think that he would show up and then poof, he was gone. It annoyed the fuck out of me and made me moodier than usual.

"Sam."

LIBERATE US

My head lifted from the bottle of beer I was nursing. I was picking at the label, the bottle half empty and probably warm by now.

"You good?" Cyrus asked, sitting in the booth across from me.

"Nope." I was damn near vibrating out of my fucking skin. "I'm not. At all."

He grunted. "I know exactly how you feel."

He wasn't exaggerating about that either. After Ainsley had almost been taken from him, he kept her close more than ever. Some would say it was him being overprotective but after she had been attacked twice, I understood the need to make sure she was safe.

After Amber and I had arrived at the clubhouse, I brought her to my room. She initiated the sex and while I insisted on letting her get some rest, she refused. So, with my kiss on every inch of her body and my cum deep inside her, I left her warmth as soon as she fell asleep.

I knew that I would have to take her back to her apartment but that could wait a couple of days. Once her scent was all over my bed, then I would take her home.

"How's Red doing?" Cyrus asked, glancing down at the beer bottle sitting on the table in front of me.

"Sleeping." I pushed the bottle toward him. "It's probably warm but you can have the rest." I wasn't feeling it and didn't want any more. What I did want was to know where the hell Price was. The father of the bastard Jaron killed to protect Piper, and who vowed revenge against Jaron and the club, was a piece of shit. Add to the fact that I had no idea what Will wanted with my girl. But I could take a wild guess and figure that shit out. As much as I didn't want to, a part of me knew exactly what Will wanted with Amber.

"Have you heard anything about Will?" Cyrus asked even though he already knew the answer.

"Nope. Nothing from him or Price. It's like they just vanished off the face of the fucking earth." I slid out of the booth, needing to do something other than just sit there. I was on the verge of losing my damn mind.

255

"Sammy." Jaron took that moment to join us. "We have news."

"What is it?" I asked, my heart jumping.

"Price was last seen with someone who fits the description you gave us of Will. I can't confirm if it's him or not, but something tells me that it is." Jaron showed me the screen of his phone. A black and white image of two men stared back at me.

My stomach twisted. I recognized Price and the other guy he was with. "That's Will. I didn't know that they knew each other. Amber hasn't said anything about it."

"She may not be aware that they know each other," Jaron suggested. "Price has been gone for awhile and he's also changed his look a bit. He's no longer overweight. So that can definitely make him less recognizable."

I thought back to what Amber told me about her and Aaron's attack. Could Price have had a hand in it? Was he working with Will this whole time and none of us knew?

"Sam?"

All of us turned to Amber standing at the entrance to the main area of the house.

"You should be resting," I said, going up to her.

"I know." She latched on to my hoodie, pulling me close. "I fell asleep and had a nightmare."

Wrapping my arms around her, I hugged her to me and kissed the top of her head. "Since you're here, you might as well meet everyone."

She nodded, chewing her bottom lip.

"Hey." I cupped her cheek, pushing my thumb under her chin and tilting her head back. "Everything will be fine. You are fine. And so are our babies."

Her eyes searched my face. Probably looking for a sign that I was lying to her. But I wasn't and I never would. I was called many things, but a liar wasn't one of them. My feelings and my truths for this woman standing in front of me, were all laid out. I was stripped bare. For her.

"You must be Amber," came a woman's voice.

I stepped aside, giving Amber a wink and running my hand down her arm.

We turned as Eve approached us with Zillah and Sara walking behind her.

"I've heard many things." Eve stopped in front of Amber. "It's so nice to finally meet you."

"It's nice to meet you too," Amber said, giving the woman who helped raise me, a wide smile.

"This is Zillah, Tray's wife, and Sara, Catch's wife," Eve told her, pointing at the other two women who had been in my life since I was a boy.

"Do you mind?" Zillah asked, stepping up to Amber and nodding toward her stomach.

Amber shook her head, grabbed her hands, and placed them on her stomach. "I'm almost five months but I feel like I look as big as a whale."

The women laughed.

"You're beautiful," I told her, interrupting their moment.

The women looked my way.

Eve glanced at Zillah and Sara before meeting my eyes.

"What?" I asked as Jaron and Cyrus came up on either side of me.

"They're not used to you having a woman here," Jaron said. "Especially a pregnant one."

I rolled my eyes. "She's not a unicorn. She's always existed. It just took me a while to find her."

Amber's eyes shone.

"You know, I'm not an overly romantic woman but…" Zillah sighed.

We laughed.

While the ladies fussed over baby shower plans, Amber quietly slid away from them and came up to me.

"Thank you for this." She placed her hands on my chest, sliding them down to my stomach before they stopped at my hips. "I've never had this. I have my mom, Shawnee, and the other girls but I've never had this with…"

My heart jumped. "You never had this with Aaron's side of the family."

She shook her head. "I wanted to, but he always made excuses. So, thank you for giving this to me."

I wanted to give her the whole fucking world but that would have to wait. Until then, we needed to figure out what the hell was going on with Will and get him to leave Amber the fuck alone.

Before I could even suggest that she go back to bed and get some rest, we were surrounded by my club brothers. They shifted from foot to foot, their bodies tense. An unnerving feeling was thick in the air as we waited for them to speak.

"Everything okay?" Amber asked, pulling her arms from around my middle but remaining close.

Thank fuck for that because I wasn't sure how I would get through this if she weren't around.

(Amber)

I wasn't sure what was going on, but I noticed how the women I had just met were suddenly no longer around. I also noticed how the guys zeroed in on us. If it wasn't for Sammy, I would have been nervous. This chapter was much better than the one Aaron had been a part of. Even though they were part of the same motorcycle club, I found the crew that Sammy was with, were nicer. They took care of their own. But I knew at the same time that if something happened to one of theirs, they would do whatever they could to avenge their family.

"What's going on?" Sammy asked, taking the question right out of my head. He linked his fingers with mine, pulling me even closer, but I knew that no matter how close we were to each other, it would never be enough.

"We have more news," Jaron said, his dark eyes flicking my way. His strong jaw was clenched tightly, and I took that as a sign. He wanted me to leave.

"Tell us," Sammy demanded, tightening his hold on my hand.

"You know the rules, Sam," Cyrus said gently. I realized then that he was the calm one, always keeping things in check and making sure no one ripped others' heads off.

"This is different when it involves Amber's late husband's brother," Sammy growled.

"Listen." I pulled my hand from Sam's and moved between them. "I know that you guys don't know me, and I also know that you are good men. What happened last night..." I shook my head. "I'm sorry for your losses. All of yours."

"We're sorry for yours too," Jaron said, the hard lines on his face, softening.

"Thank you." I took a breath, glancing up at Sammy before looking back at his family. "If you give me a chance, I can tell you everything I know. But what I can't tell you is why Will is doing this. I only know what I've been told but I haven't confronted him. I don't want anything more to happen to your club. I have a feeling you all have been through enough already."

Several grunts sounded, proving I was right.

"Sam." I turned to him. "I should go home."

"Like fuck you should." He grabbed my wrist, pulling me against him. "Not happening."

"I don't want to bring any more pain to your club. Last night wasn't my fault, but until Will gets what he wants, I know that he'll blow up everything he can to get it." I cupped Sammy's cheek. "Send some of the guys with me. Guys you trust."

"I don't trust anyone, pet," he murmured, his eyes moving back and forth over my face.

I let out a soft sigh, knowing he didn't mean that but was trying to get a point across. A point I understood.

Turning back around, I faced the men Sammy had grown up with. I recognized some from previous parties I had been to with Aaron, but I didn't actually know any of the men except for Sammy.

"I know that women aren't usually privy to club information, but I promise that if I knew what Will wanted, I would tell you." I cupped my stomach. "I just...I don't know what I'm trying to say." These men didn't know me. Sammy said he didn't trust them but how could I expect for them to trust me in return?

"Has Will said anything at all?" Jaron asked, crossing his arms under his thick chest.

"He's apparently trying to get information out of me. Information I don't have. He also wants..." I swallowed hard, hugging my arms around my middle.

"He wants Amber," Sammy said, finishing for me.

Several curses were muttered throughout the group of men.

"You have got to be fucking kidding me." Jaron took a step toward me but not before Sammy caught my arm and pulled me behind him.

"Careful, brother," Sammy growled, standing between his president and me.

"I'm not kicking her out," Jaron told him, getting in his face. "But if she stays here, we need to up the security."

"I can leave," I said, grabbing the back of Sammy's leather cut.

"You are not leaving." He spun on me. "Not at fucking all. We've had people stay here for less."

"We wouldn't kick you out." Jaron ran a hand through his dark hair. "But we do need to figure out what Will wants."

"He wants me," I muttered, pointing out the obvious. It had been something they already knew but I wasn't sure if they actually took Will seriously. I sure as hell did. As much as Aaron was an abusive bastard, Will was far worse than his brother.

While the guys continued trying to hash out a plan to bring Will down, or at least figure out what he wanted, my phone buzzed, making me jump.

Slipping away from the men, I knew I only had a couple minutes, if that, before Sammy started wondering where I was.

When I looked at my phone, I swallowed hard when I saw that Will was calling me.

I took a deep breath and placed the phone to my ear. "What do you want?" I demanded.

"We both know what I want, Amber," he said, his voice monotonous. He almost sounded bored in a way. Like he had better things to do than to try and ruin the happiness I finally found.

"Why are you doing this?" None of this made sense. Why was he all of a sudden coming around when he hadn't been after

I left the city I grew up in. After Aaron died, Will disappeared. "Why now, Will? After all of this time?"

"I was stewing. But it doesn't matter why I've waited. A little birdy told me that you're pregnant. Pregnant, Amber. Those babies should be mine."

My stomach dropped. Was this really because I was carrying Sammy's twins and not his? "You can't be serious."

"I *am* fucking serious and if you want this shit to end, you will do what I want."

"What do you want?" I whispered, gripping my phone tight in my hand.

"You know where I am, Princess."

"Please, Will. You need to stop this. Penelope died in that explosion. A member of your club died. A couple of members in fact." I didn't give a shit that I was now begging for lives I didn't know. This needed to end. "Please, Will."

"You know the only way this will end." There was some shuffling coming through from Will's end. "You know, maybe I should just keep your mom. She does look like you."

My knees buckled beneath me. "What…Will…you're not serious."

"If you don't give me what I want, Princess, I'll have to take it. And we both know what happens when I take things. Aaron especially knew. Since he took you from me."

My heart began racing, my palms sweating. I was vaguely aware of a dark shadow looming over me. "Please. You can't do this."

"Oh but I can and I already have. If you want this to end, you know what to do. If you don't…" He paused. "I wonder what the inside of your mother looks like."

"Will." My breathing came out ragged and rough. He couldn't be doing this. There was no way. "You can't. You don't…"

"Oh but I can and I have." A dark sinister chuckle left him. "You thought she was safe. It's all your fault, Princess." His laugh deepened. "Say hi."

"Amber?"

A sob escaped me as I heard my mother's voice. "Mummy. No, Will. Please. Let her go." Tears streamed down my face as I fell to my knees on the hard cold pavement beneath me.

Arms wrapped around me, a deep voice tried whispering soothing words to me but they didn't help. I couldn't focus on anything other than the fact that Will had my mom.

The phone was snatched from my hand, Will's voice suddenly booming through the speaker.

"You want to see your mom, you know where to find me, Princess. I don't suggest waiting too long either because what happened to you will be nothing compared to what I'll do to her." The click sounded around us, forcing a scream from my lips.

TWENTY-SEVEN

Amber

VOICES SURROUNDED ME BUT I couldn't make them out. The only one I tried focusing on was Sammy. He was rubbing my upper back, trying to coax me into taking deep breaths. The guys were muttering to themselves, and I knew they were forming a plan to save my mom. But they wouldn't be able to do shit. If they showed up, Will would kill her. I would have to give him what he wanted. And this would result in my first fight with Sammy.

Before I lost the courage, I garnered that anger and rose to my full height. Spinning on Sammy, my heart jumped as the guys surrounded him.

"I need a car." I held my hand out. "And keys."

Sam's eyes dropped to my open palm before meeting my gaze.

"I suggest not arguing with me right now," I told him, looking him square in the eye.

"Sammy." Cyrus went up to his side, cupping his shoulder.

"This isn't right."

"Of course it's not fucking right," I snapped. "Will has my mom and the only way that I'll be able to save her is to go there myself."

"You are not offering yourself up to him," Sammy finally said, pulling my eyes back to him.

"What the fuck do you expect me to do, Sam?" I threw at him. "If you could have done the same for your parents, you would. You know you would. Both of you would." I thrust my hand out. "I need to save my mom. Will is sick and mentally deranged." I was thinking fast, trying to come up with ideas on how my mom and I could get out of this safely.

"He's not working alone," Jaron added. "Cheesy, get her a car."

Cheesy ran off to the garage at the side of the house.

I actually thought Sammy was going to argue with him, but when he didn't and only stared at me, I wasn't sure which I preferred. It was unnerving how he could look into the deepest parts of me. The parts Aaron had me feel like I was a bad person for having. But I realized that with Sam, with the right person, those parts were beautiful. And safe.

"Leave us," Sam said to no one in particular.

"You heard him," Jaron barked. "Get in the fucking house and wait for my instructions."

The guys did as they were told and left me alone with Sammy.

Cyrus and Jaron followed Cheesy and Locke to the garage, taking all the air in my lungs with them. I didn't like the way Sammy was looking at me. It went past just being intense. It was like his eyes were searing into my soul, marking their territory, and reminding me where I belonged. He didn't need to remind me. I knew. He was my home. He had always been.

"Sam, you know I have to do this," I told him, but my voice didn't come out as sure as I would have liked.

Sammy stomped toward me. His hand reached the back of my head first. He fisted my hair, holding me in place and forcing me to look up at him. "I'll go with you." His hand dropped to my stomach. "And I don't give a shit about Will's threats. I will skin him alive if something happens to you."

"I won't be able to handle it if something happens to *you*." I gripped his hoodie, pulling him closer.

"We'll take care of this together," he said, his voice firm. It left no room for argument but I knew that Will wouldn't like it if Sammy showed up with me. Add to the fact that he had my mom, it wouldn't end well for her.

"You need to give me a head start." I pulled away from him and lifted my hand before he could stop me. "You know I have to do this. I have to save my mom."

"And sacrifice yourself in the fucking process?" Sammy yelled. "Your mom wouldn't want you to do that. I don't want you to do that. Will isn't stupid. He knows for a fact that you won't show up alone."

"It doesn't matter what she wants. What any of you want. If you could go back in time and do what you could to save your parents, I know you would." I ran a hand over my belly. "I need to do this. I need to get her back and to safety. I need her to be able to watch her grandchildren grow up. I need..." My chin wobbled, tears falling down my cheeks.

A heavy body wrapped around me, pulling me into a warmth I thought I would never feel.

Sammy gripped the sides of my head, leaning his forehead against mine. "I'll go with you and have a fucking army with us too. I'm not having you go in there alone."

"Sam."

"I can't let you go there by yourself. I can't. I refuse to offer you up to him." He reached behind him, pulling a small pistol from the back of his jeans. "Here. Take this."

"I can't. I don't know how..." The lie was on the tip of my tongue but we both knew that being married to a biker for as long as I had been, of course I knew how to shoot. Aaron made sure of it.

"Take it." Sammy grabbed my hand and placed the small pistol in my open palm. "If someone comes to you that isn't me, shoot them." He kissed my forehead, breathing me in.

My eyes welled, a single tear falling down my cheek. "My mom...she's..." The words wouldn't leave my lips but they forced bile to my throat anyway. A shuddered breath left me.

"I'm sorry, baby." Sammy took the pistol from me and spun me around. He lifted the hem of my baggy shirt and slipped the small gun into the waist of my leggings. "There's something you need to do though."

I thought a moment. "I need to call him and make sure my mom is actually alive."

Sammy turned me back around, keeping his hands at my waist. "How did you know?"

"Because I know how he works. He probably recorded her voice saying my name. I guess I didn't want to think about that and got too wrapped up in the fact that he took her in the first place when Tiny and his crew should have fucking protected her like they said they were going to." It wasn't fair of me to think it but I couldn't help it. Tiny promised me that he would look after her.

Before Sammy could comment, Cyrus came back outside, followed by Jaron.

"Sorry to interrupt," Jaron said, looking between us both. "It appears that the clubhouse in your hometown was blown up. It has Will's MO all over it. That's how they were able to get your mom. She was there."

My knees shook. "She...She was probably bringing them food. She did that often. I...My mom isn't going to make it out of this alive, is she?"

Jaron and Cyrus looked at each other while Sammy kept his gaze on me.

"You want to know my honest opinion?" Sammy asked me.

I nodded. "Yes, please."

"I think if she's still alive, she's very fucking lucky." Sam grabbed my hand, bringing it up to his mouth and kissing my knuckles. "I don't know what all Will wants but I will stand at your side and wait until you tell me that you need me."

My eyes welled. "I need to call him." I drew in a deep breath, pulled away from Sam and dialed up the man who was doing everything in his power to destroy everything I had worked hard for.

"Change your mind?" came Will's deep voice from the other end of the phone.

"Let me talk to my mom," I demanded, ignoring his comment. "Not just a hi. An actual conversation. I need to know that you didn't just record her saying my name."

"Smart fucking girl." He chuckled, the sound sending an ice-cold shiver of fear racing down my spine. "She's a little indisposed."

My eyes widened. "What the hell does that mean?"

"It means that if you don't get your ass in a car in the next two point five seconds, your mom dying will be the least of your concern." The click sounded in my ear, pulling a hard huff from my lips.

"We have to go," I said to no one specific person.

"Here." Sammy grabbed my hand and placed a set of keys in it, curling my fingers around them. "You can drive but you're not going alone."

His tone left no room for argument, so all I could do was comply and pray that we would all make it out of this.

Alive.

(Sammy)

Amber was calm. Not a lot scared me but the fact that she wasn't trembling or that her sobs and tears had completely dried up, terrified me. But whatever she needed and for however long she needed it for, I would be there. For her and our babies. No matter the cost.

She had to go to wherever Will was, but I meant what I told her when I said that I wouldn't be far behind her. I knew that she needed to be in some sort of control of the situation. After everything she had been through at the hands of her late husband, his brother, Will, and every other fucker she knew, she was the strongest person I'd ever met.

While she drove ahead of us, we stayed right behind her. Accompanied by every other biker in the area. When she had slipped out of earshot, Jaron received a call from Tiny, letting us know that they were on the way to us.

"This shit with Will ends now," Tiny growled through the speaker of the phone. *"I'm sick of his tantrums and him acting like a fucking child. It ends. Tonight."*

None of us argued with him, knowing we would need all of the backup we could get.

Glancing behind us, I saw lights gaining up on us. I prayed that it was Tiny, his crew, and every other chapter on this side of the country. He was right. This shit would end tonight.

I may have been the Enforcer, but I couldn't do this on my own. Neither could Amber. As soon as she showed up at Will's, he was going to do everything he could to make her stay with him. I wasn't sure if she was prepared for that or not, but I knew that I wasn't. Add to the fact that somehow, he was working with Price. None of this made any damn sense.

For the first time in a long time, I drove while Cyrus sat in the passenger seat beside me. Cheesy and Locke were with Amber. I didn't trust a whole lot of people but I trusted those two with my life. She had insisted on driving alone but I refused. I knew that if it got caught on camera that I was in the same car as her, it wouldn't go well. Will didn't know Cheesy or Locke, so it would have to do.

Amber drove in the car in front of us that Cheesy had lent her. This wasn't going to go down how any of us planned. But I would be there to pick up Amber's pieces because everything in me told me that her mother was no longer alive. I also knew that she wouldn't have had an easy death. If Price was involved, even though he usually went for the younger women, most were considered just girls in fact, because we were involved, he would rip her mom apart.

Literally.

I tried preparing Amber for what she could walk in on, but it didn't work. She kept muttering how her mom was still alive when we both knew that she likely wasn't.

LIBERATE US

I had seen shit. Been around the worst kind of people. When Jaron and Piper's daughter was taken from them, I wasn't sure if it could get any worse. But it could. It could always get worse. Just in different kinds of ways.

If I had it my way, I would have taken Amber out of town and driven us to my parents' cottage that was in the middle of nowhere. It was one of the safe houses that the club used from time to time and was constantly being looked after. Just Cyrus and I didn't go often because it hurt too much. Even though we were kids the last time we were there, the memories were raw and fresh in our minds as the walls bled with the tears from our past.

"This isn't going to end well," Cyrus said, puffing on a smoke. He had quit and I realized then that he only smoked now whenever he was stressed.

I was on my third smoke in a matter of minutes. It was my only vice. Chain-smoking. It was a habit I couldn't break, just like the woman I had fallen in love with.

"It has to," I said. It was all I could say even though I didn't believe those words myself.

"You honestly think she's going to be able to show up and Will's going to welcome her with open arms? This is a fucked-up idea and one that doesn't make a whole lick of sense at all." Cyrus butted the smoke out in the ashtray in the console before lighting up another one.

"Amber needs to make sure her mom is actually gone." Even though I said those words, I felt like I was using her as bait.

"She's not bait. We can't do it this way," Cyrus muttered, taking the thought out of my head.

"Then why the hell didn't you say something back at the clubhouse?" I threw at him.

He grunted. "We should be doing this *for* her. She should be at home, in your bed."

"I agree but I couldn't get through to her. The only way I could have gotten her to stay home was if I tied her up and we both know, that wouldn't end well. She's already stressed, and I didn't want to cause any more when her and the babies have already been through so much."

269

"We'll be there. Every step of the way, Sam, but we're not letting her into that building by herself."

I glanced at my brother. "I'll be there with her. Even if she fights me. I don't give a shit. She's not facing Will alone. I will be there for *her*," I told him, looking back out at the road.

"Good, but I can't lose you either, Sammy. So, we're all going to be there. All of us. And both of you can fight us. You can fight me but I don't give a flying fuck. Will and Price need to be taken out because this needs to end. We all need to move on."

I agreed with him, but I wasn't even sure if Price would be there or not. There was little information on how Will and Price were apparently working together. Even though there were pictures and security footage of them, it didn't give us a whole lot to go on. It was like as the months went by, Price became shadier.

The only thing I was certain of, was that once this was all said and done, I was going to make Amber my wife.

TWENTY-EIGHT

Amber

DRIVING TO WILL'S FELT like it took a year when really, it was only a matter of hours. I was surprised that he still did his work at an abandoned factory when he could have moved his business to somewhere better. It was like he wanted to be found after all of these years. Or he just didn't care. I was betting on the latter. There had always been something off about him. Even when we were kids. I remembered back to a time when he would torture other children just for his pleasure. Poke and make fun of them just to watch them cry. And I didn't even want to begin to think about all of the animals he hurt.

"I think there's something wrong with Will," I told Aaron, finally gathering up the courage to voice my thoughts after all of this time.

"What do you mean?" Aaron cupped my inner thigh with one hand, texting away on his phone with the other. I took a chance and glanced at his cell, knowing I shouldn't have.

Alexandra's name popped up on the screen.

He chuckled quietly to himself, probably laughing at something funny *this woman had texted him.*

I should have left him then, but I didn't.

"I mean just what I said." It was a lame reason, but I couldn't focus on what we had been talking about when I tried reading what Aaron was texting the other woman.

"I don't know what you think his issue is." Aaron stood, turning away from me but not before I caught him adjusting himself. Whatever Alexandra had texted him, turned him on. I should have been upset but I wasn't. That part of my heart had been closed off to him for awhile now. I just wished I was brave enough to divorce him.

"He's fine," Aaron added, walking away. His phone rang as he walked down the hall. His deep voice mumbling words to a woman I would never know but felt sorry for just the same.

I had mentioned to Aaron several times over the years how there was something wrong with Will, but he had brushed it off every time.

The memories hurt. Add to the fact that Aaron texted his random women right in front of me. If he would have listened to me about his brother, all of this could have been prevented.

Glancing in the rearview mirror, I breathed out a sigh of relief at seeing the cavalry behind me. Knowing that Sammy and the rest of the guys were following me, made me feel better.

He wanted to drive with me, but I had insisted on driving by myself. He wasn't going for that either, so he had Cheesy and Locke drive with me instead.

If Will saw me in the car, he would look to make sure that it was only me in it. He would be pissed that Cheesy and Locke were with me, but he would be even more enraged if Sam was there instead.

But I also knew that there was no way Sammy would let me face him by myself. For that I was thankful because I knew that my mouth could get away from me at times and especially if I said what I wanted to say.

Something told me that my mom didn't make it. Something else also told me that it wasn't easy for her. For that I would make Will pay. Someway, somehow. I would avenge my mom. I would avenge Penelope. I would do everything I could to make this right.

This world was a dark and scary place at times, but I knew that with some help, I could give my babies a little bit of light. I didn't want them coming into the world terrified that Will could still come after us.

I had never set out to actually kill him. I wasn't that type of person. Not having a vengeful bone in my body, I intended to reason with him. But that was before he took my mother.

"Deep breaths, Red."

I jumped, almost forgetting that Locke was sitting in the passenger seat beside me. He had been so quiet, lost in his thoughts. The only movement that had come from him, was his knee that wouldn't stopping bouncing.

"I shouldn't be doing this," I said, gripping the wheel tightly. My thoughts traveled back to when Sam stuck the pistol in the waist of my pants at the small of my back. It didn't make me feel a whole lot better but knowing that it was there, helped a touch.

"No, you shouldn't be, but it could be worse for all of us if you didn't show up at all," Cheesy said from the back.

The phone suddenly rang through the speaker of the car the guys had lent me. I answered, unsure as to who was calling me or who even had this number.

"Hello?"

"Hey, Red," came Sammy's smooth voice.

"God." A breath of relief left me. "I'm regretting not having you in the same car as me."

"I'm regretting not having the guys go to Will's themselves and get your mom for you. You shouldn't be doing this. Not while you're pregnant."

"I know." I thought a moment. "Listen, if something happens, I just want—"

"Don't you dare finish that fucking sentence," Sammy growled.

"But Sam, I need you to know—"

"I know, Red. I know. But nothing is going to happen. We're going to go in there and face Will together. All of us are going with you and I don't give a shit how much it pisses Will off, you are not going in there alone. We're going to get your mom, whether she's alive or not and then leave. That's it. End of. And then I'm making you my fucking wife. You hear me?"

I opened my mouth to argue but I realized something in that single moment. Sam meant what he said. It was one thing I loved about him. He wasn't two-faced or ever beat around the bush, as cliché as that sounded. He was honest. I never had to worry where I stood with him.

"We shouldn't talk about this here," was all I said.

"Nope, we shouldn't. We'll talk about it more later, but I meant what I said."

"I know." My stomach clenched. God, to be his wife. He was possessive and overbearing just by me being his girlfriend. Being his wife, would be a whole other level of dominance I had never experienced before from him, and I was so damn excited to get that side of him.

Before we could talk any more about it, a large building came into view. Will's compound sat at the outskirts of the city. The authorities had always left it alone, knowing exactly who had taken over and what went on inside of it. I always wondered how that happened and figured that Will paid them off. I didn't know what all he had his hands in or if he got help from people over the years. I didn't want to know. I knew enough already after being with Aaron.

"Red, pull—wait…" When Sam's voice trailed off, I slowed the car down.

"Don't slow down," Locke said, leaning forward. "Something's wrong."

"What the hell is that?" Sammy demanded, his voice booming through the car.

My body shook but I pressed my foot harder on the gas.

"Wait!" Sam yelled.

I slammed my foot on the brake, finally seeing what he was referring to. Lights filled my vision. A loud pop sounded in my ear, followed by another and then another. I couldn't make out what the hell was going on. Smoke started billowing out from under the hood of the car.

"Sammy," I cried, unsure if he had hung up or not.

"We need to get her out of there," I heard him yell before the line went dead.

"Stay here," Cheesy instructed before both he and Locke left the car. As soon as they did, they lifted their guns, but neither of them were fast enough. More pops sounded and both of them fell.

I gasped, my hand flying to my mouth. I didn't know what to do. I didn't know how to get out. I tried calling Sammy again on the car phone, but no answer came. Shouting erupted around me, followed by an explosion. Glancing in the rearview mirror, I saw a ball of fire behind me.

Amidst the commotion, a light tap on the window startled me. My head whipped around, and I found Will standing on the other side of the door.

"Open up," he demanded, pointing the gun at me.

"No." But even though I said that word, I knew I didn't have a choice.

"Open the fuck up," he yelled. "Or I'll kill them all and what I did to your mother, will be the least of your fucking concerns."

Not really having a choice in the matter, I opened the door when I was met with the barrel of the gun in my face.

"Hands. Keep them where I can see them, Princess."

I swallowed hard, lifting my hands and stepping out of the car.

"Good girl." The praise, coming from him, forced bile to my throat.

Will lowered his arm, pressing the end of the gun against my stomach. "You will do as I say or I'll kill them and make you agonize over your loss for the rest of your fucking life."

My eyes welled but I nodded. What else could I do? I had wanted to look around me to see the destruction and if there were any survivors. I needed to know that Sammy and his crew were okay but I had seen Cheesy and Locke go down. I just prayed that they were okay.

Will cupped my shoulder, spinning me around. "Walk," he demanded, moving the gun from my stomach to my back.

When I took a step forward, he grabbed my arm. All breath left me as his hand released my arm, trailed around to my back and lower. It stopped at the small of my back, bumping the pistol Sammy had given me.

"You think I'm stupid, don't you?" Will pulled the gun from the waist of my pants. "Now walk." He shoved me forward.

The impact had been so hard, I almost tripped over my feet. When I looked down, I realized that it hadn't been my feet that I almost tripped over but an unmoving body instead. A sob lodged its way in my throat, tears dripping down my cheeks and off my chin.

"Eyes ahead and keep walking." Will shoved the gun into the small of my back, a sharp tinge of pain exploding up my tailbone.

While he walked me to a large black SUV, I realized something.

I wasn't sure if I would ever see Sammy again.

(Sammy)

I saw him take her.

It brought me back to a time when our dad was still alive and he had just lost our mom. He couldn't live without her. Literally couldn't. Although, he never hurt himself or anything that extreme, he went through each day like he was a zombie. He took care of me and my brother only because he had to. He should have given us to Greyson and Eve. At least we would have had a better time of it. But he didn't and I couldn't dwell.

We had learned that Price had been hiding out at Will's this whole fucking time. He wasn't too far from us, and we had no idea.

There was video footage of him in another state but somehow, he made it back to this area undetected. He had traveled frequently over the years to make it look like he wasn't shacking up somewhere. He was a sneaky bastard, but he messed up. They both did. By taking my girl's mom, Will and Price were royally fucked.

Rowan had also found a death certificate for Price as well, but we all knew he was still alive. Until I watched the life leave his eyes myself, I wouldn't settle until both he and Will were gone. For good.

Now, I was like a zombie myself, seeing Will take Amber. My girl. The mother of my unborn children. The woman I was going to marry as soon as this shit was over. I willed for her to look my way but when she didn't, I had a feeling it was because he instructed her not to.

"Sammy."

"Sam."

Voices sounded around me but I couldn't make out who was saying what.

"Samson Tyler Butcher." That was Cyrus. I knew his voice anywhere, especially when he was pissed.

I looked his way, finally seeing the destruction around us.

"We need to get to Will's compound before someone drives up and sees this shit." Cyrus grabbed my shoulders. "Are you listening to me? Someone could call this in. That means police would come and your girl will probably disappear forever."

That snapped me out of it. I shoved out of his grip, pulled the Glock from the small of my back, and stomped up to the nearest victim I could get my hands on.

When I saw one of Will's men covering a wound in his side, I shoved the tip of the gun against his forehead. "What the fuck do you know?"

He stared up at me with wide eyes. "I don't—"

Before he could answer, I pulled the trigger, the sound exploding in my ears.

"Sam." Heavy hands grabbed my shoulders, stopping me from killing another. "Stop."

"Get the fuck off me." I shoved him away, spun around, and geared my fist back when I realized it was Jaron standing in front of me.

"We can fight later but for now, you need to calm down enough that we can go get Amber. She's all that matters." Jaron cupped the side of my neck. "Alright?"

I nodded.

"Cheesy and Locke." He shook his head.

"Fuck." My chest ached, my stomach filling with dread that I had put them in the line of fire. "I'll call their parents. When all of this is done, it'll be me who tells them."

Jaron nodded. "Tiny and his crew are here. We were fucking ambushed."

He continued talking but I couldn't focus.

The only thing I could see was Amber walking away with Will.

TWENTY-NINE

Amber

"WILL, PLEASE." I TRIED pulling my wrist from his rough grip, but his hold was too strong for me. "Just let me get my mom and we can leave. I'll never bother you again."

Once we entered the building, my heart started racing that I was now in an enclosed space with Will.

"Please," I begged again, hating how desperate I sounded but I couldn't help it. I needed to get my mom, whether she was dead or alive, and get out of there.

When I was alone with Will and the man I had come to learn as Price Davies, the corrupt mayor who had suddenly disappeared, I couldn't help but notice how big the inside of the building actually was. It looked like your typical abandoned warehouse. There were tables with computers on them. Some even had weapons and others had sheets over them, hiding whatever secrets lay beneath the fabric.

"This could have been different." Will's voice pulled my attention back to him. "If only you would have been mine."

"I didn't know." We had this conversation years ago. It had been the night before my wedding. Will confessed his love for me and it made me uncomfortable. I told him I was sorry but that I was marrying his brother. I thought we could have been friends, but he ended up disappearing for a while. He never even showed up to the wedding and Aaron was pissed. At me. Like it was my fault that I made Will fall in love with me in the first place.

"You did know," Will insisted, tightening his grip on my wrist. "You had to have known. How could you not?"

"I loved your brother. Will, I'm sorry. I swear that I'm sorry, but you never told me how you felt until the night before my wedding. I—" I was suddenly slammed up against the nearest wall. The impact had been so hard, my head rang.

"I shouldn't have had to tell you, Princess," he murmured, his lips brushing along the shell of my ear. "You should have known. Especially when I took care of you after he died. I saw you in the hospital too. Did you know that? But Shawnee and your mom were always there. I could never visit you alone. You looked so helpless. So vulnerable. So innocent. Which we both know that you're not." His words implied something that wasn't true.

"I woke up and I didn't remember what happened," I told him. "It took me a bit but yes, you're right. You did take care of me, but I never hinted for more."

"No." Will brought my wrist up to his mouth. "You just wanted to fuck and that was it." He bit down, the sharp slice of pain forcing tears to my eyes. "Do you remember how I held you while you cried over Aaron being dead? Do you remember how I consoled you because you lost the baby?"

My eyes widened. "How did you know that I was pregnant?" I hadn't told anyone except for Aaron. Even when I thought the baby could have been Will's, we never told him.

Will chuckled. "Just because Aaron and I hardly got along, didn't mean he never told me shit."

"He didn't announce it until that party. You weren't there. Did he call you? Text you?" I shoved against him. "Tell me."

"I hate to interrupt this little reunion," Price said, coming toward us. "But we're going to have company rather quickly."

Before I could ask any more questions, Will pulled me away from the wall and continued dragging me along with him.

"Will, please." I had to run to keep up with his quick stride but the farther we got from the front entrance, the higher my anxiety rose.

Will suddenly stopped at a door. The movement had been quick, so I ended up bumping into him. He looked down at me, something flashing behind his dark eyes. "I loved you once. Maybe I still do. But now that you're carrying babies that aren't mine, it no longer matters."

"You wouldn't hurt them." But even though I said those words, I wasn't overly sure.

"I wouldn't?" He tilted his head. "You don't know me anymore. Maybe you never have."

"Oh this is a fun story," Price said from behind me.

"Aaron was gloating how he got you pregnant. Saying that all the times we had a threesome, his boys were stronger than mine." His brows narrowed. "He was trying to make me feel like less of a man because of the shit he was saying."

"Will." I took a breath, knowing that what I was about to tell him could either work to my advantage or make things worse. "The baby could have been yours."

His eyes widened, his hold on my wrist loosening a touch at my confession. "What?"

"I went to the doctor's and found out I was three months along. We had a threesome three months before. We never used condoms, so there was a chance that it could have been yours. I told Aaron that I wanted to get a DNA test when it was possible because it wasn't fair to either of you, not to know who the father was. He snapped and..." I swallowed hard. "...he was pissed that I even suggested such a thing."

"No." Will opened the door and shoved me into the room. "You're lying. You can't mean this shit. You can't stand there and tell me that I possibly had my baby killed."

"What?" Bile rose to my throat. "What the hell are you talking about?"

Price followed us, his laughter ringing through the room.

Will shut the door, closing me in with them.

I backed up, something on the floor catching my eye. "Oh..." It was a body, and it was unmoving. Recognition dawned on me, a sob breaking through me. "Mom."

"She felt just as good as you did."

My heart sank at Price's words. "What does that even mean? What are you talking about? What did you do to her?" I screamed, rushing toward my mom's still body. "Oh, Mummy. I'm so sorry."

Her eyes were wide and unblinking. Her face was bloody and bruised. Her clothes were torn and tattered. I knew without getting the details that she was tortured and raped before she died. Sobs wracked through me.

"I'm so sorry," I whispered, brushing my hand over her eyes and closing them.

"Enough of this," Will bellowed, pulling me away from her.

I yelled, shoving against him. Before I knew what was happening, Price had my arms above my head, holding me down.

"Your mom screamed for you," Price sneered, staring down at me with his dark eyes. Eyes that held no remorse for the things he had done.

The door opened, pulling my gaze away from him.

Two more men filed into the room. Recognition dawned on me. They were there that night. They attacked me and left me for dead.

My stomach twisted, unsure as to what would happen next. Will was unstable. Price was out for blood. And these two other guys, were just there because they clearly wanted to get their fill of whatever the situation called for at the time.

"You know, I always wondered what you would feel like after you've been used up." Will pulled a switchblade out of his back pocket.

My heart picked up speed, my eyes never leaving the blade.

He ran the tip of it over my collarbone, between my breasts, and down the center of my torso. He stopped when the blade reached my swollen stomach.

A whimper left me, my breath coming out in short bursts of air. "Please don't hurt them."

"Hurt them? Nah. I'll do better than that." He placed the blade on the ground beside me. I had a moment where I thought I could reach for it, but he had been too quick. In a rough move, he ripped my leggings down over my ass and off of my feet. "Hold her legs."

"No." I struggled against him as the two guys knelt on either side of me.

They each grabbed one of my legs, spreading me open.

Bile rose to my throat, memories of that night coming back.

Price towered over me. "You remember that night, Princess? I sure do. Your husband watched you get violently fucked while *you* watched him bleed out. Do you still have nightmares from it?"

My eyes widened. "You...you were there." I recognized the other guys, but I didn't remember seeing Price. My memories of that night were fuzzy, but I knew a third man had shown up. Or maybe he had been there all along and my brain blocked it out, trying to protect me.

Price only smirked, his eyes flicking down the length of my body. "Still hot as fuck too even while pregnant."

"Hold her," Will barked, picking the blade up off the floor.

"Please, Will." His words shocked me out of my memory. "You don't have to do this."

"Oh, but I do. I want you to always remember me because no matter what happens or where I am, I will always be with you." He took the blade, bringing the tip to my inner thigh.

The moment the sharp tip touched my skin, my body tensed. I tried going to a safe place in my head. Somewhere Sammy and our children would be. But no matter how much I tried, the agony brought me back to reality.

The blade sliced across my skin, digging in deeper and deeper until a scream shattered free from my lips.

White hot pain seared into me, making my vision fade in and out.

"You'll always remember me," Will grit out through clenched teeth.

After a while, the pain turned into a dull throbbing ache. My chin wobbled with silent cries, tears leaking from the corners of my eyes. "Please," I whispered. "Just let us go."

Will cupped my inner thigh, pressing down until a rough cry left me. "Never." He squeezed my thigh one last time before finally releasing me. Our eyes locked. Once upon a time, I used to have feelings for him. But that was so long ago. Now all I saw was a monster. A vile human being who threw a tantrum because he didn't get his way.

He lifted his hand to his mouth, his tongue licking up the length of his palm. "I always knew every part of you would taste good," he told me, my blood coating his lips.

"And people say I'm sick in the fucking head." Price chuckled, releasing my arms.

I pushed away from them, curling into myself and moving closer to my mom. Even though she was no longer alive, I needed her to comfort me.

"Let's go." Will threw my leggings at me and stood, rounding up the guys before heading to the door. "You'll always remember me, Princess." Those were his final words before they left the room.

Inching closer to my mom, I checked for a pulse even though I knew she was no longer with me. "I'm so sorry," I whispered, tears streaming down my cheeks.

A sharp pain erupted through my abdomen, forcing a gasp from my lips. Cupping my stomach, I prayed that my babies were okay. I calmed my racing heart, leaned my head against my mom's side and waited.

THIRTY

SAMMY

I HEARD HER SCREAMS and I felt them down to the center of my very soul. They controlled my thoughts and my actions as I took the lead, and we went through the men who had taken Amber. It didn't matter that they never touched her themselves. They worked with Will, they deserved death.

After Amber left with Will, the rest of us tore through his men. We slaughtered, we maimed, we did shit that could put us away for the rest of our lives. But it was worth it to end Will, Price, and the other fuckers working with them. Most of all, it would be worth it to get Amber back and into my arms.

We had made our way to the compound, losing none and killing many. We had rage at our back. It was a driving force as it led us to our ultimate task.

Kill Will and Price.

Save Amber.

And bury her mother along with our own.

"Price is mine," Jaron said, pulling me from my thoughts. "If he's here, I want him." He scratched his temple with the barrel of his pistol. "You know, Piper's told me that I've been on edge lately. Maybe this is what I need."

Death and mayhem. It was what a lot of us needed. But for me, I just needed to take Amber and get out of there. I needed to make sure that she was safe and that our babies were okay because without any of them, what was the point?

"How many do you think are inside?" Jaron asked, pulling his second piece from the back of his jeans.

"Will, maybe Price, and who knows who else," I answered.

"We'll go in the back," Tiny told us, heading toward his crew. "Get Amber," he yelled before rushing off to help his brothers.

Another scream sounded from inside the building, pulling me forward.

My name was called out, but I had enough with the waiting. Barreling into the building, I was stopped short by the vast expanse before me. No one was around and the screams had stopped. I was vaguely aware of the guys coming up behind me.

Taking a step forward, a door in front of us opened, revealing Will, Price, and two guys I didn't recognize. Everything in me told me that Amber was in that room.

Will noticed us first, a slow grin spreading on his face. "It's about time you joined us."

"Leave him for me," I told Cyrus and Jaron. "I need to make sure Amber's safe first."

Both of them nodded.

"Get your girl, Sam," Cyrus said. "We got this."

Not waiting for Will, or Price, or the other two fuckers to say anything, all of us stalked toward them.

Will held a switchblade in his hand, which only pulled a laugh from my lips.

"Bringing a knife to a gun fight, is not the brightest move on your part, buddy." I leaned my head from left to right, a hard crack rippling down the length of my spine at the impact.

The guys rushed past me, forcing Will and the others back. While they did that, I was able to enter the room that I could only assume held Amber and her mom. But I wasn't prepared for the sight that lay before me. Amber was lying on the ground, her eyes closed. A bundled heap was beside her. It was still and unmoving.

"Red." I rushed to her.

She lifted her head, her eyes landing on me. "Sam," she cried.

"Fucking hell, you're okay, baby." I fell to my knees in front of her, giving her a once-over, making sure that she was in fact okay.

Her chin wobbled, tears dripping down her cheeks. "My mom..."

"I'm sorry." I took off my leather cut and wrapped it around her shoulders.

She hugged it closed, bringing the collar up to her nose and taking a deep inhale.

"Let's get you out of here." I helped her to her feet.

She winced at the movement.

"What is it?" I asked, concern for her well-being twisting at my gut.

"He cut my inner thigh. I passed out after he left and then woke up and put my leggings back on. He came back in here and threatened to do more but he only wanted to watch me cower. He wants me scared of him. But he...he cut me, Sam. They held me down while he carved something into my thigh." She held onto me and looked down at herself.

I was going to kill him. I was going to rip his head from his scrawny neck and piss down his throat. Amber was wearing black leggings and I couldn't see any of the damage Will had caused, but I would get her checked out once we got out of here. "Let's go. I'll get you looked at and make sure that you and our babies are okay."

She nodded. "Sam...I..."

"I know." I wrapped my arm around her shoulders and led her to the door. Opening it slowly, I saw two prospects who belonged to Tiny's Chapter standing back, waiting for instructions. "I need you both to grab Amber's mom." I nodded toward her unmoving body on the floor. "She's gone but you need to be gentle and show her respect."

"On it," they both said at the same time, entering the room and doing as they were told.

Once Amber and I were out of the room, that's when I heard the commotion. Fists were flying, gunshots rang out, and more bodies fell. Death permeated in the air, and I had a feeling I would be consoling Amber for the rest of our lives. She didn't deserve this shit. None of us did.

Every time a shot went off, Amber jumped in my arms. I needed to get her out of here, but I also needed to help my brothers at the same time.

Everything next happened quickly. It was like it came right out of an action movie. Carnage and mayhem lay before us as the guys who were still under Will's thumb, were killed off one by one.

Even though Will's men were now taken care of, there was no sign of him, Jaron, or Price.

"Where's Jaron?" I asked Cyrus.

He wiped his mouth with the end of his shirt, licking his tongue along his split lip. "Fucker got me with a ring." He scowled. "Jaron is..." He looked around the room. "I don't know where he is."

My stomach did a flip. "We have to find him."

If we didn't, there would be no way we could go home to face his parents and Piper. We might as well all be dead in that case.

THIRTY-ONE

JARON

"**I'VE BEEN WAITING FOR** this moment," I sneered, looking directly at the man who had taken me from my fiancée and daughter.

Price chuckled, crouching low. "So have I, Jaron. I've been meaning to avenge my son's death."

"You said he wasn't your son," I reminded him, lifting the gun higher.

His laugh deepened. "True. He wasn't. But I did help raise him. So, he was my son in a way. Even though he was a pussy. Took after his mother that way. It doesn't matter. I'm here. You're here. Let's get this shit done and over with."

"No guns," I told him, placing my pistol on the ground and kicking it away. "I want to feel it when you die."

Price's smile fell. He charged for me.

I didn't move. I would. But not yet. When his body connected with mine, we went down in a pile of limbs. He got one punch in before I had him on his back.

Straddling his chest, I grabbed the collar of his jacket. "Killing you would be too easy. You should rot in prison like you tried making me do."

Price didn't even bother struggling. He only laughed, peering up at me. "It doesn't matter. I have nothing left."

"You have power and money. Isn't that what you've always wanted? This whole damn time?" It was almost like he was just giving up.

"Like I said, it doesn't matter."

"No." I lifted off of him. "You're going to fight me. I'm done having to worry about Piper looking over her shoulder. I'm sick of this shit. You either fight me or I'll give you to Sammy."

"And what's he going to do?" Price pushed to his feet, brushing the dirt off his knees. "He's too focused on his little family. But I wonder if he knows how Amber and I know each other." Price ran two fingers along his mouth. "I still remember how she felt. I remember how she choked on her blood when I was balls deep inside of her—"

A hard yell left me as I charged for him. My fists landed against his face. We fell to the ground once again. He tried blocking me, but my rage controlled my actions. It was like I was looking down on myself, watching me take the life Price never deserved in the first place.

His laughter rang out, proving just how sick and twisted he truly was. "Hit me harder, Jaron. Come on you fucking bastard. Hit *me*."

His words pissed me off but what made me even angrier was that he wouldn't fight me back.

"Brody was more of a man than you could ever be," I told Price.

The laughter stopped, his dark eyes turning cold.

Before I knew what was happening, I was on my back.

"I wonder if Piper thinks of me when you're inside her," he growled, spittle landing on my face.

"Why would she?" It took all of my strength, but I was able to shove him off of me and take a step back to collect my bearings. "She only thinks of her man. Her only man."

Price ran toward me, snarling and snapping like a fucking dog. Looked like I hit a nerve.

When he was close enough, I geared a fist back and lifted it with all of my strength. I poured all of the rage, the fear, the pain both Piper and I had felt over the years, and channeled those emotions into that punch. When my fist connected with his nose in a smooth uppercut, his body flew back.

When he landed on the ground, he was unmoving. I rushed to him and looked around the vast room, expecting his men to come and surround us. But when it remained just me and Price, I knelt by his still body.

His eyes were open. His chest rose and fell, a gurgled sound leaving him with every breath. He was choking on his blood just like he made Amber do.

"I hope you rot in hell," I told him.

"I...hope...you...join...me," he said between ragged breaths.

"I've already been there. There's nothing worse than you taking my daughter. But never again, Price. You won't hurt anyone else." Before he could get anymore words in, I pinched his nose and covered his mouth.

He struggled under me, gasping for the breath that I wouldn't let him take. He deserved pain and suffering but I didn't have a lot of time. As much as I would have loved to see Sammy rip him apart, I needed to do this on my own.

Price Davies had hurt both of our girls in very different ways.

Once he was unblinking and still, the life no longer inside of him, I released him and wiped my blood coated hands on my jeans. Opening and closing my fist that had connected with his face, I waited for the tinge of regret. My knuckles throbbed but other than that, I didn't feel anything. No pain. No remorse. Nothing for the man who died by my hands.

"Jaron, there you are."

I turned as Tiny came toward me with a few of his guys following behind him. Instead of answering, I looked back down at Price's still body. A part of me wished that he would jump up and let me take his life all over again. But he didn't and I couldn't.

So instead, I walked away from his body and sent up a silent prayer and thanked whoever decided to listen that I finally killed the man who had tried taking everything from me.

THIRTY-TWO

Amber

I KNEW THAT SAMMY was out for blood. I got it. I did. But something had already happened to me. That was enough because I wasn't sure what exactly Will did to my inner thigh, but he carved something into it. My mind wracked with what it could be but at the same time, a part of me didn't want to know either.

Hugging Sammy's leather cut around my shoulders, I breathed in the scent of him.

He caught the movement, looking down at me over his shoulder. Something flashed in his brown eyes. Something dark, something sinister, something I needed and craved. Something we would explore later. But he was right. Right now, we needed to find Will or else this would never end.

I tried not looking around us, but it couldn't be helped. There were bodies. Everywhere.

"Is this who you're looking for?"

I turned at the question coming from behind me.

One of the guys in Tiny's crew was holding Will by the

scruff of his neck. He shoved him forward, making him almost trip over his feet.

"How did you find him?" I asked, my voice shaking and not as strong as I wished it was.

Will glanced my way, a slow grin spreading on his face. I didn't like that he scared me or how much he enjoyed it.

"We found him lurking around the back. He was on the phone with someone, asking for a ride or some shit," Tiny explained, coming toward us.

Sammy grabbed Will and threw him up against the wall. "Did you have fun causing all of this chaos? So many men died because of you."

Will only chuckled.

"Did you have fun messing with my girl?" Sam bit out through clenched teeth.

The laughter leaving Will was evil and vile. "Just wait until you see what I carved into her skin."

White hot rage coursed through me. I took a step forward when a hand landed on my shoulder. I looked up, finding Cyrus beside me. He didn't say anything as he slipped a gun into my hand.

I was thankful for that single act of kindness, since Will had taken the pistol Sammy had originally given me.

Sammy pulled his arm back, landing his fist into Will's stomach but that move only seemed to make him laugh harder.

"You're a sick son of a bitch," Sammy threw at him, pulling him back to his feet.

"You obviously haven't seen what's on her thigh or else I wouldn't still be alive." Will looked my way. "Did you show him? Did you let him see how I carved my—"

A gunshot boomed through the air, making me jump. Will's eyes widened, blood sputtering from his lips.

Sammy released him, letting his body slide down the wall.

Will cupped the side of his neck, red liquid seeping from between his fingers.

I stared at him as he slowly died in front of me. I noticed then how my hands were lifted with a gun aimed right at Will. I pulled the trigger. I didn't even remember doing so.

Sammy came up to me, wrapping his arm around my waist and whispering soothing words in my ear as he took the gun from my shaking hand. He handed the pistol off to whoever was standing beside me. Maybe it was still Cyrus. I couldn't be sure. All I could focus on was seeing Will now sitting on the floor, his eyes vacant of all life.

"I didn't want him to finish his sentence," I heard myself say. My voice sounded far away, like I was hearing myself through a tunnel.

A deep voice barked instructions, but I couldn't help but watch the scene unfold before me. Will was gone. It was over. All of it was over. Finally. After all of this time.

I was lifted off my feet, my body wrapped in heavy arms as I was carried away from the mass carnage.

Once we were outside and the sun beat down on my face, a sob escaped me.

"Let it out, Red," Sam said gently, carrying me in his arms. "Let it all out."

I latched on to him and cried against his chest.

It was over.

I lost my mom in the process, and I would never forgive myself because of that. But at the same time, I knew that she would be happy I no longer had to fear that Will would come for me.

(Sammy)

I could feel her soul shattering in my arms. Amber was breaking before me, and I didn't know how to help her through it. Maybe she needed to do it on her own. But whenever she needed me and however, she needed me, I would be there. With open arms. Whatever she wanted, I was there.

I placed her in the back of the SUV I shared with my brother and leaned my forehead against her temple.

Thankful the SUV was still driveable even though it was shot to shit by Will's men.

I breathed her in, the sweet scent of her skin calming the racing nerves rushing through me. I almost lost her. I almost lost her and our babies. We lost men. Cheesy and Locke were so damn young, they never deserved this. My chest tightened as I tried thinking up ways I could gently let their parents know what had happened.

Will fucked Amber up and I wasn't sure if she would ever get through it, but I would help her. Always. Forever. No matter what and no matter the cost. I would help her with whatever she needed.

When I went to pull away, she whimpered. "Shh…" I kissed her head. "I'm here. Not going anywhere, pet. Just giving you some space."

She shook her head. "I don't need space. I need to go home. I need to bury my mom. I need…Oh God, Cheesy and Locke…did they…are they okay?"

I shook my head. "I'm sorry, pet, but they died with honor."

Tears fell harder down her cheeks. "Are you okay?"

I stared at her, taken aback by her question. There she was, sitting before me, crying and losing pieces of herself, but yet, she still asked me if I was okay.

"You need to get checked out," I said instead of answering her. We would take her to a doctor we knew that worked out of the Mayhem's Revenge clubhouse. Hospitals could be dangerous. Especially when, depending on the injury, they could call the police. Amber had been through enough. She didn't need to go through that.

"Don't close the door," Amber said. "Please."

"I won't." I turned as Cyrus, Jaron, and several of the other guys came toward us.

"I've called the cleaning crew," Jaron said. "We've lost…" He shook his head. "Fuck…this…"

Cyrus wrapped his arm around his shoulders. "I know, brother. I know."

Jaron took a deep breath. "Price is dead." He shook out his hand. "It was almost too easy but fuck me, was it ever satisfying. Tiny's prospects have Amber's mom. We'll give her a burial and a funeral."

"We'll put her with our parents." I looked at Amber. "If that's okay with you."

She nodded. "I would like that."

"Is that okay with you?" I asked my brother.

"You don't even have to ask me, Sam." He clapped my shoulder. "Ever. We can bury Cheesy, Locke, and everyone else, at the same location. Like always." He ran a hand through his hair, a deep frown settling between his brows. "Fuck, I have to tell Ainsley about Cheesy. This is going to hurt."

"Be there for her," I reminded him. "She'll need you."

He nodded.

I slipped into the back seat with Amber. "We need to go see Ricky and get Amber checked out."

Cyrus nodded. "I'll drive."

He went around to the driver's side of the SUV and Jaron slid into the passenger seat.

Before I closed the door, I saw Tiny, some of his crew, and the other guys who had been under Will's thumb.

"I need a minute." I left the SUV and went up to the guys who helped us save Amber. "Tiny."

He stopped by a navy-blue SUV, looking at me over his shoulder.

"I know you were close with Amber's mom too, so I'm sorry for your loss, but thank you for helping us." I stuck my hand out. "I mean it."

He returned the handshake. "You take care of her and don't let her be a stranger."

"I won't." I looked around us. "Where's your president?"

"Laying low after being a bad boy." He opened the back door to the SUV and pulled out a leather cut. Slipping it on over his shoulders, the president patch sat on the left breast.

I chuckled. "I had no idea."

"Not many do. The previous president was shady as fuck. So, we kicked him out. And looks like I moved up in ranks." He winked, grinning.

"I'll bring Amber by soon and we'll meet up for a beer," I told him, backing up.

"I like that idea." He nodded once. "Take care of her."

I would. More than he would ever know.

THIRTY-THREE

Amber

WE WERE FINALLY ON our way back to the clubhouse. I craved Sammy's bed, needing to wrap myself up in his sheets and everything that smelled like him. He was tense beside me, not saying anything since we left the Mayhem's Revenge clubhouse. My thigh was mangled thanks to Will but what bothered both of us the most was the actual word that Will carved into my thigh.

We hadn't talked about it, but Sammy punched a hole in the wall when he saw it.

Will.

Four letters.

Four letters carved deep into my skin that would eventually heal, scar, and be there forever. A constant reminder that he would always be a part of my life even though he was now dead and gone. We also didn't talk about the fact that I pulled the trigger that ended his life. Sammy seemed to care more about the word in my thigh than the fact that I had killed someone.

I had met Ricky, a wonderful older man who was a doctor in

his previous life but still kept up with his medical practice for those in need. I learned that he didn't just help bikers but anyone who couldn't afford insurance or was down on their luck. He had a whole medical room set up at the Mayhem's Revenge clubhouse and to say I was impressed, was an understatement. He did an ultrasound on me after taking care of my thigh and told me that the babies were healthy and strong but for me to take it easy for the rest of my pregnancy. He didn't say I would have to go on bed rest but if I remained stressed, I would have to. Now that Will was no longer around, I could finally relax. Or try to at least.

While Cyrus drove, Jaron sat in the passenger seat and Sammy sat beside me. His hand was cupping my good thigh and he was looking out the window.

"Sam," I finally said, the silence unnerving.

His dark eyes shot to mine, but he never said anything.

I stared up at him, wishing I could tell him something that would make him feel better. That would make both of us feel better, but I wasn't sure what I could say. Instead, I looked down at his hand on my thigh. His finger reached out, brushing along the other one. Although I had a bandage wrapped around it, I could still feel his touch. And even though it was gentle and soft, it spoke volumes. More than our words could ever say.

My throat burned past a hard lump.

Finally, after what felt like forever, the clubhouse came into view. I needed a shower. I needed sleep. I just needed to move on and past the shit show that had been this day.

"Jaron," I blurted.

He turned, his eyes meeting mine. "Yeah?"

"Are you okay?" I knew Piper would take care of him, but I still needed to know.

He gave me a small smile. "Yeah, I am. Thank you for asking. Are you okay?"

"Ye—No." I picked at a fuzz on my leggings. "I'm not."

Sammy wrapped his arm around my shoulders, pulling me into his side. "I got you and I will take care of you. If you want to just sit in silence, that's fine and I will do that. Just do it with me, Red. Don't shut me out."

LIBERATE US

My chin wobbled, fresh tears rolling down my cheeks. I huffed, roughly wiping them away. "I'm sick of crying," I mumbled.

"To be fair, you are pregnant with twins," Cyrus pointed out. "Your hormones are going to be extra crazy right now. Besides everything else that's happened of course."

"Thank you. All of you," I said as we pulled past the gates and into the long driveway that led to the large house.

Cyrus parked the SUV, his eyes catching mine in the rearview mirror. "We'll talk later," he told Sammy. "You need some rest, Amber."

I nodded, following Sammy out of the back of the vehicle.

"I just got a text from…Krew, Tiny's prospect," Cyrus said, coming around to our side of the SUV. "They brought your mom to the funeral home. They'll get her taken care of, but I imagine you would want her to wear something of her own."

"Yes, I would." I grabbed Sammy's hand. "We'll have to go to her house." I started thinking of all the things I needed to do and people I needed to contact. "I don't know how to do this."

"I'll help you." Sammy brought my hand up to his mouth. "We all will."

"He's right." Cyrus gave me a small smile. "I never met your mom and I only just started getting to know you but you're family, Red. And you're carrying my nieces or nephews or one of each."

I laughed lightly, wiping away a lonely tear that ran down my cheek. "Thank you. We can start planning tomorrow, but I would like my mom to be buried at the same place as your parents. She said she had friends back home, but I think they were just using her. I should have gone home. I should have done a lot of stuff but now I can't. I—"

"You need some rest," Sam said, his tone leaving no room for argument.

"I need a shower first." I looked down at myself, wishing I could have changed so many things, but I couldn't, so I would have to move on. I was just thankful that our babies were okay. They were safe. That was all that mattered.

THIRTY-FOUR

SAMMY

AS SOON AS I left my bedroom, I let out a heavy breath. It was like all of the weight from the night came crashing down on my shoulders whether I wanted it to or not. I leaned against the wall, sliding down until my ass hit the floor.

Rubbing the back of my neck, I blew out another breath. She was fine. They were fine. Our babies were strong. My girl was strong. It only made me feel a little better as the minutes ticked on. Amber had become quiet. Ever since she slipped into my shower and started the water, I could hear her muffled cries as she tried keeping them at bay, but it didn't help. *I could hear her.*

"How's she doing?"

My head lifted, finding Cyrus coming down the hall toward me.

"I don't know." I leaned my head back against the wall, bringing my knees up to my chest. "She's quiet. I'm not used to her being quiet and I don't like it. I tried getting her to talk. About shooting Will. About her thigh. About her mom.

Just…about something…but she's closed up."

Cyrus sat on the floor beside me, mirroring my pose. "She needs time."

"Will carved his name into her thigh," I blurted.

My brother stiffened beside me, his gaze searing into the side of my head.

"Shit." Cyrus blew out a slow breath. "Listen, I know you haven't asked for advice but I'm going to give it to you anyway. First off, you need to be patient."

I grunted.

"Second, whatever she wants, whether it's to talk or just sit there in the dark and be quiet, she's going to need you to be there with her."

"I don't want her to shut me out." I looked at him then. "I can't handle it if she did."

"It wouldn't be intentional, Sam. But she has to figure out how to deal with this on her own too. Our women are strong. They don't want to have to depend on us to take care of them. As much as we insist on trying."

"She hasn't said much since we've been…home…" Was it even her home? Was that the issue? Maybe I should bring her back to her apartment. Or better yet, I could bring her to her mom's sooner than she planned. I could drive and she could sleep.

I jumped to my feet.

"Sam?" Cyrus followed suit.

"I'm going to do everything you suggested. I'm going to wait until she's ready to talk but I'm…" A thought crossed my mind. That single thought made my stomach flip. "I'm not waiting to marry her."

A slow grin spread on my brother's face. He pulled me into a hug, clapping my back. "It's about fucking time."

"You wouldn't be pissed?" I asked him, knowing that he was planning his own wedding with Ainsley.

"Not at all. Jaron and I never thought you would find your person anyway, so I'm happy for you and will stand by you."

My chest tightened. "I love you, brother, but I think…I think I'm going to take Amber to her mom's place. It's her childhood home. But that would mean…"

"You want to transfer to Tiny's chapter?"

"I think it might be best. Not that I want to move away from you of course but I need to do this for Amber. And it's only a few hours' drive. But if Jaron agrees to it…"

Cyrus smiled, hugging me again. "I only want what's best for you and I get it. I would do anything to make Ainsley happy and if it meant moving across the damn world, I would."

"Why are we hugging, and why am I not included?"

Cyrus and I turned to Jaron coming down the hall toward us.

"I wanted to make sure you were good before I went home," Jaron explained. "Piper insisted that I check on you all first."

I held my arm out, keeping my other wrapped around my brother's shoulders.

Jaron closed the distance between us, allowing us to wrap around each other in an awkward group hug.

"I love you guys," he muttered.

We stood like that for a few minutes, hugging and embracing each other. While Cyrus was my brother by blood, Jaron was just as much a part of our family. They were my life, and I would lay down mine for them without any hesitation at all.

"I want to transfer," I blurted.

Jaron leaned back, staring at me.

"I want to take Amber and move her home. I think being in her mom's house will be good for her." I didn't want to leave them and knew that I would see them often. It wouldn't be the same but I had to do this. "If Amber decides that she wants to move back here, I'm fine with that too. I just…"

Jaron pulled me back into a hug. "You don't need to explain. I get it. Let me make some calls."

"You would do this for me?" I asked, my voice thick.

"Of course. Now go to your girl," Jaron said, pulling away from us. "And marry her already."

"Are you both sure you won't be pissed?" I needed to make sure there would be no animosity between the three of us before I made Amber my wife.

"Never." Jaron clapped my shoulder. "As long as we're both there, I don't give a shit when you marry Amber. I'll also call Tiny and see what he says about you transferring to his chapter. We do need to vote about this and then they'll have to vote too but you're lucky you stayed on his good side. I think everyone will agree to it. But he could make you start out as a prospect if he really wanted to."

"I know. I'll do anything and I really don't care about starting out at the bottom again. As long as Amber is happy, that's all I want."

"I'll set it up." Jaron looked between us. "It'll be odd as fuck without you here but don't be a stranger. That's all I ask."

"Never." And I wouldn't. They were my family. Even if both of our chapters agreed, I would always come home.

Most clubs made you start out as a prospect again. The big ones anyway. But Greyson had changed some of the rules over the years. As long as you kept your nose clean so to speak and both chapters agreed, a transfer could happen.

"Take care of your girl, Sam," Cyrus said as he walked away.

They headed back down the hall, talking amongst themselves about their own weddings and how they planned on buying something special for their fiancées. The moment I was once again alone, I slipped back into my bedroom.

Amber was sitting on the edge of my bed in one of my t-shirts, looking at her phone. Her head lifted, her eyes finding mine. "Just reading the last texts between me and my mom." A shuddered breath left her. "She offered to come see me after I told her I was pregnant. I should have said yes."

My stomach twisted. Shutting the door behind me, I went up to her and knelt at her feet. "Marry me."

Her eyes widened.

"I mean…" I shook my head. "No, that's exactly what I mean." I hooked my arms around her waist and gently pulled her off the bed and down onto my lap. "Listen, I love you and I'm so fucking sorry for what you've been through. I don't expect you to want to talk about it. If you want to speak to a professional, I'll help you get that set up. If you want to fuck until the walls shake, I'll help you. If you want to just sit there in the dark and not say a single thing, I'll help with that too. But no matter what you want to do, I am not going anywhere. Am I bothered that Will…" I looked down, not even realizing that my fingers were lightly brushing the bandage wrapped around her inner thigh. "Yes, I'm bothered. I won't lie to you, Red." I met her gaze then. "But I don't want you thinking that I love you any less because of what he did. I don't want you thinking that I don't want to touch you, make love to you…" I leaned my forehead against hers. "…kiss you, all because of what he did. None of it is your fault."

Her shoulders shook with silent sobs. Throwing her arms around me, the cries deepened, her body trembling against me.

"I'm not okay," she whispered. "I'm not. I've tried faking it. But I haven't been okay in a long time."

"I know." I ran my fingers through her damp hair and held her head while I looked deep into her eyes. "But I'm here and I'm not going anywhere. I haven't been okay for a long time either. Losing our parents fucked me up. But you…being with you, falling in love with you, getting you pregnant…you are my strength, pet. You are the reason I'm not so damn moody anymore. You are the sunshine in my darkness."

Her chin wobbled, her eyes welling with fresh tears. "Yes, I'll marry you."

A shiver rippled down my spine at her words. "Good." I kissed her hard on the mouth, tasting the salt of her tears on my tongue. "Oh, by the way, we're not waiting to get married."

Amber gave me a small smile. "Let's give my mom and the guys the service they deserve and then I'm yours."

Standing with her in my arms, I placed her gently on the bed and laid down beside her. Not giving her a chance to say any more, I crushed my mouth to hers.

She sighed, cupping my cheek and for the next couple of hours, that was all we did. We held each other, touching and kissing between our words.

When I first met Amber, I thought she was just an unhealthy obsession. But little did I know at the time, that she was exactly what I needed all along. Now I understood what Jaron and Cyrus went through and how they felt. While every relationship had their moments and issues, I made a silent vow right then and there to never not tell Amber how I felt.

She was my liberation.

She made me realize that even though my parents were gone far too soon, I could still open up and allow myself to love. Amber did that without even realizing it. We went in wanting some fun, only to fall in love in the process.

Because of her, I was no longer scared of giving pieces of myself that only she ever saw. She kept them safe within her clutches and gave me pieces of herself in return.

It would take a while, but Amber would heal. Mentally and physically. And no matter what, I would be there every step of the way.

By her side.

As her lover.

As her husband.

And definitely as her Dom.

EPILOGUE

Amber

SAM AND I GOT married a couple of days after we buried my mom and members of his club. I was with him when he had told both Cheesy's parents as well as Locke's. It was something I never wanted to experience ever again. But my respect for Sammy grew then. He didn't want to tell them over the phone. So, we drove hours to both sets of parents and delivered the news.

With all of us pulling together, they were both beautiful ceremonies. I never had a chance to talk to my mom much about Sammy before she died. I knew that she liked him, but I still had never been sure if she thought he was right for me. She never said in that motherly tone like she had with Aaron. Maybe that meant she wasn't worried about it. I chose a good one. Finally.

While I was Sammy's first wife, he was my second husband. Technically anyway. But I looked at him like he was my first. Aaron had been a part of my life when I was young and naïve. Sammy was now a part of my life when I was older and stronger.

Although I had days where I didn't feel too strong.

During the funeral, I broke down and begged for my mom to come back to me, which caused stress on the babies, and I was put on instant bed rest.

Sammy never left my side for those remaining months of my pregnancy. Shawnee and Emma came to visit often. The first time I had seen them after the explosion at the club, was weeks later. Our little reunion resulted in tears and apologies. So many tears shed between us and while I was sick of crying, the tears lifted some of the heavy weight that had rested on my shoulders ever since Will came back into my life unexpectedly.

"I should have tried harder to find out what Will had wanted," Shawnee said through her tears. *"I'm so sorry, Amber. I'm so sorry."*

"Don't." I hugged her to me and reached out for Emma.

We huddled close, the three of us whispering and muttering words of strength and encouragement, even though we didn't feel them at the moment.

"I love you girls," I finally said, pulling away from them. *"Please don't be strangers."*

"Never." Emma wrapped an arm around Shawnee's shoulders, pulling her closer. *"We're here for you."*

Shawnee kissed her cheek and covered my hand with hers. "We are."

"Are you two a thing finally?" I asked, hoping they were.

"We're taking it slow," Emma told me. *"But yeah…"* She smiled at Shawnee. *"We're a thing."*

"Finally." Shawnee sighed. *"Although, you do need to get some tattoos and piercings."*

We laughed and continued talking about their new relationship and Shawnee's obsession with ink and piercings.

The hairs on the back of my neck suddenly tingled.

Sammy stood at the door to our bedroom. He gave me a smile. In that single moment, with him and my friends, I finally felt like we were all taking a step in the right direction.

One night, Sam and I were sitting on the couch at my mom's place, facing each other. He was holding our son and I was holding our daughter.

After my mom's funeral and our small but beautiful wedding, we moved back into my childhood home.

He had been given the approval from both his original chapter and Tiny's chapter and the transfer was made. He remained an Enforcer per Tiny's request.

We were slowly changing things to make the house ours, but it made me feel closer to my mom in a way. It had been Sammy's idea and I fell in love with him even more because of it.

"I still can't believe we made these beautiful little humans," I said, resting our daughter on my lap.

"I know." Sam hugged our son to his chest. We had named him John after his father.

The twins were born a month early and spent a couple of weeks in the NICU as a result. We finally brought them home a few days ago and have been snuggling them ever since.

Our daughter, Kyra, started fussing. Her little body wiggled, flailing her arms wildly. I laughed lightly, lifted her into my arms, and began to nurse her.

Sam moved to the spot beside me and kissed my temple. "I love you and I'm so damn proud of you."

It had been the same thing he said every time I nursed the twins. John was easy but Kyra was a stubborn little thing. Sam joked that it was because we named her after his brother. I wanted the twins to be named after the people we loved, so I had Googled a female version for Cyrus's name and Kyra popped up. It was an easy decision after that and one I would never forget when I asked Sammy about it.

"You want to name our daughter after my brother?" Sam asked, his voice thick as he stared down at our little girl in his arms.

"I do." I cupped his cheek. "I love you and I know how close you are with your brother and Jaron. I also know you miss them." It was constantly at the back of my mind that maybe one day we would sell my mom's place and move back to Sammy's home. It would be the least I could do for him. "I figured we could name our son and daughter after both of them and my mom."

A shuddered breath left him. "I like that idea."

Johnathon Jaron and Kyra Andrea Butcher.

They were going to grow up to do amazing things.

Once we put the twins to bed later that evening, Sam and I sat together on the couch. It had been something we did quite often. Just sitting there. Touching, holding, being together. No TV. No music. No talking. Just pure silence.

He would never know how much these little moments meant to me. After everything that had happened with Will and Price and the scar on my inner thigh as a constant reminder, Sam and I never took these moments for granted.

"I love you," he whispered, breaking the sweet silence.

I snuggled into his side, pulling the blanket up and around us. "I love you too." I looked up at him then. "Thank you."

He frowned. "For what?"

"For being persistent back in the beginning. For being patient with me. For making me fall in love with you and for giving me a family."

He cupped my chin, pushing his mouth against mine. The kiss was soft but firm, reminding me how far we had come.

"No, pet," he nipped my bottom lip. "Thank you."

A sharp twinge erupted through my lip, sending a hot shiver down my spine. "You know." I waggled my eyebrows. It had been a long while for us. He was letting me heal from the C-section and didn't want to push me too soon.

Sam smirked, a wicked glint flashing in his eyes. He pushed me back onto the couch and knelt between my legs. He pulled my sweatpants down my legs and brushed his thumb along the scar in my thigh. The word was faint but both of us could see it. Even if it disappeared completely or we covered it up by a tattoo, we would still know that it had been there once upon a time.

While Sam spent the next little bit making love to me slowly, he never removed his hand from my inner thigh. It was a silent reminder that Will wouldn't have control over us even though it had been his intention when he dug his knife into my skin. Instead, Sam ran his mouth and tongue over the light pink scars, murmuring every so often that I was his.

When we finally made it to bed, Sam was running his fingers lightly over my hip. We were facing each other, completely naked and bare.

"I think I want to start seeing a therapist," I blurted.

Sam's fingers stopped in their path.

I looked at him then, almost expecting him to ask me why I would need to when I had him, but as his fingers started moving again in their light feathery touches, I realized that I was wrong.

"I'm proud of you," he said, kissing my forehead and then my nose.

"You are?"

"Yes." He gave me a small smile. "I've been wanting to suggest that you see someone because I can only do so much. I want to eventually take you to a BDSM club as well and dive deeper into that lifestyle with you but for now, I'm enjoying what we're doing."

"Me too," I whispered.

"But speaking to an unbiased person is a good idea. So, I'll be there every step of the way. If you want me to join you, I will. If you want to go to these sessions by yourself, I'll drive you and wait in the car. If you find that it's not working for you, I'll support you. No matter what."

"God." My eyes welled. "How am I so lucky to get my second chance at happiness?"

Sam pinched my chin, tilted my head back, and kissed me softly on the mouth. "I was young when my parents died but I still remember how my dad treated my mom. I always vowed to be the same way. It just took me awhile to find my person where I actually wanted to be that man for her."

"Am I your person?" I asked even though I knew I was.

Sam chuckled, pulling me into his arms and rolling onto his back with me straddling his waist. "You've always been my person." He sat up, leaning against the headboard. "I know I can never replace what you had with Aaron. I also know that while you had your problems with him, you did love him at some point. I don't want to take his place. I just want to be your now and your forever."

"You are, Sam." I kissed him hard on the mouth. "You are."

"My forever," he repeated, slipping his tongue between my lips.

My forever.

J.M. WALKER

THE END

The Next Generation Series:

https://www.aboutjmwalker.com/next-generation-series

ACKNOWLEDGEMENTS

Oh Sammy. Although he's a twin, he is nothing like his brother but at the same time he is. Taking care of his girl is all that matters to him, which is exactly like Cyrus, but his special kinks are far different than his brothers. And man was it ever fun to write.

Angie: Even though you weren't able to help with this one, it feels weird not including you in the acknowledgements. So here I am, including you. You've been with me since my very first book. You loved, disliked, reminded me that sex does NOT need to be a major plot point and more. I really can't thank you enough for sticking by me all of these years. You're one of the good ones. I love you, FS!

Thank you to Jennifer and Christina for always helping me fix my many issues, timeline problems and inconsistencies. You girls mean so much to me. I really can't thank you enough.

Thank you to Joanne, my wonderful editor and friend. I feel like you know this world as much as I do, probably even better than I do at points. We're almost done this series and I can't wait to work with you on all the future crazy ideas I have.

Thank you to my Jems: I really couldn't do this without your support. Sammy is a fun one and I hope you enjoyed his story as much as I enjoyed writing it.

To the authors, bloggers and readers who shared my cover reveals, release information and more: Thank you for making this book community being the amazing thing it is.

We are now book 8 into The Next Generation Series but the ride isn't over!

JM

ABOUT

J.M. Walker is an Amazon bestselling author who also hit USA Today with Wanted: An Outlaw Anthology. She loves all things books, pigs and lip gloss. She is happily married to the man who inspires all of her Heroes and continues to make her weak in the knees every single day.

"Above all, be the HEROINE of your own life..." ~ Nora Ephron

Find me!

https://linktr.ee/authorjmwalker